Craig J. Black is the alias of Paul Gibson. Paul grew up in the North East of England with his parents Craig and Annette and his brother Lee. He currently resides in Yarm, England with his lifelong partner and best friend Paul. Paul is passionate about writing and has a vivid imagination which brings his words to life.

From an early age, Paul has always been creative and fulfils his artistic expression through various outlets. Supported by his family and fans, Paul enjoys taking people on an emotional journey with his writing.

You can learn more about Paul, or if you wish to contact him simply visit www.craigjblack.com and go to the contacts page.

THE BLOODLINE:
FORBIDDEN HUNGER

*Ruby,
Best Wishes
Craig J. Black*

CRAIG J. BLACK

THE BLOODLINE:
FORBIDDEN HUNGER

Vanguard Press

VANGUARD PAPERBACK

© Copyright 2016
Craig J. Black

The right of Craig J. Black to be identified as author of
this work has been asserted by him in accordance with the
Copyright, Designs and Patents Act 1988.

All Rights Reserved

No reproduction, copy or transmission of this publication
may be made without written permission.
No paragraph of this publication may be reproduced,
copied or transmitted save with the written permission of the publisher, or
in accordance with the provisions
of the Copyright Act 1956 (as amended).

Any person who commits any unauthorised act in relation to
this publication may be liable to criminal
prosecution and civil claims for damages.

A CIP catalogue record for this title is
available from the British Library.

ISBN 978 1 784651 96 1

*Vanguard Press is an imprint of
Pegasus Elliot MacKenzie Publishers Ltd.*
www.pegasuspublishers.com

First Published in 2016

**Vanguard Press
Sheraton House Castle Park
Cambridge England**

Printed & Bound in Great Britain

Acknowledgments

I wish to thank everyone at Pegasus for your hard work. Also, to my amazing Production Coordinator Jasmine. You have been wonderful.

Dedication

To my dad, Craig.
For your love, bravery and support, and most of all for being my father.

To my mam, for supporting me and reading my material.

Also to my partner for putting up with my late nights. Thank you for your support and love throughout.

Thank you to my dear friend Tony.

Contents

Prologue..19

Chapter 1 ....

   The Beginning.. 31

Chapter 2 ....

   The River Dour 51

Chapter 3 ....

   Catherine.. 80

Chapter 4 103

   Catherine.. 103

Chapter 5 122

   Fugloy Island.. 122

Chapter 6 131

   My Empire 131

Chapter 7 138

Council... 138

Chapter 8 149
The Army 149

Chapter 9 158
The New Recruits 158

Chapter 10 170
The Burning Escape 170

Chapter 11 181
Eleanor's Choice 181

Chapter 12 196
The Burning 196

Chapter 13 206
Trapped 206

Chapter 14 216
The New Council Member 216

Chapter 15 225
Philippe's Return 225

Chapter 16..237

   The Truce.. 237

Chapter 17..249

   My Decision.. 249

Chapter 18..260

   The Pain 260

Chapter 19..267

   My Sacrifice... 267

Chapter 20..273

   There is Light.. 273

Chapter 21..285

   Surprise 285

"Behind closed eyes,
Lies a wide–awake gaze"

Sensei Paul Milburn, 5th Dan Aikido

*Welcome to
The Bloodline,
Amelia*

Prologue

It was the year 1589. My mother Amelia Mireille was living in France with my father Jean Paul, in a quiet village just outside of Pertuis. She was six months' pregnant with me at the time. My parents heard whispers throughout the land that disease was ravaging entire villages and consuming people's lives, yet they did not attempt to leave.

When the unnamed disease arrived, it consumed most of the village and killed my father in the process. Distraught by his passing, my mother fell ill, and was taken care of by my grandmother, Zanette. She moved from a nearby village to care for her, and it is from her that I know the story of my birth. To speak of how she watched helplessly as her daughter writhed in agony and was taken from us so quickly always brought tears to her eyes, and so I did not often ask.

About a month had passed when my mother, by now heavy with child, saw her leg bore the bites of a flea. As the days passed it was obvious she had caught the disease. People were calling it *la peste Noir* as her skin greyed and black cysts appeared on her body, she felt her unborn child move strangely within her. Something was happening to me inside her belly, something unnatural. Sudden, sharp convulsions accompanied a tearing pain inside. She suspected that I too had contracted this deathly plague. Petrified and knowing she had little time, she begged my grandmother to save her unborn child. This, she knew, would kill her and that she would never see me grow up. She was however, more fearful for my life than her own.

My grandmother did as requested and cut me from her own daughter's belly. As one can imagine in a small, remote village ravaged by *la peste*, an infant born too soon was unlikely to survive but my grandmother performed her tragic duty well. Although I was born nearly two months early, and it was highly likely that I had contracted the disease, I somehow emerged alive. Zanette, not knowing if I would survive at such a premature age, placed me into my mother's arms and whispered into her ear, "You have a beautiful little girl, my darling." My mother weakly opened her eyes, stared down at me and, in a whisper, named me Zanette Amelia Mireille.

My mother died soon after, leaving me in the care of my grandparents. Given what remained of a village eaten up by disease, my grandparents knew they had to get me as far away as possible from the infection that was sweeping around us. Across the field, the *Peste* had taken an entire farming family. There they found an abandoned horse and cart and, loaded up with the barest chattels and provinder, they took me across France to a town called Provence were she and my grandfather Augustin raised me.

Augustin was a tall, slim man with curly, dark hair and green eyes with a few wrinkles around them. Grandmama, with a loving smile on her face and a twinkle in her eyes, always said that he was the handsomest man in her village. He had given her a red ribbon for her sixteenth birthday and they had become betrothed.

I stayed in Provence, living in a small wooden house by the side of a vast forest a couple of miles away from the centre of the town. My grandmother was strict but caring and taught me everything she knew, as schooling was hard to come by. She would take me on long nature walks and tell me all about my mother when she was a little girl, and the mischief she would get into. We would laugh together and she always made me feel like I had a connection to my mother, although I had no memory of her. But it also made me feel sad that the life I should have had with her was taken away from me. I suppose I felt angry at the world: that this could happen to such a lovely warm family and close community.

I remember one morning in my sixteenth year. My grandfather had taken me on one of his long hikes around the forest, pointing out all the spectacular specimens of creatures and flowers. I was never really interested but it made me happy to be with him and gave my grandfather a warm, happy glow to teach me things that he had repeated time and time again on our walks. It was approaching dinnertime and the sun was setting behind the trees so we decided to head back to the house. I was in for a big surprise as we entered the front door and grandmother was waiting with a homemade birthday cake. I had completely forgotten that it was my birthday and it gave me a warm and exciting feeling. I ran to my grandmother and embraced her. I breathed her in so deeply that I can still remember the smell of cooking on her apron, a mixture of sugar and spices. I was truly happy and content in our little dwelling. It comprised of an open area for cooking and sitting, a large area to sleep that was split in two by a piece of material so I had my own space, and a small wooden table and three chairs. It was basic, but when the embers glowed in our small–bricked fireplace, it created a warm and relaxing homely feel. I felt like I was home.

The following morning, I left my grandmother to go fetch some fresh water from the spring that was a couple of miles through the forest and which opened up to a beautiful clearing.

On some days I would sit for hours looking into the clear pools and seeing my reflection, my long, blonde hair shimmering in the crystal waters, big bright blue eyes and skin as white as snow. I was a slim, tall girl with a shapely face and blonde ringlets that flowed down to my waist. My grandmother always said I looked like my mother but with more symmetry and a beauty that she had never seen before. Gazing at the shallow sparkling waters, I imagined my mother's face staring back me: all the things she would say if she had still been with me. I felt my stomach tighten and my eyes starting to flow with tears. I sat wishing I knew her and the more I thought about her, the more I felt cheated.

I was so engrossed in my own thoughts that I didn't notice that several hours had passed and I was now so very late. I sat up suddenly and went to gather my shawl and fill the pail with water. Grandmama wanted it this morning, I thought suddenly worried.

As I made my way noisily out of the stream, I didn't hear them approach. A snapping twig made me whirl around. At first though I thought it was my grandfather looking for me as time had passed so quickly. However, when I turned around, three men stood before me dressed in filthy hunting clothes. The first man to approach me was a tall stocky man with grey hair and a long beard, carrying an axe. An enormous belt around his waist concealed a giant knife, the handle protruding. He had a scar that ran across his left eye down to the end of his mouth. He said:

"My, you seem a long way from the town. What's your name?"

I felt uneasy as the two men behind him stared at me with a look that made my blood run cold. I said:

"It's Zanette." Thinking quickly, I added, "My grandfather and I are collecting fruits for my grandmother."

The man who was closest to me said,

"You're a very pretty little thing aren't you? Maybe it would please you to let me and my men to sit with you while we wait for him. We have been working all day, with no rest."

The man moved over and stood in front of me but didn't sit, instead staring down at me with a gleam in his eyes that told me to run. I said

"I'm afraid I must go. I'd better find my grandfather – he's highly protective of me. Good day to you all."

I was about to move around him but he placed a hand on my shoulder.

"Stay here child – we can play a game if you like..."

I could feel my stomach churning and my eyes starting to fill up as fear passed through me.

"By my faith I must go, sir. I pray. Pray, sir!" I begged him.

The second man, who resembled the first and could have been a brother to him, carried a brace of dead rabbits. He stepped closer to me and said, "I'm afraid we must insist."

Before I knew it, the one in front pushed me to the floor while the other two grabbed an arm each side of me. I started screaming and crying out for someone to help.

"No one can hear you my child. Such a pretty thing... and, I would guess, untouched..."

All I could do was try to plead with this man . "Please, no!" I said shaking with fear. The man stood and took off his jacket. I could feel my nerves jumping in my body and my face was soaked in the tears that streamed down my face.

"Now, now, little one – this will be over sooner if you don't struggle."

Before I could say another word, the man on my right forced some rags into my mouth whilst the one on my left raised his fist and hit me across the face. I fell to the ground, a blinding pain landed on the side of my head. My face lay in the damp soil. The last thing I remember, as darkness crept into my world, were the opaque eyes and distended mouths of three little dead rabbits...

*

I woke up lying by the side of the spring, my clothes ripped open, a burning sensation between my legs. I looked down to see they were covered in blood and there were red blotches of hand marks all over my thighs. I started to cry again, bringing my knees up to my chest and hugging myself. I could feel the coolness of the evening sky as the sun had almost disappeared behind the trees. I felt so ashamed and scared. I stumbled to my feet and went to wash my legs in the spring. I had the deepest feeling that I had been punished for an unknown misdeed. I waded deeper into the spring, unable to wash away my feelings of devastation. Intensely I poured through my memories for what I could possibly have done to deserve such an attack. I kept thinking to myself, is this my fault? It must be my fault. Had I done any single thing, however small, to encourage them? I lay down in the water, unsure whether to stand up ever again. My mind was in turmoil, turning over and over until I thought I might run mad with it all. It would not stop. I could not make it stop. I let the cool waters flow over me and prayed to God for His love to come for me.

*

I was suddenly aware that I was late. Very soon, if I did not return, my grandfather would be out looking for me. I was determined that he would not find me like this. His frail heart would surely break. It was only the thought of my beloved grandparents that gave me the strength to lift myself out of the water. The blood was gone but I was not sure if my feelings of revulsion and dirt would ever lift from me.

Still shaking and unable to walk very well, I managed to tidy myself up and stumbled all the way back home, outside of myself, as if in a dream, a very dark dream. Every creek of a tree and rustle of leaves made my heart beat so fast I thought I would pass out again. At that moment I had never felt more alone and scared in my life. I recited aloud my prayer over and over, *"If I should die before I wake, I pray the Lord my soul to take…"*

I resolved not to tell my grandparents what had happened. Would they even believe me? I cried anew at the thought of their sorrowful eyes, seeing me differently.

*

I was suddenly at the front door and it was as if I could only vaguely recall my journey there. I stood quite still and gathered myself. I tied my hair back and forced a smile as I entered.

I was met immediately by the sight of my grandfather sitting at the table, his head shaking in his hands, wailing:

"Why her, why not me?"

Again panic rose in me. I slowly walked in, closing the door gently behind me. My grandfather looked up, his eyes red and puffy. He moved his chair back to walk over to me. I stood with my body jumping and finally said:

"Grandpapa, what on earth is the matter?"

My grandfather looked at me, took hold of my arm and steered me to a chair by the table.

"Sit down child I have some terrible news."

I sat down with my eyes fixed on his. He couldn't meet my gaze but stared instead at the back of the house where we slept. The curtain was pulled round their bed and I could hear what seemed to be my grandmother coughing, yet she sputtered loudly and strained to breathe. *Oh God – is that Grandmama?* I thought. I looked up to see my grandfather had taken a seat on the opposite side of the table with his hand stretched out. I took it, and he squeezed my hand, gently.

"Your grandmother has had an accident today whilst out at the market.

"She collapsed and, and… They brought her back here and laid her on the bed. There's a physician from the town examining her."

I could see by the look in his eyes that my grandmama must have been in a terrible state when she arrived back home.

"Grandmama! Will she recover?"

For the third time that day my eyes, already sore from crying so much at the spring, started to fill up again. I heard the curtain draw back.

"Monsieur Mireille?"

My grandfather pushed his chair back and stood up facing the doctor.

"How is she? Will she recover?"

The physician looked at him for a time before answering. He was a small, rounded man with short hair and a brown beard slightly peppered with grey. Sweat was smeared across his brow. His sleeves were rolled up and blood covered his hands. Small red droplets had sprayed his shirt. My heart lurched as I realised my grandmama had been coughing up blood.

"I have done everything I can for her, but I am told that when she collapsed in the market, a wooden barrel broke her fall, piercing her chest. I'm afraid there is not much more I can do. I have cleaned her and dressed the wound. Her breath shortens as her chest fills with blood

"... Monsieur Mireille, you must prepare yourself – it is only a matter of time before she drowns from this fluid..."

My grandfather went white and was fixed to the spot, staring at the doctor. Finally his legs seemed to give way beneath him and he fell to his knees. He reached out for support, and caught the doctor's leg. "Pray – there must be something you can do, you can't just leave her to die!"

"I'm sorry, Monsieur Mireille, there is nothing more I can do. I really am most deeply sorry."

The doctor broke free and walked towards me. "Take good care of him my dear," he spoke softly.

And he was gone, softly closing the door behind him. My grandfather sat on the floor, a look of despair covering his face. I was frowning in confusion.

"Why was she at the market? I was getting the water. I said I would bring her the water..." My voice trailed off.

I whispered, "Oh sweet Jesus in heaven, what have I done? I should have come straight back this morning." I ran to my grandfather's side and held onto him. "Grandpapa, it is my fault! I was out too long. She shouldn't have gone all the way to the market. Her heart wasn't strong enough. Grandpapa! I'm so sorry! I'm so sorry."

"Now, now child..." was all he could softly utter as he stared, in a trance, in the direction of his wife.

pa, let me help you up. You must go to her. She

andfather looked up at me, nodded and pushed up from the floor, steadily moving towards the closed curtains around the bed, as if unready to face what he would find there. I sat back on my chair, staring at the low flames of the fireplace, not knowing what to think... I felt numb, lifeless. I turned to look at my grandfather now at my grandmother's side, holding her hand and smoothing her hair back from her face. I had never seen anyone lie so still as she did that day. My grandfather laid his head down on the bed, cradling her hand and sobbed quietly.

My grandmother was so quiet. Occasionally a crackle could be heard. It tore our hearts to hear her struggle to breathe and we knew her time was short. We both wept in silence not wanting her to sense our sorrow in the final moments of her life. She only had the strength of a few hours before slipping away later that evening. We continued to pray after she had gone until the light appeared at the window. A new day was beginning but we could not bear to face it. Our hearts had been laid at her side the previous evening.

*

My grandfather was never the same. Part of him could not let grandmama go. It was as if his spirit walked away with hers, their vows unbroken, even in death. He would not leave the house, did no work, and did not hunt for food. He barely spoke and I couldn't bear to look into his eyes and see the hurt there, a hurt that I felt responsible for. I realised that I would have to find my own source of strength in order to support him. At the age of sixteen I was looking after my grandfather and my home all on my own. He would sit and stare for hours at the empty fireplace. Days passed where he hardly ate or said a word. The days turned to months; the seasons came and went.

*

Little by little my grandfather started speaking again as his spirit returned to the present, to our little cottage, to life. I hated to see him like this and my worries for my one remaining relative overshadowed the passing of my grandmother. I felt that I had hardly mourned her because there was always work that I had to do, otherwise I do believe we would have perished that winter. Perhaps I was still in a state of shock, putting all my own cares to the back of my mind and going through the motions of a life, hoping for some light to return to it.

Time passed in this way uneventfully. I continued to look after us both, cooking, cleaning, chopping wood and hunting food. I had never returned to the spring since that terrible day. It took all my strength to leave the cottage for the few essentials that we needed to stave off hunger. I kept to myself, somehow frightened to look people in the eye, as if by doing so all the pain would pour out of me in a loud, black torrent of despair. I now went to market to quickly collect water from the well, and returned home as soon as possible. It was a journey longer by three miles but I preferred this to the thought of ever going back to the spring. It was tiring, but over time, it slowly began to give me some small sense of freedom from my own worries about Grandpapa and provided a break from my chores at the house.

I was usually so tired by the end of the day that I too would only eat a mouthful before falling into a slumber down on my straw bed, too tired to think or plan the days ahead.

Chapter 1
The Beginning

Zanette Amelia

It had been just such a day in midwinter. I had fallen into a deep sleep one night, when something awoke me from my slumber...

It was the dead of night. I stood listening to the sounds of the forest as the moon shone *through* the treetops and the clear sky above showed off the distant stars. I became aware of hearing the smallest sounds. I was surrounded by a cacophony of movements of animals and insects, shuffling and crawling, seeking food and a mate. I heard hogs grunt, bats call, moths kiss the air with their wings, the glissando of spiders at their tapestries.

A soft wind raised my skin and arose in me a shiver. The night embraced me, closed my eyes and wrapped me in its damp, earthy perfumes as I breathed. My senses popped with the sweet, raw smell of prey. I felt truly alive. My nose traced streams of the aromas in the air; my dark, wide eyes darted back and forth to pinpoint the direction of the mesmerising scent. I began to run. I felt at one with the energy of the Earth, as if she were giving me her full power. Her energy pulsated through the forest and into me as if we were the same animal. Blood coursed through my veins as I leapt through thickets and over fallen branches, their thorns and bracts tearing my skin as I pushed undeterred through overgrown ferns and slipping through the trees until I arrived at an opening.

A man stood alone and still, staring away from me into the dense woodland. I couldn't see his face. His scent was rich and my mouth flooded with expectant saliva. I was momentarily confused at my feelings but at the same time it felt normal, right. I stole up behind him, but he didn't even turn. I noticed the forest around me became eerily quiet, no mouse shuffled, no fox leapt, no sound could be heard except the clear, stark thumping of his heart.

I felt my mouth open and down came long slender fangs. I ceased seeing him as a person. At that moment he meant one thing only to me: food. I stroked the back of his neck and inhaled his deep, musky scent, yet still he did not move. I felt my hands wrap around his throat to pull him closer. I squeezed tighter and heard the rasping of liquids rushing up and down inside his neck. I leaned into the sound of the rhythmic beat calling out from his body. Only then did his head turn towards me. I knew the face only too well. The intense noises of the forest at night ceased in an instant as I froze in shock... "Grandpapa!"

My eyes flew open and I found myself in my bed, just as I had been. The horrible vision scuttled away. Shocked, I sat up and calmed myself, relieved it was only imagined, and now at an end. I felt a chill and reached down to pull up the blanket. As my arms brushed past my nightgown, I suddenly felt the cold, wet cloth. My heart started to beat faster as I quickly became fully awake and leaned over to light a candle at the side of my bed. Squinting in the bright light, I saw a great pool of crimson – blood covered my nightgown. I felt a scream rising but held it down for Grandpapa's sake. I jumped out of bed, shaking with fear. Open–mouthed in bewilderment and feeling faint, I pulled out my nightgown to see the extent of the blood. It ran from the neck to hem. Panicking, I moved my hands around my body through the soaked gown but I could not feel any injury – no cuts or wounds, and no pain coming from any part of me. I lifted my nightgown but my legs were clean. I ran to the kitchen to get a cloth, feeling sick at the smell.

Images rushed into my mind of that day at the spring and the passing that same day of my grandmother. I shook with fear, not knowing why these images were in my head, and what on earth had happened to me to end up this way. And what of my beloved grandpapa? Had I harmed him too?

Out of the small kitchen window, I noticed the moon. It was a clear sky and it shone through, reflecting my face in the glass. It was then I noticed it. With horror I saw my face around my mouth was also covered in blood. I stared at myself, wide–eyed, trying to imagine what could have happened.

My grandfather stirred in his bed. Thank God he was safe. But a thousand questions flooded into my mind. What kind of monster was I? What had I done? Who had I hurt? I peered out of the window to see if I could see anybody lying hurt outside, or any evidence at all of my terrible deeds, but there were none. No trace at all of anything unusual. I shook my head, confused.

I found a cloth, dipped it in our pail of water, quietly wiped my face and body and changed my nightgown before my grandfather saw the horrorful sight. Luckily he didn't get up, just murmured,

"Zanette is that you? Is all well my dear?"

"Yes Grandpapa – quite well – I wanted a little water, that is all. You go back to sleep."

He didn't say anything after that. I heard him turn over and fall back asleep.

Still confused with what just happened – and how it could have happened – I went to lie back down. I could go and find out tomorrow. I placed the covered nightgown and cloth under my bed and laid back, wondering what had just happened to me. I would have to go to the river to wash it tomorrow. I stared up into the darkness, unable to sleep, desperately reaching for explanations… Perhaps I had bitten my tongue or had a loose tooth? There was some pain in my upper teeth. I tried to reason it away, but I could not convince myself.

I was still awake when the sun started to rise. I decided to get up and make breakfast before my grandpapa woke up.

That day things went on as normal. I went to explore our surroundings for any trace of a fight, a dead animal, or an attack, at least some blood, but I found nothing. Only my mouth felt somewhat bruised. I took my nightgown to the river. It washed away any trace of blood, and I could imagine once more that I was just like everyone else.

I arrived at the market mid-afternoon to fetch more water and exchange food for the firewood that I had chopped the day before. As I filled my bucket at the well, I once more became aware of a growing ache in my mouth. It intensified within a very short time until I felt like my gums were on fire and being ripped open. The feeling was excruciating. Suddenly dizzy, and fearful of fainting, I sat at the well with a cloth to my mouth. I noticed there was blood on it. I swilled my mouth with water but the pain grew until it was blinding.

I decided to quickly make my way to the home of the physician to ask for help but there was nobody in. I was dizzy and scared and sat down at the threshold as my legs began to give way. I didn't know what was happening to me. All of sudden a woman approached me from behind and said:

"Are you quite well, my dear? You look like you are in pain?" She was a young woman, perhaps ten years older than myself, with brown hair tied back and carrying a basket of vegetables under her arm.

I jumped at her question. I was still so shy of talking to others. "I–I seem to have a problem with my mouth – it's very painful…"

The woman put down her basket and knelt in front of me, saying, "Let me have a look, dear."

I recoiled from her touch but, after another surge in pain brought tears to my eyes, I opened my mouth whilst she looked inside.

"Goodness dear your top gums are red raw – you must have caught them on something very sharp…"

As I looked at her, something made me think of Grandmama. Perhaps it was her warm eyes, a kindness that I recognised.

"Would you like me to walk you home, you look like you could use the help?"

I shook my head as the pain began anew. "No – it is nothing – thank you. So kind of you to ask. But I'm sure I'll shall be well."

"Very well dear, you make sure you go straight home and rest. You don't want any dirt in your mouth. Keep washing it and if it gets any worse come and see my husband."

I looked up at her. "Your husband?"

"Yes dear – the physician."

Feeling overwhelmed with memories, I started to cry.

"My dear what on earth is it?"

I blinked back the tears. "I believe I have already met him. He came to see to my grandmother who passed away shortly afterwards."

The woman stroked my cheek, pushing my tears away and moving tendrils of my hair aside. For a moment, I could have believed it to be the touch of my grandmother. All my tension vanished as I let in her warmth and compassion.

"Oh, my dear. I'm so sorry to hear that." She embraced me warmly.

"There now, my sweet. It is a terrible thing losing a loved one. Life has a strange way of running things. The older you get, the more thankful you become for what you have, and how important family is." She dabbed my tears away with her kerchief and I began to breathe more calmly. "Don't forget, there are many here who will help, should you require it."

She gave me a warm smile before disappearing into the crowd. I didn't even notice that the pain had stopped in my mouth. I collected the water and headed home.

The next morning I awoke to sounds coming from the kitchen. I got out of bed and pulled back my curtain to find my grandpapa cooking breakfast. I stared at him in shock. He turned and said:

"Breakfast is nearly done. Come my beloved girl: sit and I'll serve up."

Still startled by what I was witnessing, I wondered if I was still asleep and dreaming.

"...with me?"

I blinked and found my grandpapa staring at me, holding out a bowl of porridge. "Sorry?"

"Are you still with me?"

I looked at him and blinked. "Oh yes, of course – sorry I must have been day dreaming." I was walking to the table when everything seemed to fall away into blackness...

*

"Zanette! Zanette! Oh God – please let her wake up. Zanette can you hear me?"

I awoke to find I was lying on my bed with my grandpapa sitting beside me, a cool damp cloth in his hand, pressed to my forehead.

"Zanette! Thank God. My sweet girl – are you back with us again?"

The room came back into focus and I could now make out the concerned face of my grandfather. I smiled at the sight, still a little drowsy. "Yes I think so – what happened?"

"You fell in the kitchen. You must have hit your mouth, little one.

"There was some blood. I shall bring some water. Rest here." He headed to the kitchen.

But something was wrong. I could feel it within me. The room was spinning, my eyes lost focus and the light was so bright I had to pull the covers over my face to hide from it.

"There we are – some fresh water!"

"Grandpapa. It's the light," I said, "it's blinding me."

I could hear him move around the room and pull the curtains around my bed. "How's that?"

I peeled back the covers to find the room was dimmer. Grandpapa stood over me with a cup of water. "Much better thank you."

"Here have some water, you took a nasty fall back there."

I sat up and swilled my mouth out first before having a drink.

What on earth...? Is she unwell? Maybe I should get the doctor or ...

'Swounds! I don't know what to do....

"You don't need to do anything, I'll be fine."

He looked at me for a moment. "I didn't say anything..." I felt very puzzled and watched his face while he stared at me with worried eyes.

What if her head has been hit too hard and she fades away?

"Of course I won't fade away! I'm just a little woozy, that's all."

My grandpapa came closer to sit next to me and placed the cloth on my forehead. "Of course you won't what, child?"

I looked into his eyes and I could see that he was puzzled as well. "Fade away. Trust me I shall recover soon enough."

He stood up sharply, suddenly serious, and a little afraid. "Zanette... I never said that out loud... I only thought that."

I looked at him and pulled myself up resting on my elbows. "I'm sorry, Grandpapa, I don't understand?"

He turned and wiped his own brow with the cloth before facing me again. "Zanette I'm going to try something, so just stay still for a moment..."

I looked at him and wondered to myself if his concerns were finally getting to him.

What is your favorite colour my little squirrel?

I giggled and smiled at him. "Squirrel? Erm, blue I think, why?"

He just stared at me, still serious, and my smile faded.

"What is it, Grandpapa?"

"Zanette... I – I don't know what's happening to you but I asked that question in my mind only. I did not say it aloud. I wonder if your fall has done some damage. I mean it's... impossible... It has to be... it's impossible."

"What is? You're not making any sense." I was starting to worry about him but then I remembered. I had been looking at him the whole time and could swear that I did not see his mouth move. No... This couldn't be right. "Grandpapa I... I..."

He moved towards me, when, from nowhere—

"Aaaaargggggghhhh...!" I moaned in pain again, suddenly.

"Zanette? Zanette!" he cried.

The pain ripped through me like a hot knife stabbing my body. It felt like my skin was on fire. My eyes burned with a sensation I had never felt before. My mouth sprang open to reveal two long teeth pushing their way through my gums. I tasted the blood in my mouth and it made its way down my throat. My body arched and convulsed on the bed, my hands and feet clenching as the pain rippled through my body. I felt as if every muscle was being pulled on the rack. The pain was overwhelming. My heart pounded so hard and fast in my chest that I thought it would spring out of my body and smash into the wall. I couldn't hear or see anything. All I knew was the pain. *Oh God – what's happening to me?* I thought.

It seemed to go on forever. I was panting hard, and sweat poured from my brow. Now I was crawling around the bed, trying to find a position that would lessen the agony. I was suddenly hot, suddenly cold and shivering. I covered myself in the blanket and tore it off again, when the next minute, just as quickly, the heat overwhelmed me. It shot through my arms and legs and I collapsed, still struggling to pull in deep, heavy breaths through my mouth. I prayed that it would end, or that the Good Lord would spare me the torture and take me to Heaven there and then.

"Grandpapa! Grandpapa!" I sobbed.

He clung onto my still body, trying to keep me alive and safe."My darling Zanette. Lord save her! Oh my darling girl!"

And then, just as suddenly, it stopped. I dropped out of wakefulness like a stone in a stream and fell into a deep sleep, exhausted.

*

"What do you think Doctor? She's been like this for some time now."

"Monsieur Mireille, I can't answer that at the moment. She seems so pale and thin. Her skin is like paper. She appears to have lost blood, yet I am unable to determine where it has gone. I'm afraid this is in God's hands now."

Again this man has been in my home and still has not helped us. First my wife and now my granddaughter. Why did I bother?

"Will you wait with us? Will you take a drink of water, Doctor?" *I hope not!*

"Erm, no... Thank you. I will leave you to tend your granddaughter."

I haven't the faintest idea what caused this. Maybe growing pains? A bit extreme though... It will be a relief to leave this house and this demanding old fool. How should I know what's wrong with her? The silly thing probably ate a toadstool. I shall give an excuse: He'll never know.

"I will look into this matter further."

"Very well Doctor. Thank you for calling."

Now get out and stop wasting our time you mountebank! You charlatan!

"Can you find the way back to the road?"

"Yes I'll be fine thank you. I'll see you soon, Monsieur Mireille."

Thank God he's gone what a waste of time... I should never have invited him here.

"Zanette, my child? Zanette...? Can you hear me?"

I became aware of something cold and wet on my forehead and came back to wakefulness. Grandpapa was wiping my brow. "Grandpapa – I... I... feel strange..."

I opened my eyes to see him, still sitting at my side, holding my hand. I looked around the room, my vision dim and blurred at first as I slowly grew fully alert. Then out of the dark monochrome suddenly a shock of colour flooded my vision. I could feel my eyes focusing as they swept around the room bringing everything into view with sharp detail.

I could see the woodworm moving in and out of holes in the roof and smell the damp, woody shavings they left behind. Lint would flicker in my vision and I could see the shape and colour as it passed. I saw every line around Grandpapa's face, every pore. I could even see his transparent warm breath as it escaped his mouth and disturbed the air in front in ripples. I heard his eyes blink and the heavy beating thud of his heartbeat, racing.

"Thank God, I thought I had lost you. Let me look at you. How are you feeling? Oh...! But you look... different, Zanette – your eyes are such a piercing shade of blue... glowing, in fact... I have never seen eyes like that before. And somehow you look all grown up, so very strange, more like a woman than you did only a few short days ago." He looked so worried and I could tell by the expression on his face that something must be wrong in the way I looked.

"Days?" that caught my attention. "What do you mean days?"

He looked at me and said,

"My child, you have been in a deep sleep for three days. We could not wake you. If it weren't for your heart beating, I swear you looked... well... You looked pale and were as still as stone. I thought the good Lord had taken you from me. For a moment, at least."

I could hear his heartbeat starting to slow and return to normal. I shifted up onto my elbows again and placed a hand on his face. He flinched and raised his hand to cover mine. "My God dear – you're freezing. Let me get some more blankets."

I took my hand away as he stood. "Grandpapa I'm fine, I'm quite warm."

He turned and stood looking at me. "How are you feeling?"

I sat there thinking for a moment and finally said, "I feel more alive, energetic."

He turned towards the kitchen. "I'll be right back my child; I'll get you some water."

I watched as he went to the kitchen, poured a cup of water and brought it back to me.

"There you are. I'll make you something to eat. You must be starving." I took the cup of water from him, placed it to my lips and took a sip. As soon as the water touched my lips, my body started to shake. The taste of the water was foul yet I could smell how clear and fresh it was. It made no sense.

"What is it Zanette? What's the matter?"

I placed the cup back in his hand and said, "I'm sorry, I can't drink it – it is turning my stomach."

He looked at me and then sniffed the water. He placed the cup to his lips and took a sip. "Tastes fine to me. I wonder if some delirium has come upon you?" He bent down and placed a hand on my forehead.

"You are still so cold, my child. Perhaps I should recall the doctor." He bent down to kiss my cheek. I felt my heart starting to beat faster, as if the dread fever may come upon me again. Somewhere I heard a heartbeat. My memory of the events that followed haunted my mind with dark nightmares for decades afterwards. I felt as if I was somehow a witness to the terrible event, as if I had moved aside and another being had stepped in and taken over my body.

As his face approached, my eyes fixed on the vein in his neck. It seemed to be pulsating right off the skin. I felt my mouth starting to water, my lips being forced open by my growing teeth. I felt the soreness that came with it as they sliced through my gums and continued to grow. The smell of him overpowered me. I was covered in a cloud of sweet, tangy scents buzzing around me, drawing me in. I could feel the hypnotising rhythm of the blood pumping through his body. My back arched as if a magnet was pulling me towards him.

He looked into my eyes as he leaned in to care for me and immediately stopped, quickly jumping back. "Zanette – your eyes! What's wrong with your eyes?"

He looked terrified but all I knew was how famished I was. The burning sensation in my throat was as dry as if I had been wandering lost across parched sands and had had no water for days. Every part of my body cried out wildly, aching for food.

"Your eyes are blood red... Your... My God! What is wrong with your mouth? Your teeth!"

I didn't hear his words: I focused intently, closely following his movements, as if he were my prey.

This isn't right – I need to get help. She must be possessed. Why is she looking at me like that?

I slowly rose from my bed and stood listening to his thoughts.

Oh God! Run! Run now and get help! Get to the door!

My eyes were fixed only on him as he hurried away. Something in him must have recognised the danger of staying by my side. He looked terrified. I knew he was also scared for me because he didn't know what was happening. But neither did I. My mind was filled completely with one thing only – the need to feed. It felt like I was existing purely on instinct and didn't have control over myself. I was a prisoner in my own body, watching and feeling everything that was going on around me. He turned and ran for the door.

Stop! I called out in my mind. My thoughts seemed to come together in what I could only term as my will. It felt like a strange surge of power flowing out of me and into the room. It took a lot of my strength as it left my body. What I was willing to happen using only my thoughts was indeed happening here in front of me. Grandpapa stopped. He was a few feet from his escape, and stood motionless, staring vacantly ahead.

I found myself moving towards him with the intent to feed. It felt so natural to me. In the furthest part of myself a faint voice protested, but was ignored. I stood behind him lowering my head to his neck. I placed a hand on his head and tilted it to one side. I sank my teeth into his neck. A sudden rush of hot blood filled my mouth. I felt empowered as it moved quickly around my body. The taste was exquisite and addictive. I drew more and more from his open neck. I felt delirious, carried along by the experience when suddenly I became aware of what I was doing. I pulled back, awake and present, my entire body shaking.

My grandfather slid to floor, lifeless. "Oh my God what have I done? Grandpapa!"

I knelt down and turned him over. His eyes were frozen open in fear. I couldn't hear his heartbeat.

"Grandpapa... Oh God – please let him recover! Grandpapa!" I cried out, shaking him. Nothing. He didn't move. My eyes filled with tears and the feeling of utter dread filled me. I had killed him. My own grandpapa... the most loving person in my life. My mind flooded with memories of my beloved grandpapa, his constant presence, always by my side, teaching me, guiding me, protecting me. I had repaid his deep love of me by ending his life.

I stepped back in disbelief, shaking, staring at his lifeless body by the door. I couldn't move. I was frozen in shock, all my nerves jumping as realisation spread through my body in jarring ripples. I stood there and time stood still. The room was beginning to get dark and I could see light escaping behind the trees outside the window. I didn't know what to do to. I knew if I went to get help I would receive the punishment I truly deserved. Yet something held me back, rooted to the spot. A creeping devastation crawled over my flesh as I stared ahead in shock. I heard the long howl of a wild animal in the surrounding forest, moaning quietly at first, then building into a loud cry of deep pain and realised with fright that the sound was coming from within me.

I now had nobody, no family, and no friends, thrown into a situation I didn't understand. What was wrong with me? I couldn't believe that I had done this terrible deed – not to him – my only flesh and blood. My God – that word – blood, it made me shiver with repulsion. Was he right? Am I possessed? Yet I knew I wasn't an evil person: I loved him dearly, I couldn't be. On some level though, I had been aware of my actions. My mind raced back and forth, twisting in agony at the nightmarish memories that now polluted every part of it. I could find no hiding place from it. I couldn't come to terms with it.

I felt like I had divided into two people. I was the person I remembered as a young girl, growing up and carefree, in love with my life at home with my grandparents. And then, after that day at the spring, after the passing of my grandmother, another half of me had begun to develop.

She was afraid and quiet. She was sad and couldn't make friends. She couldn't bear to leave the house for very long; she worried about her grandfather departing this life and leaving her completely alone.

It was as if evil had pierced the furthest reaches of my deepest being and had now grown to take hold of my heart, and control my life.

I began to burn with fury at the injustice of this wicked part of myself. Where had the carefree little girl gone? I used to be so happy. We did not have a great deal but we always had so much love, such laughter. Now I had nothing. I had nobody. It had all been taken away from me. Now I felt as if half of me had died and was haunting the other half. I imagined all the damage I could bring down upon the heads of the men who had attacked me. Once more I found myself churning with vengeance. Curses spat from my mouth as I called forth the wrath of the elements, of thunder, of lightning, begging them to assist me in my quest to torture, to maim these evil dogs. They had ended my life as I had known it. I screamed with rage and felt the whole cottage shudder.

The twin spirits of hot rage and squirming fear wrestled inside me. I grabbed a burning length of wood from the fireplace and started to light the little wooden house that I had lived in for so long. Fire quickly swept through the building, filling the air with smoke. Surrounded by a circle of fire, I took a look at my grandfather and noticed something shining around his neck. I pulled off the necklace and slowly laid his head back down. I kissed him on the forehead for one last time.

"Forgive me, dearest Grandpapa." I left and did not look back.

I ran towards the dirt road a few miles ahead that led to the centre of town. Behind me I could hear the roar of the fire as it consumed my childhood home, and my beloved grandpapa.

The sun had already set by this time and the cool air flowed around me, the gentle breeze sweeping the tears from my eyes. I remembered all the things we used to do together, just we three: my grandpapa, my grandmama and me. I had with me only the clothes on my back and the necklace, which I vowed would never leave me.

I look back now sometimes, trying to remember everything that happened all those years ago. Perhaps things would have been different if I had lived the life of everyone else, if I had known my mother and father, married at sixteen, had children... Recalling memories from over 400 years ago takes time. My youth was eventful: too eventful. It was over too quickly and I found myself alone. Knowing what I know now, I can only guess at the events that triggered me to change, to grow, perhaps even to evolve? I am jumping ahead. I have not told you about how I became the way I am today.

You will recall the terrible disease that spread through my village. As my mother carried me, she became infected and naturally thought her child was in danger of being consumed by the ravaging menace. Yet I survived. My grandmother always told me it should have killed me. This she did not say to hurt me but with a look of wonder in her eyes at our good fortune, especially in the face of tragedy. She said I was special, like a miracle from God. I know that her goodness led her to come to this conclusion. She could not have understood the darkness that was present at the very beginning of my creation.

As *la peste* made its way into every cell of my mother's body, I now know with certainty that I should have become infected. But, instead of killing me, I believe I adapted to it, grew with it, used it to give me strength. It was a virus that would survive at all costs. It made me thrive, as it had thriven throughout the whole of Europe and Russia. The heavy price that I had to pay was my mutation. I was changed as a result, into something that was not fully human. Just as those who were bitten became sick, I became that sickness in human form while still in my mother's belly.

I still seek answers even after all these years. I was often told in my youth that I possessed a power and beauty that mesmerised people. At the time, I found it flattering. I remember that day in the market when I encountered the physician's kind wife. It never occurred to me until now that I was being stared at in a strange way by the people standing by. I thought they were concerned for a girl with a bleeding gum. Anyone might stare when someone is in pain. With experience, I believe they stared at me because I was different. On the outside I appeared to be like them yet there was something, some quality they couldn't quite name, something beautiful and strange…

And so I came to leave my home burning behind me, and headed away from Provence, travelling north on foot and being offered the occasional ride along the way. All I wanted to do was get as far away as possible. I wasn't sure what my plan was, I just left and travelled day and night, sleeping under trees and in barns that I encountered. I did not sleep really, but spent my time in thought, coming to terms with the past.

The urge to feed that I had first encountered at home became more and more frequent. It was a compulsion I felt little ability to control. This left a destructive trail behind me.

It was when I reached Amiens in northern France that I heard villagers were following my trail believing that *la peste noire* was once again upon them and seeking out the source. In truth it was I, feeding and leaving the bodies wherever I found them. Perhaps I should have hidden their remains but I did not think to.

From Amiens I moved further north to the docks in Brittany hoping to find a way out of France and into another land where I might be able to start a new life. I kept myself to myself and changed my name so many times that I almost lost myself in the process. My identity was fluid as I lived lie after lie. In one town I was the sole survivor of a village near Paris. In another I was searching for my father, the Compte. In a time when people rarely ventured away from their birthplaces, I was forever searching for a persona that would not arouse suspicion. I hoped that changing my name frequently would keep me safe by ensuring that any pursuers would find a cold trail as each identity disappeared.

By the turn of the year 1606, I arrived in the town of Brittany after travelling months on foot never tiring, never sleeping, just feeding and walking. It was a strange feeling never getting tired or wanting to sleep. I looked back on my old life in Provence and remembered how exhausted I had been at the end of the day, of how I fell immediately, soundly asleep until the dawn woke me. I used to yearn for an hour longer to rest, yet now I required none. On the contrary, at nights I seemed more alive, sharper and more focused than during the day.

At Brittany docks I managed to talk my way on board a ship bound for England. I was to cook one hot meal a day for the sailors in part payment of the passage. It was a daily struggle being on board with a captive crew yet being unable to feed on them. To do so would quickly result in discovery and my swift death. Over the past few months, however, I had managed to control my thirst, not completely but enough that I could get through one day at a time without pouncing on anyone and giving myself away. I noticed that I was losing strength as the days passed. Trying not to feed was tormenting my body and not eating was making the crew mildly suspicious. By now an accomplished liar, I waved away their questions by saying I ate in the galley. In reality though, it was getting to the stage where I had to do something or I would have passed out...

One day the grasping sensations that stalked my mind and wrung my stomach were so all–encompassing that I finally took desperate action. The galley, where I cooked the meals, was regularly visited by rats. I lay in wait and flung my knife at one. It pierced the neck through and pinned the scavenger to the floor. I fell upon its stinking wet body, sucking its thick, still–warm blood into my mouth like it was nectar. It was foul and the act filled me with revulsion but had I not taken this course, I might have starved.

Chapter 2
The River Dour

Zanette Amelia

We were on our last few days' voyage to the River Dour, which later came to be known as Dover, home to majestic white cliffs that tower commandingly over the Channel.

It was 1606 and I was in my eighteenth year. According to the calendar chart on board ship, I noticed it was a few days short of my eighteenth birthday. I did not care enough to have kept a record: one day was much like another. Given the events of the last couple of years, I felt that time was of little importance. I managed to get by on the ship with very little to sustain me. When we finally docked I couldn't wait to get on to land to feed. It seemed to me that every person that passed within a few yards of me smelt divine.

I caught a ride with a sailor from my ship into town where he dropped me off just outside an inn. It was rather late and the clouds were forming overhead. A trickle of rain started to drop from the sky but I knew I must feed soon. I waved the sailor off and walked the streets of Dover looking for an easy kill.

I have turned into someone unrecognisable from who I was even three years ago. A consummate liar, a vagabond, a thief and at my lowest level I am a killer. Even after two years, killing people still evoked in me a sense of shame. I hated the thought, the admission that I was a murderer. I kill people for food. I used to try to justify it, to help me feel better about it. *At least I do not kill people out of anger or on a whim. I kill because I have to in order to survive.* Yet it is a hard compulsion to carry.

As the light faded and darkness spread across the town, I saw a young, thin beggar standing alone on the street, his hand held out, his eyes cast down at the ground and knew I had found my prey. I always go for the most vulnerable. They are weaker, easier to control and sometimes don't even put up a fight. The shadows, and my speed gave me an advantage. He never had a chance. Before he even knew I was there, I was on his throat, piercing his grimy skin, covering his mouth to stifle any noise.

He went limp very quickly, giving in to my superior will, as if I had done him a favour by choosing him to feast upon and ending a miserable existence. What saviour could do more? So I fed and it was just like the first time: the warm liquid rushing into my mouth, the power coursing through my veins, until my scalp, my fingers, even my toes tingled with pulsating energy. My strength returned quicker than it left me.

As time passed I became faster, lighter on my feet. There was no excess fat on my body, just sleek, sculpted muscle. I easily outran both humans and animals. My presence alone was enough to stop them in their tracks. My senses became keener as I became aware of a potential quarry, long before they were aware of my presence. No longer was I burdened by being at the mercy of my emotions as, growing in strength, I found I did not need them. I no longer needed fear and I felt like the situations were few that I couldn't overcome physically. The previous worries I had about my family disappeared, as I no longer had one. Anger was superseded, as people were unable to effectively wrong me. I had put all such feelings aside in favour of my growing powers. At least, I thought I had.

I spent some nights in Dover staying at the George Inn. I funded my stay by taking the money of people I fed on. It wasn't a lot, but it got me by.

I was walking through the streets one day and turned into Castle Street. I stopped in my tracks when I noticed Dover Castle sitting high on a stronghold as the focus of the town, its walls and square turrets a powerful defence against those who would try to attack this country. I remember thinking to myself, *one day I will have a castle and riches.* Of course there would be those who said that thoughts like these are simply silly daydreams. But such people did not know my will to power. Such people did not understand that I would never be weak again, never be the victim again, never have to bow and scrape to fit in. I knew with my whole being that I would have my own castle one day. I would have riches and servants. My determination would assure it. No one would get in my way. Let the naysayers come. Let them try to breach my walls.

It was then that I became aware of a unique scent, something I had never encountered before. I turned to see a man looking at me from across the street. He was smartly dressed in a black suit, white shirt and black shoes. It was a very plain outfit but yet it made him look very attractive. He was tall and slender with dark, short hair, parted at the side and a small, neatly groomed moustache. He was lightly sun–kissed, with green eyes and strong features. He walked over to me.

"Good afternoon, my lady."

"Good afternoon, sir," I said, taken further aback by just how attractive he was closer to me.

"I see you're admiring our beautiful castle. You must be a visitor. Have I guessed correctly?"

Trying to get my thoughts together I simply said, "Yes." My attraction to him had obliterated anything clever, witty or interesting that I might have said and I reprimanded myself, searching my mind for something better to say!

"My dear lady do you speak English?"

I frowned at him. "Yes of course I do, why do you ask such a question?"

He just stood smiling.

"I believe you're from France, are you not?"

"Why, yes I am. Is my accent so strong that you recognise it?"

The man came closer still and this time I again perceived the scent – a sweet, heady smell – that of his blood, which carried the smallest hint of plum. It was the strangest aroma I had encountered.

"Forgive me, I'm Jonathan Walker. Delightful to make your acquaintance."

I looked at him and I could feel my heart beating. This time it was not through hunger. "Charmed, sir."

He looked at me with those beautiful green eyes and said, "May I enquire as to your name?"

I couldn't breathe. A thousand different images swirled through my head. "Pardon me, Mr Walker, my name is Zanette, Zanette Mireille."

He smiled at me again. "What a beautiful name you have. It's a pleasure to meet you, my lady."

I smiled back and turned my head so he couldn't see me blush. Was I really blushing? Where was the strength I had been feeling only minutes ago?

"Please – call me John," he added.

"Very well, John. Well," I gasped for air. "It was lovely to meet you. I must be on my way."

He looked at me with a comforting smile. "May I have the pleasure of walking you to your home? It can be rather dangerous here at night for an unaccompanied young woman."

I remember thinking to myself that in all likelihood his concerns were groundless, but instead I found myself beaming, "Thank you that is very kind."

We walked down Castle Street and chatted about anything that came to mind. I didn't even notice that I had walked past the inn at which I was staying. The sun was setting and at that moment I realised that in my heart, an all–consuming feeling for this man was battling with a growing need to feed.

I said, a little too quickly, "I'm sorry but I must leave. Thank you for walking me back but I really must go." I walked rather quickly away from him.

"Wait – may I see you again?"

I stopped and turned to face the man, pausing briefly as I asked myself if I dared to do so. "Very well. I will be at the George Inn tomorrow evening."

Before he could say another word, I disappeared down a nearby alley.

That was close! I thought. Only then did it occur to me that I hadn't heard his thoughts while we were walking. I began to wonder if he did not think that much of me... *No doubt I will find out tomorrow...*

*

Jonathan Walker was left standing at the side of the road, watching the lady until she was out of sight. He had enjoyed a pleasant, though brief, stroll. *Very pleasant*, he noted, before walking home.

*

I moved swiftly to the docks and hid myself behind some large crates. I stood and watched ships docking and putting out to sea, my thirst getting stronger moment by moment. I watched various people as they moved around the docks, here, two sailors carrying a large heavy wooden chest, there, a young family all holding hands and asking directions of a ship's master. Again I looked for that solitary person... Being a lady on her own in a port, I had not long to wait before I heard the words I knew were coming, "Hello lovely lady."

It was a sailor walking alone on his way to the docks. I moved closer to him, smiling, not saying a word. The smile on his face suddenly disappeared as he saw my eyes.

"My lady – you don't look well – allow me to fetch help."

I didn't move. Inside me was a force building up, an energy I knew I could use to my advantage. It propelled out of me and across to where the sailor stood. It forced him to his knees. Like the others before him, he didn't move, nor did he speak. He did only as I willed. Speech was no longer important; I could project this power at will. The clouds where gathering far above our heads and I heard a slight rumble of thunder. The rain started, slow at first, then more and more heavy. I approached my prey and fed. This time I easily disposed of the body. I carried him to the dockside and slid his body silently into the water. He floated for a while before finally sinking to the depths. *This is going to be a lot easier*, I told myself, knowing now what I was capable of. Looking back I can see now how each small step of my journey led to a small loss of my humanity. At the time I could not, or perhaps would not, see it. All I thought of was survival. It was an instinctive existence, I was like an animal; I had little room for moralising.

*

Jonathan or John as he liked to be called was a Colonel in King James' army. He was a lot older than Zanette, being fifteen years her senior, though he did not seem it. He achieved the rank of general early in his life. He was an only child and an orphan, both his parents having passed away many years ago from fever. It made him sad that he had so few memories of his upbringing. He was sent away to school and then entered the army at fourteen. As a Colonel he enjoyed more opulent quarters away from the rest of the cavalry on site. He was not short of money; his parents had bequeathed him a good amount that provided him with comfortable surroundings. At thirty-three he longed to share his life with someone but had either been on assignment in foreign countries for the King, or had felt nothing the few times he had chatted with the daughters of suitable dignitaries.

The day he had met a beguilingly beautiful French lady called Zanette, however, he felt his fortunes changing in respect of love and family.

John found himself mesmerised by Zanette's unusual beauty. As he walked the short distance back home he thought about this striking young woman's engaging smile, her long blonde hair and piercing blue eyes. He had never seen anything like them. It had been a very ordinary walk to clear his thoughts. He had not planned to walk down Castle Street particularly. His leave for a few days had started and he ventured out to wassail with the other fellows. His duties in the Army were usually his priority and very often he had no desire to fraternise afterwards. What a strange day. Strange, but good.

*

I was sitting in the bar of the George Inn. It wasn't very busy that night, only a handful of people and a maidservant delivering drinks and collecting empty flagons and cups. I sat at the back of the taproom in a small cubicle. From there I could see the main doors and waited to see if John would come.

"What can I get thee?" A rough voice bellowed from above me. The serving woman stood with her hands on her hips, her cheeks bright with rouge. She was a small, round woman of around forty years old, however the strain of a hard life and too much beer had ravaged her face until she looked – at best – threescore.

"Just some water please." I looked up at the maidservant.

"Listen love I don't know where you're from but round here water doesn't pay the landlord."

The maidservant placed her hand on the table and leant in towards me. I must admit all I could smell was beer.

"A small cup of cider will be fine."

She walked away without saying another word. This place was certainly no castle. Everything was made of wood. There was a low light, leaving plenty of nooks dark enough to remain unseen. The shady clientele did not move from their mugs of ale, just stared at the liquid as the level went down, or gazed off into the middle distance and avoided eye contact. There was no interaction at all. It was as if a spell had been cast over the room. A loud thud pulled me out of my trance and I looked up to see the maidservant had slammed down my drink.

"I suggest you drink up and leave: we don't want any of your sort hanging around here. The men in here have enough money to pay for a good few drinks. I'm not having you taking any of it from them for a quick scuffle around the alleys. Do you mark my words?" her deep voice rasped.

I looked up at her and felt my face starting to rush with blood, my fingers curling underneath the table.

"Did you hear what I said?" she repeated.

I stood from the table, the energy inside filling me up with rage and wanting to burst out to crush this sour pudding that may once have been a woman. I projected the energy and it flooded out of me to surround the waitress, and beyond to the limits of the room.

"Now listen to me. You are to walk away and don't look back. If I catch you but *once* looking in my direction, you will have decided your fate for you."

The waitress, stunned, turned on her heels and slowly walked away towards the bar.

"Good evening, my lady." I turned to find Mr Walker, standing there with his coat in his hand and a hat in the other.

"Good evening, Mr Walker. I didn't see you come in"

He looked from me to the catatonic maidservant. "John, please," he reminded me. "Is everything well? You seem a little uneasy. Was that maid bothering you?"

I looked at him and then to her. "No, not at all, she was just bringing my drink."

For a moment he looked at the maidservant, who seemed to be avoiding his gaze. "Excuse me, if you wouldn't mind, I would like a large whisky."

The maidservant, in her aversion to physically facing me, didn't even acknowledge him.

"Please have a seat."

John seemed uneasy himself at this point. "Where are my manners? Please, Miss Mireille." He indicated the seat next to me. I glanced over to the bar and took my seat. He sat on the adjacent chair.

"Please, call me Zanette."

He smiled, which broke the spell suspending the room and in turn made me relax and smile back. "Very well, Zanette."

I stared at him for a short while before I realised that neither of us was talking. "I... I hope you didn't find it too difficult to find me."

"Not at all. I must pass this place nearly every week."

We sat chatting and exchanging life stories, some of which I admit I had to cover with untruths. He didn't seem to question what I was saying so I carried on. It was so easy to talk to him and I happily told him some of my past, some stories of my family and where I had lived in France. We did not notice time passing so quickly, or the bar slowly emptying of people. I became aware of a tall gentlemen hovering near us politely coughing, but reluctant to speak. Eventually he uttered, "Begging your pardon, sir, we are wanting to close up for the night."

John looked at him and smiled. "Yes of course." The man backed away. We stood together John and I, putting on our cloaks. "Would you like to join me for a picnic by the river tomorrow? Weather permitting of course!"

Without hesitation, I answered, "Yes, I would love that dearly." But then realisation hit me. Picnic? I had to do what I could to minimise the problem of not eating. "You'll forgive me if I don't eat very much. It's just that I'm quite particular… and I have such a small appetite…"

He just winked at me and said, "I'll have them prepare only the best and maybe then you will be tempted!"

We departed after that, making arrangements to meet at the river's edge at noon the next day. He offered to walk me home, so I confessed that I was staying here in this lowly place in a room above the bar. It didn't seem to matter to him. He gave a polite bow and left. I slowly made my way out of the bar and up to my room. I waited there for a while until all the lamps downstairs and up had been extinguished and I heard no more the footsteps of people making their way to bed. I then went out and fed.

It seemed like a long night, as if the sun was still enjoying his dream of yesterday and did not wish to rise. I was totally smitten by this man and couldn't wait for tomorrow to come. I sat on the edge of my bed looking out of the window, watching the clouds move by and the moon dance in the clear sky. It was a magical night and I began to feel at home again.

For the next few weeks we courted and I was blissfully happy to be with him. We never did make that picnic as luck would have it, as the heavens opened and it stayed like that for a several weeks. One fine Saturday afternoon though, we were strolling by the river when he stopped and turned to face me, suddenly serious and apprehensive.

"Zanette, my love, these past few weeks have been the most joyful of my life. You have my heart. I have a question to ask, and I have great hopes of a positive outcome." He knelt down on one knee. I started to breathe heavily, in anticipation, as I knew what was coming. "Zanette, would you do me the great honour of becoming my wife?" I was filled with emotions swimming through my heart and head. I stood there, staring at him, as if in a trance, overcome with delight and love. Yet, at the back of my heart, were the inevitable traces of darkness. I would later be distracted by concerns about my past, but for now I couldn't be gladder. A smile flew across my face as Finally, I answered him. "Yes! I would love to marry you. Yes."

I could see the delight in his eyes and he must have sensed too how happy I was. The very next month we married in a small church in the north of Devon, in his boyhood village. Not many people came and, as I didn't know anybody in England, nobody sat on the bride's side of the church. One or two old friends and men from his regiment were there.

The time for truth telling came later. On the day of our wedding, John told me that as he was a general in the army, he went where his orders commanded, from assignment to assignment. It meant moving around regularly, with no one place to call home for any length of time. It also meant that he could be away for long periods. I was a little disappointed that he had not told me this prior to our nuptials, but I nevertheless contentedly returned to the celebrations.

Shortly after we were married, he was posted to the north of Scotland and of course I moved with him, sailing north after our return to Dover.

We were happy. For a while at least.

*

John bought a cottage for us to live in, a lovely building of stone near the town of Halkirk in north-east Scotland. It had two floors. Two large rooms made up the downstairs: a big kitchen area and fire at the rear, a large sitting area and parlour and stairs in the middle of the house leading to a sleeping area above. The view from our doorway was entrancing, one could see for miles as we lived in the middle of a field with a dirt track that came up to the house.

The village wasn't far, just a couple of miles away. It had a handful of houses, a drapery, a smithy, and a small inn. There was a daily market. For the most part, I was in charge of the running of the house, and I happily made myself busy in making the soft furnishings and little touches that I thought John would like. It reminded me of my days looking after Grandpapa. If I felt lonely, it was only briefly, and I would go out into the woods or go to market to distract myself. When he was home though, my whole world was complete and we lived in love and contentment. I cooked for him and he ate every morsel. I prayed it would continue forever.

There was, however, the matter of my true nature. I was mostly able to hide it, except when I had to feed. When John was home, I always insisted on eating in private. My excuse was that if anything didn't agree with me, I didn't want him to see it as it affected me. He was surprisingly understanding about this, and would laugh at me, "You eat like a little mouse, my sweetness!"

We lived happily in Halkirk and even to this day not many reside there. It was a challenge to feed with it having such a small population, and so I had to travel farther afield for my meal. Given my newfound energies, however, this was a simple matter. In the middle of the night, when I was sure John was asleep, I would quietly tiptoe out of our bedroom and thence outside. I was able to run a few miles in minutes. I was a good hunter now and it was merely a functional part of my life.

And so my life continued in a similar vein for a few years. Sometimes finding stray humans was hard, especially in freezing weather, when most of the living had retired to their firesides or their burrows over winter. I didn't want to eat too close to the house in order to avoid panic in the village and suspicion falling on me, so I would often feed on the blood of animals. Chickens were a good idea because foxes were always blamed for their deaths. With the livestock from the local farms, people speculated about wolves rumoured to be in the area, rumours I had had a hand in spreading. Animal blood though was not ideal. It was thicker and tasted foul, often congealing in my mouth and leaving a metallic taste that would take days to get rid of. It kept my strength up, though it did not deliver the type of power I was used to. Still, it tided me over until I could safely procure human blood.

I was out one night looking to feed when I smelled a man walking through a field ahead. He was alone and singing quietly to himself. I kept low and approached stealthily until I was close enough to smell his blood. I had the downwind advantage and it was a fairly clear night. I could smell him, and my body quickened at the scent. My heart pounded in my chest and I was salivating as my nostrils widened, inhaling the stream of air linking him to me. I moved closer still to him, not making a sound. I throve on hunting and although I could easily have drawn him towards me using only my mind, the pursuit of prey made me feel alive, using all my senses like a being from the kingdom of wild beasts.

There were some trees nearby and a dirt track road just after that. I suppose that's where he must have been heading.

He was a small man, balding and round, and perhaps in his early fifties. Finally, intoxicated by thoughts of his blood bursting forth into my mouth, I could not stop myself and leapt onto his back. He tried to shake me off but to no avail: I clung on all the harder. He spun this way and that, sweating and grunting loudly, frantically trying to shake me, flailing his arms, unable to prise me from behind him. I enjoyed playing with my food, the sport of it. He turned his head. One clear sight of that expanse of neck and I could hold back no longer. My teeth slid out and down I went. Sinking my teeth into his neck, I could feel liquid running though my veins as it quenched my thirst.

"Stop!" My meal was interrupted by a shout.

I snapped out of my euphoric frenzy and looked up to see a woman heading from behind the trees holding what looked like a musket. "Stop beast! I warn you!"

Clouds passed away from the moon, throwing a huge stream of light down on us. The woman stopped, suddenly terrified as she took in the scene. Her ebullient courage seemed to drain from her as her eyes beheld me. I seemed to be a woman, yet I had the mouth of a wild animal, covered in dark liquid. Her eyes moved from my glistening teeth across to him, clinging onto life. Before I could summon enough energy to stop her, she aimed and fired, hitting me in the shoulder. I fell back from the man and blood spattered his face as he fell to the ground on top of me. The woman was upon me by this point pointing the gun towards me and shouting, "Callum... Callum? Please answer me, husband. Can you move?"

The man looked up at this woman, nodded and slowly rolled off me and to his knees, crawling away as quickly as he could.

"Move and I will open fire!"

The rising tide of energy inside me had slowed with my injury. Yet I released it and it flowed over the woman. The woman dropped the barrel of the gun and stared straight ahead as if in shock. I rose to my feet looking at the wound in my shoulder. It seemed smaller than it did a moment ago. I turned to the woman. "You will lift your weapon and place it near your mouth. On my command you will fire."

I walked towards the woman. From the corner of my eye I saw the man lying on the ground convulsing and shaking. I could hear his heartbeat racing, his eyes wide in terror. Teeth clenched, his hands balled into fists as his back arched. Then slowly all his muscles relaxed and he lay still. I moved closer to him and saw his eyes were wide open. I couldn't hear his heartbeat and assumed he had gone. Another dead one.

I faced the woman who was still standing there awaiting my command. I could feel my energy force give a little around her and drop slightly. Her head began to move, I could see her eyes blinking now and looking directly at me but her body stayed the same. I looked up to see her face streaming with tears and terror in her blinking eyes, as if she knew what was about to happen. I looked at my shoulder. In the minute or so since taking a shot there, the wound had healed, leaving only a rash-like mark where it had been.

I could feel the anger in me build once again that someone had dared to interrupt me before I had completed my feed. I looked her in the eye and, without a second thought, a single word emerged from my curled lip.

"Fire," I said, softly.

The woman did her utmost to resist my will but she was so much weaker. The energy inside me strengthened around her and compelled her to do as I asked. Another loud bang pierced the darkness. The woman's lifeless body flew back several feet before coming to a stop, her gun hitting the ground beside her.

I heard a noise behind and quickly turned to behold a most surprising sight. The man was standing now, his eyes red. His hair had grown long, thick and dark, he appeared to have shed weight and he looked perceptibly younger. He held himself straight and bowed his head towards me. "What is thy Will, my lady?"

Astonished, I didn't know what to say or do. I looked at him for a moment trying to divine how this had come to be... *He seemed to be like me, but how? How did he not die? Surely he could only be like me if he had the same blood as me. Yet he was most definitely an ordinary human when I attacked him. He had their smell; his blood was of their kind. Could he have somehow developed into a being like me? Could I have caused this? Could it be our blood had mingled? Had the spray from my shoulder wound landed in his torn neck and transformed him? My mind raced in bounds into the future. If I can create one like myself, then perhaps I can create more. How would this be of use to me?*

I needed time to digest this new information. I needed a plan. Firstly, what was I going to do about this man? "What is your name?"

The man straightened up. "My name is Callum Lucas McNeil. People call me Callum, my lady."

I couldn't help but think that there was a whole different future that I could create and control. "Callum. Who do you follow?"

"I follow you, my lady," he said calmly, as if awaiting orders. *Could it be true?* I seemed to have created an obedient servant. I realised at that point that my will still covered us. I pulled it back in, seeing the man's eyes turn from red to brown in the blink of an eye.

Callum looked over at the woman a few feet away and immediately became more animated. "What did you do to my wife?" He now appeared confused and scared, as if returning to his more human self.

He looked pleadingly back at me. "What's happening to me?"

I explained to him who I was, although I could not put a name to what I was. I explained how I had come to be the way I am and that he now had the same condition. He looked white, not moving for a moment, before falling to his knees and crying out for his wife with tears streaking the dirt on his face. He went to her and knelt at her side, embracing her and crying. For several minutes he sat with her corpse, attempting to piece together the shreds of material from her torn blouse to cover her wounds. Silently, he lowered his head to hers and appeared to be saying goodbye with a kiss.

Time was moving on so I approached Callum to part him from his wife. It was then I noticed that he was not kissing her but was face deep in her wound, licking the blood around neck and shoulder. As he heard me he turned sharply with bright red eyes, like a discovered wild animal.

"Thirsty... I need... I need!"

"You need to feed," I said "Come with me and we will see what we can do."

He looked up at me and then down to his wife. There was the briefest glimmer of attack in his eyes as he looked from her to me. But he stood and dropped his wife where she lay, saying, "Yes, my lady."

It was as if all emotion had washed away from him, as if somehow his wife was no longer an important part of him anymore. He seemed to have no feeling towards her after that and did not mention her again. He was looking to feed and be by my side. Perhaps the blood that lingered in his veins compelled him to follow and obey me.

That night I showed Callum how to hunt and to cover his tracks. He swore an oath to keep the secret and be loyal to me. He told me that he would stay close, should I require his assistance. He went running off into the night while I headed home and back to the bedroom, before my husband awoke.

The night had been extraordinary. A lot had happened, new things that I never thought possible. With time to think before dawn arose, a plan began to take shape. I could turn more people so they could be like me. I could command them to do exactly what I wanted. I would have my castle! I would have servants! I could own a village, a town, even a country if I so desired! The possibilities seemed endless. I could build an empire! No human would be able to stop us. If our plans became public, however, they would certainly try. It was imperative that the matter was kept secret.

As the nights passed I became closer to Callum, discussing my plans for an empire. He became, as you might say, my second in command. He would seek out new people and report back to me with his findings. I didn't want to create any more like me so close to home however and there were too few people to choose from. I decided to send Callum on a quest around England and make a note of people worthy to be in my secret family, and he left that morning. His mission was to find people of wealth and power and send the names to me so that I could consume them for myself.

A few weeks had passed and I hadn't heard from Callum in some time. I began to think that something was wrong until I received a note that he was heading back up with urgent news and that he would arrive in Halkirk in a fortnight, and not alone.

Meanwhile I had been feeling somewhat sluggish. My husband had been posted to France for a campaign two months previously and I was expecting him to return presently. I found myself lying longer in bed, not wanting to get up or even hardly move as my strength physically wasn't there. I had even been sleeping a little, something I had not done in years. I had been feeding as normal but this only seemed to cure me for a short period of time.

It was early spring and I managed to get up and dress to wait for the arrival of John who was coming home that day. I waited outside the house on the porch looking for signs of my husband when I heard a familiar voice cry, "Zanette!"

I turned to see where it was coming from. I could mostly see for miles around. I could see no one on the path but my sight was obstructed by trees in several areas around the house, and a hill further back. Again it came, "Zanette! Zanette!"

And then, emerging from the trees, I saw John walking towards me waving his hands in the air. I waved back and started to run to him. I was half the way to him when I started to feel dizzy and light headed and suddenly I went down.

I could hear John's voice in the background talking to someone in the room. "What is wrong with my wife, sir?"

A second man said, "Mr Walker I assure you, she is in good health. Mrs Walker is doing quite well, I promise."

Mrs Walker. Yes that's me. It still sounds strange. Mrs Walker... I thought, drowsily.

"Mr Redman please..." I opened my eyes to see John was standing at the bottom of my bed with an elderly man in a dark suit. He had a shock of red hair with grey sideburns that formed a beard at the chin. He was a smart man.

"Ah Mrs Walker. How are you feeling? You took a nasty fall outside." I looked over to him. "I'm feeling a little…" I felt my body suddenly convulse. My stomach churned and before I could stop it, I vomited black liquid onto the sheets.

"Oh dear it seems it won't stay down."

I blinked and look up at him. "What won't stay down?"

The man was busy rustling around inside a bag when he looked up. "Nothing to be alarmed about, Mrs Walker, just a little medicine to help calm your stomach."

My stomach was aching, for the first time since I could remember.

"Mr Redman as I was say—"

"Yes, Mr Walker. Your wife is fine, and so is the baby."

Baby?

"Baby?"

"Why yes Mrs Walker, I thought you would have known, I believe you to be around four months' gone by the feel of things, although I can't be more definite. It's God's divine timing," he chuckled.

I looked over to John who was smiling down at me and his smile spread over my face, too. I was going to be a mother! It took a while for it to sink in. The more I thought about it, the more pleased at the idea I became. Any other plans, however sizable, left my mind entirely. All I could do was think how wonderful this news was. *I'm going to be a Mother!*"

"Thank you Mr Redman for seeing to her at such short notice." John did not once take his eyes off me, even while talking to the doctor.

"Not at all General Walker. Congratulations to you both. I'll come back in a few weeks to oversee your wife's progress, if that is what you both would like."

I looked at the doctor and realised I was still beaming with the news.

"Thank you so much – that would be wonderful."

"Very well my dear. Ease up on your duties and get plenty of rest.

"You're going to need it."

I didn't hear what John said to him after that, I was too busy thinking about the beautiful child growing inside me. The physician waved at me and disappeared through the door before John, who stopped to look back at me, a warm smile covering his face. He sighed happily and followed the doctor out.

I'm going to be a mother, finally, a mother.

Days passed by, John and I went out to the village to spread the joyous news of our forthcoming child. Everyone seemed so happy for us. I forgot my plans for empire and put aside what I truly was. It felt blissfully normal, and that was what I craved. I wanted to have a life like others have. I wanted to be a wife and a mother and raise our children. I wanted to grow old with John by my side, and see our grandchildren playing outside the cottage. Living here, I felt like I was home again, with a family on the way, a wonderful husband and a lovely home. I was already starting to think up names for a baby: Zanette for a girl or Augustin for a boy. I was filled with joy, a feeling I had not experienced so profoundly for a while.

I did not want it to be tainted in any way. I did not want to think about the dark desires that sometimes overtook me in vulnerable moments. I put the dreams of hunting and killing out of my mind the instant I awoke from my recovered ability to sleep. During waking hours, I denied any thoughts of needing to feed. I put my true nature to the back of my mind and kept myself busy preparing our home to welcome our baby. I would not allow the darkest parts of myself to be expressed. Perhaps I could conquer this with willpower: if I wanted normality enough then surely it could be mine.

The following week John was summoned to London regarding a mission he would soon be part of. Although I wasn't privy to the details,

I was sure John would tell me about it later, when he arrived back home.

It was beginning to get dark when I realised that the need to feed was becoming so very strong inside me that it leeched into my every thought. I had denied myself for a number of days. Now my mind was filled with routes to kill. I could go into town. I could seek out a traveller although there were very few lone travellers that wandered so far north.

With my growing belly though, I wasn't going to be able to travel very far, which made things harder.

I couldn't stand my racing mind any more. I had to hunt. I had to feed. I opened the door to leave and found Callum standing there, a woman draped limply over his shoulders, hardly breathing. I could hear her heart beating, so knew she was holding onto life, just. I invited him in. He placed the woman on the floor and sat in the chair near the unlit fireplace.

"Who is this?" I asked, looking from one to the other.

"It's food my lady. I thought with your husband being home you might not have had time to go out hunting."

That was true. I didn't have a lot of time, especially with the news about the baby. If I but turned over in bed, John would wake to see if everything was all right. "That is so kind of you. You just caught me – I was about to go and hunt. This will be much better, thank you."

"Not at all my lady."

Before I knew it, I was kneeling over the woman pushing her onto her back and exposing her neck. I felt my fangs slide forth and emerge from the corners of my mouth. I leaned over and sank my teeth into her flesh. The woman quickly opened her eyes in shock and attempted a scream before fainting. As I drank I could hear her heartbeat steadily slow, before coming to a stop. I lifted my head and wiped the remaining blood from my mouth with a handful of the woman's dress.

"Is she dead my lady?" I looked over to see him standing over her, seemingly puzzled.

"Yes, why?"

"I can still hear her heart beating."

I knelt down to listen to the woman's chest but she was definitely gone.

"She has gone, Callum."

He continued to stare at both of us with a furrowed brow. "I hear two heartbeats, my lady."

For a moment I didn't understand. "Oh Callum, my dear man, that second heartbeat lies within me! I'm pregnant!"

Callum looked at me and smiled. "My lady, I am pleased for you. John must be excited. Sorry, I mean Mr Walker, please forgive me."

I nodded and walked past him to take a seat. "Callum, would you get rid of that please?" I said, pointing at the corpse. "And then perhaps you would tell me your findings, although I must tell you that all I can think about is my growing baby. Nothing else is as important to me as my little one."

"Of course, madam," he nodded. He told me about his journey down to the north of England, looking for suitable candidates for me to turn. Most of them were men in power and wealthy landowners. Although he did well, exactly as I requested of him, I felt my plans must now be set aside for the time being, given my condition. I was about to give my husband an heir. My energy was unstable. My unborn child was not only feeding but was consuming energy more quickly than I could restore it. My own energy would not settle.

Until I could once again control myself, I sent Callum on a quest to find a secluded piece of land for me. I gave him no particulars on the type or size of land, only that it be remote. To be frank, I wanted him away for now. Again he did as I asked.

I noticed a strange effect when he left. I found I could sense his location, as if some cord connected us wherever he journeyed. These small changes in me happened more and more frequently. My hearing was keener but, as with all my abilities, I often felt very drained if I tried to use it to its full capacity. The baby feeding on my energy was taking its toll. A further drain on my energy was my growing worries about the baby. What if the child were like me? That single question roamed my mind like a cutpurse, robbing me of the joy of my condition, and of my peace. I tried my utmost to banish it from my thoughts.

I generally rested for most of the day, going out to feed every other night. It was difficult to hunt whilst in my current state and sometimes I went without feeding for a few days.

A couple of weeks later I received a note sent by messenger from my husband. It read:

My darling Zanette,

How I have missed you! I think of naught but my little Scottish family up in the Highlands. My term of office is presently coming to an end. While I await my new command, I shall be with you, my love.

I am on route to you even now and I bring with me a companion.

I have missed you dearly. I should reach you at the end of the month.

Fondest love, John.

A companion? As the days passed, I wondered who his companion was. *Could it be a relative – someone from his friends or family in the south-west maybe, or an enlisted man under his command?* Perhaps it was important and had to be kept secret. *Perhaps it is someone of rank!* In the few hours of strength I had daily, I busied myself cleaning and arranging the house to make it perfect as I eagerly awaited John's return with the secret visitor.

It was night and I was sitting next to fireplace, watching the embers burn softly, sometimes dozing, and occasionally gazing out the window as the first light of morning appeared. I heard footsteps coming from outside and went to look, hoping it wasn't Callum back too early with the results of his search.

I opened the door to see John walking up the dirt road with a young girl I guessed to be around ten or eleven years old. John walked up and embraced me gently. "My darling I have missed you so very much." My eyes darted from him to the girl standing behind. She wore a long, dark coat with wooden buttons, curly brown hair down to her shoulders with freckles on her face. She was sweet, I suppose. John could see what I was looking at and turned to place a hand around the girl's shoulder.

"Do forgive me darling. Allow me to introduce my daughter. This is Catherine."

My eyes quickly snapped up at John. "Daughter?" A hand flew to my belly as my heart lurched in pain. John looked at me, pushing the girl behind him. He could tell I was surprised and I wasn't afraid to show it.

"Catherine." My teeth clenched as I said her name.

"Yes, Zanette. This is my daughter. I shall explain."

I could feel my fangs pushing down on teeth causing an aching feeling inside my clamped mouth. "Please do!"

John didn't move his eyes from me. "Catherine dear: go inside and help yourself to some food, while I talk to your stepmother."

Stepmother. A title bestowed on me before I even knew the role was mine. Before I was a mother to my own child. I felt even angrier at that thought.

"Zanette can we sit inside and talk please?" I nodded but didn't say a word, just went through the door and stood with my arms laid over my belly, holding my breath.

He followed me inside. "Zanette please, we must talk. I need to tell you about my past."

I didn't move, just stared at him. "Evidently." I hissed.

"Very well," he said, looking nervous. "Catherine is my daughter. Long before I met you, long before I fell in love with you," he said, resting a hand on mine, "I was briefly married when I was twenty to a woman called Ruth. We were only together a short time before she fell pregnant with Catherine." His eyes misted over. "She died giving birth to her..."

John put his face into his hands and started to sob. "I couldn't tell you because I couldn't bring myself to let Ruth go. Catherine reminds me of her so much. She has been staying with my cousin Elizabeth in London.

"Elizabeth essentially brought her up but I support her financially." John lifted his head to look at me.

"Why didn't you tell me this before we married? I thought you went to London so regularly because of your orders. You lied to me, John."

John turned his head towards the fireplace. "I didn't know how to tell you. So many times I wanted to but I never seemed to find the words." He placed his hand over his mouth, tears welling in his eyes.

But I wasn't feeling sympathetic.

"I went to London to see my daughter! Elizabeth has raised her to be kind and well mannered. She reads poetry and can cook. She is growing into a lovely young girl, a real blessing." He paused, searching for acceptance in my face. "I would like you to be a mother to her, Zanette. You could grow to love her, as I do. Zanette, can you forgive me for my deception?"

My breathing grew deeper and faster. "Excuse me. I need some air." I began to make my way out of the room. I thought that going for a walk might calm me down. I was in an angry, dark mood. It surprised me how dark my thoughts became, and how quickly. *I should be helping, calming him down, not rushing out.* As I reached the door, I turned towards him. "What about the Army?" I asked. "Was that also untrue?" John made his way over to me until I held up my hand up to stop him.

"Well?"

His head sank in shame, his eyes looked up at me, sadly. "I have not been in the army for some time. I resigned my commission, using the time instead to visit Catherine. I am really and truly sorry, my love."

I could feel my blood rising to the boil. "You left me for four months; I thought to go to France but that was a LIE! Four months!"

John stepped back a foot. "Yes, I admit it was a lie but with reason – Catherine was very unwell. For months she did not appear to be improving and I could not leave her."

I turned and walk to the front door. "I must think and clear my mind."

John walked behind me. "Can you forgive me?"

I turned sharply on my heels and stared straight into him. "You expect me to forgive you? The one thing I was looking forward to you have taken away!"

John looked up, confused. "What?"

I felt my teeth grind. "Without my knowledge you have thrown me into motherhood before I have even given birth to my own child. You have deceived me since we married. Is there anything else you wish to add to your list of lies?"

Before I allowed him to answer, I stormed out of the house, slamming the door with such force that a crack appeared at the top. I ran into the fields, tears streaming down my face. My head was aching with pressure and my chest unable to draw in enough air. I needed time to think. For my own child's survival, I also needed to feed…

Chapter 3
Catherine

Zanette Amelia

That evening I stayed outside, travelling for miles to feed and resting frequently. I didn't know where I was heading; I was too busy trying to think. I had to decide what I was going to do next. I couldn't bring myself to go back home, not just yet.

I sat for long periods, watching the moon start her journey across the sky, wondering how I didn't know, why he hadn't told me. I could hear people's thoughts; I could control them at will, so why not John? It never occurred to me that I couldn't hear him. I never once tried to control him as he had always made me so happy. Now that was all in question. All my hopes and dreams with John now seemed suspended by a single thread.

Yet despite everything, all the anger and hurt, I still loved him. I kept thinking back to the night we were married, the way he made love to me. Holding me so tight and breathing me in. I loved the touch of his hands that caressed my back as we danced, his hot, moist lips kissing my neck sending shivers down my spine. He made my toes curl with excitement. I could be vulnerable again. I loved the way he protected me and made me feel safe in his embrace. Yet now, I doubted him. I felt that it was all a lie. I felt used and betrayed. All the emotions I had put away years before were welling up inside me and running wild.

I mulled things over in my mind as I walked. To re-energise myself and to give myself a treat, I hunted. As I had several hours but could not run far I followed the scents left on paths and bushes until one in particular remained, drifting onwards into the Highlands. At last I found the source: a man of about twenty years' old asleep under a hedge near Loch Calder, a knapsack under his head as a pillow.

Prone, he was entirely vulnerable and ripe for the plucking. He looked physically strong and was probably travelling around with the season, seeking work in the fields. I did not wake him as I pushed his dark, straw-coloured curls to one side and slowly moved in to bite. Indeed, he sighed contentedly, and seemed to be enjoying whatever dream he was having. He stirred sharply though, as I broke the skin and bit deep into his flesh – but by then it was far too late to struggle and he soon went limp as I drew out his power mouthful by mouthful.

I finished feeding at my leisure and, standing, took in the glory of the wilderness and felt its energy being absorbed through my skin. I had not felt so alive and powerful in months but it had taken me so much longer to walk here. I turned back towards home to try and save whatever was left of our marriage.

*

I reached the outskirts of Halkirk and walked up to the dirt track leading to our home. I stood watching, smelling the air, my ears reaching for any sound that would tell me that John was out looking for me. Sure enough it came. I couldn't see him but I could hear him shouting my name over and over again. My knees felt weak at the sound of his voice.

I slowly retraced my steps along the track.

A rumble of thunder broke out and a surge of power filled the air. My eyes easily adjusted to the dark. I could often see even better in the dark than during the day. At night the whole of our surroundings seemed to come alive and I could hear the sound of the grass moving with the wind, the song of a meadow, field mice turning in their sleep. An old fence that separated the fields creaked and repeatedly smacked one of its desiccated posts against another, like two hollow bones. I felt calmer all of a sudden, as if my emotions were just another element of the growing storm whirling around me. It was only a few hours ago that I was consumed with anger towards John, but now I had the need to see him, I longed for him.

Why had I been so cold towards him? He was scared. I should have been more understanding about what Catherine had been through: I too had lost a mother and been raised by others. In her young life she had been parted from her only parent more often than they had been together. Yet my mind returned to the fact that John had lied to me. To my face. For years. He should not have kept such things from me. Yet still, I needed him, and he needed me.

I reached the house as John walked around the corner of it. He stopped for a moment to gauge my reaction. I smiled and he ran to me, embracing me so gently and I let him, folding my arms around him and breathing him in.

"I'm so sorry my darling, I will do whatever it takes to make you happy again. I know what I did was wrong and I want to make it up to you, just tell me…"

I placed a finger to his lips and whispered, "Come inside, we can talk about this later."

He took my hand and we walked into the house together staring at each other and almost forgot about Catherine. Almost.

In the lounge, I took a seat by the blazing fire that John had built for my return. He knelt in front of me, still holding my hand. A creak came from the landing and I could hear a smaller, faster heart beating at the top of the stairs. John didn't seem to notice until I looked in the direction of the staircase.

"What is it?" he asked.

I looked to him, and in a soft voice I said, "We have a visitor."

John moved across the room and beckoned his daughter down the stairs.

"Catherine, I would like to introduce you to Zanette, your stepmother."

I could hear Catherine making her way down the stairs. "I don't think she likes me, Papa."

John looked at me. He didn't say anything but his expression told me he wanted me to try and make an effort to welcome Catherine. So I made my way to the stairs where Catherine was standing halfway, holding onto the rail to steady herself. I took a deep breath and smiled. "Nice to meet you, Catherine. Please come join us. I would like to get to know you."

Catherine didn't move until John waved her. "Come on Cathy, don't be rude."

Catherine climbed down the last few steps and took hold of her father's hand. John steered her to the lounge and sat on the other chair. He gathered her over and she leaned against him. She fell against his chest, sleepily and his arms cradled her while she peered over the top of his arm towards me. I knelt down at his side and leaned in.

I couldn't fight my nature though. The sweet smell of her blood rushed through my nose and I could feel my mouth begin to water. I swallowed, and tried to push it down. "Catherine – that's a pretty name."

She looked at me and smiled, "My Papa chose it."

I smiled back, looking from her to him. "Is that so? Well, he made a good choice."

Catherine lifted her head and looked into my eyes. "What lovely eyes you have."

I placed a hand on her cheek, softly. "That's very kind of you to say, child."

She giggled, "Your hands are cold."

I took my hand away and placed it my lap "It is chilly this evening." I looked up at John and smiled. "She is very sweet."

He looked into my eyes and smiled back, relieved. We spent the evening chatting and I exchanged stories with her about my life; the things I got up to as a child. This made her giggle and seem more at ease with me.

Deep inside me though, I could feel something wasn't right. I knew we could never be close. I tried and failed to feel settled with Catherine becoming part of our family, but I was jealous of the bond that she and John had and I hated that fact that I was being pushed aside, along with our growing baby.

Resentment grew inside of me each passing day. I watched them from my rocking chair on the porch as I knitted clothes for our baby, each stitch a spiteful knot. They were always playing together in the field, running and laughing. I smiled sweetly to mask my anger. I peered at their every move, like an infirm old cat, unable to pounce and end it. As my belly swelled further, so did my growing feeling that something had to be done about this interloper.

John had been so distracted since her arrival that he hardly spent a minute with me without Catherine interrupting. I made up my mind: she had to go. John was mine and only mine. I was not prepared to share him with someone who reminded him so much of his late wife. And so I waited. Now was not the time to do anything about it, but it would be soon. I rested my head against the porch chair and closed my eyes against the sunset, a faint smile playing on my lips.

It was a waning moon that night, but still bright enough. John slept by my side. I heard a noise downstairs. As I slipped out of bed, I expected that John would wake as he had been doing, to make sure I was not unwell. Since the arrival of Catherine, however, this had stopped. He would spend hours playing with her, brushing her hair, making posies from wild flowers or taking her to watch the baby rabbits growing. I could feel the darkness building inside me. I went softly to the landing to see what I could hear.

A voice whispered up the stairs. "It's me, my lady."

Callum had once again come with his findings. I slowly walked down the staircase, stepping around the creaky boards as I descended. "Well met, Callum. What news do you have?"

Callum retreated back out the front door, whispering, "May we talk outside my lady? The thumping of heartbeats in this house is distracting."

I had grown used to it so that I no longer noticed unless I listened for it.

"Of course."

I followed him outside and onto the porch. I looked up to make sure no one was watching from the windows.

"My lady, I have a found a dwelling for you on an island not far from here. It is unpopulated and so it should be easy to lay the foundations of your empire there."

My first thought was of John. I could not leave the love of my life.

Then I considered Catherine. The plans flooded back into my mind.

"Very well... Where is this island you speak of?"

Callum pulled out a piece of rag with what looked like a map of several rocky islands drawn onto it. "It's an island called Fugloy many miles north of here in the Faroe Islands, my lady. It is small but I believe it to be deserted, apart from sheep and birds. It is reckoned to be reached in two full days and two full nights with a full sail."

I was stunned. I had not been thinking much about these plans since I found out about my condition, yet since Catherine's arrival, I was only too happy to consider this desolate place where I could grow my kingdom. Many images raced through my mind: the gathering place of my people, ships sailing north, filled with human cargo, all waiting to do my bidding... Was it possible? Was this where my empire was due to start?

Callum continued. "The problem I have encountered is finding a ship to take us there. Luckily, I have befriended a captain whilst on my journeys and with your help, my lady, his ship could be our vessel to and from this place."

I considered it. "Bring him to me Callum. I think the sooner we start, the better."

Callum smiled at me and bowed his head. He was on the point of leaving when he remembered something. "My lady – I was unsure if you had fed lately, therefore I took the liberty of bringing you something to sustain yourself."

The thought of feeding made my body ache and my mouth water. I could feel the blood run through my veins in anticipation of a meal.

"She is around the back of the house, my lady. Once you are finished, I will dispose of the body."

Callum escorted me to the young woman, bound, gagged and unconscious on the floor. She was no more than eighteen and slender with pale skin. Broad, petulant lips framed her rag-stuffed mouth. I knelt and tilted her head to one side, moving her pale hair to one side. The swollen vein in her neck seemed to pulsate a rhythmic message to me:

Here I am – here I am – take a bite… My fangs slid quickly out from my mouth. I lowered my head and was about to bite when I looked up at Callum.

"Perhaps I will not kill this one. I think I will turn her into company for you. Why kill them when I can control them?"

Callum smiled and bowed his head, agreeably. "Very well."

I lowered my head and sank my teeth into her neck. I would feed enough to satisfy my basic needs and then give her my gift. My nostrils filled with her scent as I buried my teeth into her vein. The blood ran through me filling me with an energy I was not accustomed to lately – that of the female. It was a heady mix, feeling her earthy, sultry energy blending with mine and I found myself wanting to drink in much more of her. It was almost hard to stop but I forced myself and broke free.

The rushing of adrenaline flowing around my body lit me up with life. I raised my wrist to my mouth and bit into the flesh. The pain surged up my arm, and I couldn't help but suppress a scream. I lowered my wrist to her neck and allowed my blood to flow over her wound. The flow stopped as my wound quickly began to heal, but it was enough to have the desired effect.

The woman's body started to move strangely, undulating back and forth.

Suddenly her body arched as she started to convulse. Her eyes opened wide in terror and she let out a deep, muffled moan, her face twitching in confusion. I could see the red appearing in her eyes as she joined our exclusive breed. Gradually, her writhing lessened and she fell still. She breathed heavily, looking from me to Callum. She yelped, louder this time as, during her transition, the rag had slipped from her mouth and lay wet on the ground. She tried to move but her bonds reined her in, whereupon she let out a scream for help. Callum hurriedly blocked her mouth with his hand, pushing her down against the cold soil. I focused my energy and allowed it to rise, releasing it over her defenceless body.

She became quite still, her eyes wide open.

"Now listen to me, you will be quiet, do you understand?"

Callum drew back his hand. She looked up and replied, "Yes."

I knelt down beside her and looked into her face. "You have been given a gift and you will obey me. Do you understand?"

A second "Yes."

I stood looking down at her "What is your name?"

"Jane McCloud, my lady."

I looked to Callum and asked him take care of her. "Of course, my lady."

I moved away from her towards Callum. "Untie her: she will not be a nuisance now." Callum bowed his head and did as he was asked.

I took in the scene of my achievement and a proud smile rose inside me. I had a second follower to assist me. My plans were becoming more real to me. I tilted my head back and closed my eyes, and exhaled a satisfied sigh, absorbing the energy of the moonlight on my face. My tongue passed over my fangs, wiping away the blood as I beamed. A gasp broke the silence. As one, Callum and I looked up at the window above us. "Catherine."

I felt no fear upon our discovery. I knew what I had to do. I shot a look at Callum. "Hide. I'll deal with this." I made my way back around the house with determination written over my face, and, if I'm honest, a little glee. Callum pulled the girl out of sight.

I came softly through the door to see Catherine on the landing screaming, "Papa! Papa!"

I heard the banging of footsteps as John struggled to wakefulness and came marching out of the bedroom. "What's going on? What is it Catherine?"

He looked down the stairs to see me in the doorway. "What on earth is going on?" Catherine turned and ran into her father's arms. "What's the matter darling?"

The girl peered from around her father's arms and looked down to me: "She was outside, hurting that poor lady!" Her voice was shaking as she spoke. Her father held her close.

"What is she talking about Zanette? What were you doing outside at this time of night?"

"Look out the window Papa – she's there! She's down there!" Catherine pointed down near the window to where I had stood with Callum less than a minute previously.

"I can't see anything, Cathy."

"She was there, Papa, with a man!" John looked at me.

"The poor love. Perhaps it was a nightmare. Her first night in a strange house... I couldn't sleep, so went to take the night air. But I was alone, little one, quite alone." I smiled kindly at her.

John took hold of Catherine and knelt down on one knee to face her.

"Oh sweetness, you had a bad dream. Let me tuck you up. Come along."

John stood up and, taking hold of her hand, started to walk back to her room. "But Papa..." she insisted.

John turned his head towards her. "Now, now Cathy. We shall have no more of this silly talk."

Catherine's gaze was fixed on me as she walked back to her room hand in hand with her father, until she was out of sight. I turned around to close the door and caught sight of Callum leading the new recruit, Jane, towards the trees at the far side of the field in front of my house. I headed for the stairs as John appeared at the top.

"Are you quite well, Zanette?" He came down the stairs to meet me and held my hands looking into my eyes. "You should never go out at night on your own, my dear Zanette. It's not safe for you. It is only by God's grace that you were unharmed yesterday." He took hold of my hand and proceeded to escort me up the stairs and back to bed.

The next morning I waited until John left the house. He was heading into town to get me some flour from the store. I was no longer able to lift the sacks myself. In the kitchen area I found Catherine sitting at the table, eating bread. As I approached, Catherine froze. I walked around her to face her. "Good morning, Catherine."

She sat and stared at me, not saying a word. I turned away from her to go to the cupboard when Catherine said, "I saw what you did last night." I stopped in my tracks. A pause. I turned to look at her.

"Sorry, dear? What was that?"

"I said – I saw what you did last night."

I moved closer and sat down opposite her, resting my elbows lightly on the table. "I'm not sure to what you are referring."

She looked at me and pulled her hands away from the table. "I saw you hurt that lady, and when my Papa comes back I will tell him everything I saw you do."

"Is that right? Your father never told me you had such an imagination." I pushed the chair back and stood to look at her. The energy inside started to build. I released it to surround Catherine. Something was wrong though. I could not sense her. I tried forcing more energy towards her. Still nothing. I pulled it back in and sat down, feeling extremely weak, and trying to understand why this had happened.

I felt something inside move. I looked down at my stomach and realised it was the baby. I had not felt my child move before! I quickly forgot what I was doing, mesmerised by my little baby's tiny movements, already making her – or perhaps his – presence felt inside my stomach. A scream broke my reverie. I looked up to see Catherine had left the kitchen. I followed her, at my own pace.

Catherine stood in the corridor, her back to me looking at a figure in front of her. It was Callum, eyes red, fangs down. Jane was behind him.

She was about the same height as Callum with long straight, white hair. Her eyes burned bright crimson. Her fangs were down and she was staring intently at Catherine.

"Oh, I'm glad you've met. But of course, you already know my friends, don't you?"

"This is Catherine. She's ever so curious. Like a cat. A little, nosey cat."

Catherine whimpered and ran for the stairs, grabbing the railing to pull herself up. In a blur of speed, Callum appeared in front of her. Jane followed to come up behind Catherine, stretching her arms from banister to wall. Catherine was trapped. She span around, tears streaming down her face. "Are y–you going to kill me?"

I walked to the side of the banister and rested my arms on it for support. My strength had dipped after I released it in the kitchen. Only slowly was it now returning.

"That depends on you, dear child."

Catherine faced me. "What do you want of me?"

"If you say one word against me, dearest Catherine, I'll make sure you never see your daddy again!"

I was suddenly interrupted by a searing pain coursing round my body. I dropped to my knees, panting and crying out. My hand flew to my stomach. With the other I clung on to a step, my strength ebbing away further. The pain was excruciating. It felt as though my unborn child was trying to get out. In a searing moment of insight, I realised that the baby was hungry! I hadn't drunk enough blood from Jane and was dangerously low. If I didn't have more soon my baby would die, and there was no supply for miles around... except... My eyes alighted on Catherine.

I could feel my mouth watering as I heard the beating of her heart flood my ears. My fangs began involuntarily to protrude. I looked to Callum and then to Catherine. Callum grabbed the little girl by the arms. She was utterly terrified, and let out an ear-piercing scream so loud the chickens outside began to call and scuffle in distress. "Let me go! Let me go – please!" she wailed tearfully.

I let go of the step and crawled around to the front of the stairs. Jane had moved from where she was and stood over me, helping me to my feet.

Other sounds were obliterated by Catherine's cries for help. I slowly climbed the stairs, one by one, my gaze focused on Catherine's neck. Finally, I reached her and placed my hands either side of her face. I whispered into her ear.

"I'm about to give you a gift Catherine, a gift of life. You will be by my side forever."

Catherine looked pleadingly into my eyes, but I ignored her, tilting her head with my hands. I slowly leaned forwards towards her neck and sank my teeth in.

"STOP! What are you doing?"

I whirled around to find John in the doorway, his eyes fixed on Catherine's neck. He froze, taking in the scene. He dropped the sack of flour, which spilled around him in clouds. Jane began to move in his direction. "Get back, demon!"

Jane turned to look at me and paused, just short of John. "Stop." I ordered. "He is not to be harmed."

John saw Catherine being held firmly by Callum. She was still breathing, but gasped as he saw she was covered in blood. "Let her go, damn you!"

I turned to Callum and then back to John.

"John, darling – you mustn't worry so much. This is just our game. It is not how it appears!" I easily lied to him.

I descended the stairs and stood behind Jane. John saw my teeth and the thin line of blood falling down my chin and dripping onto my gown. "What are you? Stay away from us Zanette! You were going to kill her! Release her immediately!"

I stared into his eyes. My stomach churned with conflict as a battle raged inside me between who I used to be and who I was now. I could feel a rising tide of tears, tapping into a somehow ancient sadness. "John – please let me explain." I felt clearer now and more human.

John started slowly moving towards the sitting room, never taking his eyes off us. "I won't say it again. Let her go!"

I turned to Callum and nodded. Callum let go and Catherine ran down the stairs, her face flushed with tears. She clung to John but he pushed her behind him as he backed into the parlour. His hand moved behind the doorframe and he pulled out a sword. Jane edged forward fangs down, eyes red. She looked like a wildcat, ready to pounce.

Callum came down the stairs and stood by my side awaiting orders. "Get out of my house!" John bellowed.

"John – please listen!"

John turned to face me, red with anger and fear for his firstborn. "I want nothing more to do with you, whatever you are! You are an abomination! Call them back or I swear – I will be forced to defend myself!"

I stepped forward at that, determined to halt any fight. John sliced the air in front of him, nearly catching me with the blade. I stood back. Jane leapt forward. Her throat met John's blade in mid-air, slicing it open. Blood flew out of her and life fled. Her limp body fell to the ground, a dark pool forming around her. Callum was about to leap forward when I placed a hand in front of him, stopping him.

"John you need to understand I wasn't going to kill her, I was giving her a gift…"

John clenched his teeth. He held a hand behind him, shielding Catherine from any attack.

"It's not a gift. Creatures like you are not gifts! You are against God's will! I want nothing more to do with you – or that thing growing inside you!"

I could feel my blood starting to rise again. How dare he call our child a thing! I stepped forward, prepared to vehemently defend our child and change his mind. At that moment, I felt the worst pain of my life shoot through me and down my spine. Agonised, my every fibre on edge, I looked down to see John's hand holding a sword through my stomach. I screamed in agony but it was not at the excruciating physical pain, it was the certain knowledge of where the blade had landed.

My baby! My baby! I looked up into his wet eyes, his stare boring into me. I felt my little baby jerk and convulse. And then... Nothing...

"No–o–o–o–o!" I screamed. "No–o! You wicked murderer!" I hit him with my fist but it landed weakly against his chest.

I started to cough and saw a red cloud. Large droplets of blood flew out of me and landed in the pale flour still lying on the ground. My legs refused to support me and I fell to the ground. Callum caught me. He dragged me outside. John followed. I looked up and caught his eye.

"I will let you go while I protect my daughter, but – as soon as Catherine is safe – I will hunt you down! I promise you this – the next time we meet will be your last. I will destroy you!"

Callum dragged me backwards through the fields. I fell in and out of a deep sleep, catching glimpses of woodland, hearing a rushing brook some distance away, before blackness finally fell like an arras curtain. When I did wake, the hurt inside was indescribable. I felt my world crashing around me. I felt like my life was ebbing away. My body was in so much pain, I felt sure I would die. Again, I fell away into the deepest, darkest abyss.

Callum carried me to the undergrowth in the nearby trees. I heard his voice in the distance. "My lady – we have to get your baby out or it will kill you."

I came to, wild-eyed and raving, my eyes flaming with hurt and anger. "You will not touch my child! He is strong! He will survive to breathe air!" I held my belly tight with both arms. "He is strong! He will thrive…" I cried to the heavens, as if this would somehow make it so. Again, the menacing cloak of pitch wrapped itself around me.

I dreamed I had been buried. All the pain had gone. I was with my little girl. We flew over a fence into a field full of bright flowers. A chorus of birds sang happily above. Animals surrounded us. I carried her in my arms and we walked, her golden curls bouncing and shining in the sun.

She put her finger on my forehead. "Look Mummy you can see me!" She giggled and I saw a mouth full of milk teeth. And then she was running ahead. "Not too far, beloved," I called. I could see her nowhere.

"Beloved?"

Light pierced my eyes as they opened, and I winced. "My lady?" Callum stood quite still for a moment before leaning forward and bending on one knee. "My lady? I can hear only one heartbeat."

I screamed in pain. This could not be happening. *My beloved girl.* My eyes felt sore with tears; my mouth was dry. My whole body ached to feed to try and repair the damage. I looked up at Callum and nodded that I understood, weeping. I closed my eyes trying to block the pain, the overwhelming emotional pain. I had lost my baby. I felt empty and again alone.

"My lady, there's not much time. The baby must be removed or you will die."

I nodded numbly and braced myself for what was about to come. I never in my wildest imaginings thought that pain like this existed. Callum slowly reached a hand into the wound made by the sword. He pulled out a purple and red mass of flesh. He then lowered his head and started to bite through the cord that joined me to my baby. I could feel every bite in my heart. The pain was so unbearable and finally I lost the will to stay awake...

*

I awoke in a different place from where I fell. I was surrounded by rocks and birds and could hear the sea not far away. Callum was in front of me holding a young man in his arms, unconscious. "You need to feed, my queen."

I raised my head to accept the offering Callum had brought me. I was wrapped in a blanket. I stopped short. *Queen?*

"Queen?"

Callum came closer and lowered the young man to the ground. "Yes my lady. You were the first like us, and so you are Queen to all of us."

I never really thought about being a queen... I, a queen... It would take some time to accustom myself to the sound of it. *Queen.* It had a pretty sound to it, like a bell ringing in the heavens.

Callum succeeded in his task of finding a sailor to take us to the Faroe Islands. We were warned, however, that no one lived there that the weather was highly unpredictable. He advised us that the seas could get rough around the shore and that it might take some time to get ashore. He did as promised and we boarded his small ship, a vessel with about twenty or thirty hands. After some suspicious talk that we had not brought much with us, we set sail for Fugloy.

Callum and I kept below decks listening to the banter of the crew above. Occasionally we heard a knock on the door of our quarters, offering food and drink. We refused, explaining that we had brought enough to get by. The crew seemed suspicious but we kept to ourselves as best we could. At night we went on deck to see what progress they had made but we were surrounded by sea, with no land in sight.

My wounds healed by this time and my stomach showed only a faint scar where Callum had torn it apart. I had lost a lot of blood but I was able to regain my strength as Callum had brought me a regular supply of waifs in preparation for our voyage.

It was getting late so we decided to head up to the decks and take in the salt air. A sailor stood by the side smoking a pipe and looking over the ocean. He wasn't a young man, being around sixty, with a grey cap and long white beard. He dressed in a rough cotton shirt, with navy breeches and a waistcoat to match. He turned and watched us approach.

"A fine evening for sailing, my lady."

I looked around at the calm waters, the moon shining overhead, with only the occasional wispy cloud to break her view. "Yes it is."

He turned fully and rested against the side. "Amis is the name."

I smiled and offered my hand. "Amelia." I didn't want anyone knowing who I was or where I had come from so in that moment, I chose to use my middle name. "This is my companion... Lucas."

Callum looked at me, then to the sailor and offered his hand.

"Amis." He raised his pipe to his lips and began to inhale. "Do you come far?"

I diverted my eyes and looked at the moon. "We are from London."

The man lowered his pipe. "I must ask. It seems passing strange to be going to such a remote place. Is there a reason for this?" Amis stared at us waiting for an answer.

"We have been told what a beautiful place Fugloy is. I wish to spend some time there, to paint flowers and convalesce after a recent illness."

Amis seemed skeptical but nodded out of politeness. "Very well." He walked past us towards the door that led below. "I am pleased you got away from the strigas!"

We looked after him. "The strigas?"

He placed a hand on the doorframe. "Aye, the strigas: dangerous, mad creatures of the night. Death has been stalking the lands of the north of Scotland for some time. People have gone missing and there is no sign of the wild beasts who committed such devilish acts."

I looked at Callum who stared right back at me. "Then we are indeed blessed."

"Good night to you both."

"Good night, Amis," I replied, softly. Callum nodded and looked out across the ocean. Amis disappeared below until only we two remained on the deck.

"My Queen why are we using our middle names?"

"Callum, from this moment on we must be Amelia and Lucas. We don't want people following our trail. I don't want John to know our whereabouts. Besides, I feel… different. This is the start of my empire. What happened can have no place in my life now. I cannot speak of it further, my pain would be insurmountable. I have lost everything. Nearly everything," I added, realising that in Callum, I had a devoted servant.

Callum bowed. "As you wish my lady, but does he not know your middle name?"

"No, Callum. I don't think he ever knew it. However he knows my maiden name, so we must use caution when using our names. I shall use the name Amelia Mireille and shall honour my family's name."

Lucas nodded. "As you wish."

Given the unsettled weather, we spent a few more days aboard than expected. We were informed that we were awaiting the seas to calm so that we could transfer to the island. The captain informed us that we would be taken to shore by rowboat, due to the swells. I had formed a plan to change those on board. Perhaps I should have done this while we were sailing. I wasn't sure.

As promised, we were taken ashore on Fugloy Island accompanied by two crew who took turns rowing. They asked us how we were going to survive on Fugloy, where we would stay and what we would do for food, as supplies to the island were not frequent. We explained that we had a shipment bringing supplies. They didn't seem to believe us.

We arrived on shore and made our way inland. It was a chilly afternoon and the clouds above were heavy. The crew returned to the ship.

So here we were, Callum and I, on our own on a deserted and wild island in the middle of the northern seas. "Now what do we do?"

Callum faced me. "My lady, I believe an old man lived here but has since passed away. We can use his dwelling for now. I'm afraid it's some distance, but we should be there in less than a day."

I considered this for a moment. "We can reach it in a few minutes if we use our strength."

"With all due respect, my Queen, you are in no fit state to tap into your energy. We should save our energy until we are able to feed on a regular basis."

He did make sense. "How are we to acquire what we need with no way of getting back to the mainland?"

Callum walked ahead of me. "The captain I told you about is meeting us here in two weeks, bringing everything we need. He is expecting payment when he arrives. We will require your ability to control him then, my lady."

I couldn't believe how efficient he was in arranging all this in such a short space of time. I was very impressed. I did as he suggested and followed him over the land to the place we were now going to call home. We trudged slowly ahead, occasionally speaking, but often I was left to my own thoughts.

My mind quickly went back to the terrible events at the cottage in Halkirk. My heart filled with sadness and anger when I thought of the innocent child that John had killed, of my home and everything I had known for the past few years coming to an end in a single night. I had lost everything in less than an hour. I now think that two lives ended that night.

I thought of my baby, of how I would never see the child grow up or get married. My arm held my stomach as we walked and again, the tears came. I knew in my heart that having another child would be impossible. In all likelihood I would never now be a mother. John: the name made me angry. How could he have done this to me? He didn't give me a chance to explain. He struck me and viciously killed my child.

This was not the man I met all those years ago. John made sure I knew from the very start that Catherine came before me, before us. He put her before me!

My heart felt as heavy as black lead. The pain was so overwhelming I thought it would shatter. In fact, from that day on, I resolved to use my pain to build up my strength. Rather than giving into it and crumbling away to nothing, the scars that had littered my heart since I was a girl gradually hardened into shields of protection. My strength was growing. I knew I could be invincible if I conquered my past. It was going to take some time, though.

John's final words to me stalked my mind: "I will hunt you down and destroy you!" Instead of feeling afraid of John, as I might have done in the past, I knew that single-mindedly pursuing my plans would destroy him before he realised what was happening.

I had to build and build fast…

I vowed to myself that he would never hurt me again, that I would not allow anyone ever to hurt me again. I vowed that the world would suffer at my hands for everything that it had made me suffer. I vowed that I would have vengeance against those who had hurt me. I vowed to defeat anyone who stood in my way. My time was coming! I, and my kind, would prosper! And it would be soon!

Chapter 4
Catherine

Jonathan Walker

I awoke to hear Catherine screaming outside of my room.

"Papa! ... Papa!"

In a panic, I stumbled out of bed and turned to shout *Zanett*e! but she wasn't there. Fear gripped my mind as screams bounced off the walls. *My God! What on earth is happening?*

I ran to the door and flung it open, almost taking it off its hinges. On the landing I found Catherine staring down the stairs. I approached her and looked down to find Zanette standing in the doorway. I turned to Catherine and in a panicked voice.

"What's going on? What is it, Catherine?"

I felt winded. She turned and bolted into my arms. She was shaking, her tears staining my chest. I could hear her straining to catch her breath.

"What on earth is going on?"

I felt her head move and peer over my arm towards Zanette. I looked down at my wife. "What's the matter darling?"

Catherine was trying so hard to control her voice. "She was outside, hurting that poor lady!" she sobbed.

I stared at my wife and placed a hand on Cathy's head, softly stroking her hair, trying to comfort her.

"What is she talking about Zanette? What were you doing outside at this time of night?"

Before Zanette had chance to speak, Catherine pulled me towards the window. "Look out the window Papa – she's there... she's down there!" She pointed out of the window towards an empty dark patch behind the house. I squinted to try and see what she was pointing at, but couldn't see anything.

"I can't see anything, Cathy."

She turned and looked at me. "She was there, Papa! With a man!" I turned my head towards Zanette, still holding Catherine as she cradled into my chest again, still sobbing.

"She must have been dreaming, dear. I was outside but it was because I couldn't sleep, so went to take the night air."

I looked at Zanette for a moment. Something wasn't quite right, something in her voice...her eyes? Was she lying to me? In the dim light cast by the moon, did I see her cheeks were a little flushed? I turned back to Catherine and knelt down in front of her, holding her with my arms.

"Oh sweetness, you had a bad dream. Let me tuck you up. Come along."

I held her hand and rose slowly heading for Catherine's room.

"But Papa!" she insisted.

I turned to her. "Now, now Cathy. We will have no more of this silly talk." I continued to her room. As I was laying her down, "Papa, I swear I saw her and that man. She was kneeling over a woman lying on the ground."

I pulled the covers over her and tucked her in. I swept little tendrils of hair aside from her pretty face. "Come Cathy, back to sleep. We can talk more about this tomorrow. Now get some rest darling."

She turned over, away from me and I stood gently, and quietly walked out of the room.

I was curious to find out what Zanette had been doing outside; perhaps the baby was making her unwell. But Catherine has never lied to me before, I thought. Perhaps Zanette was right. Was she only dreaming after all? Yet what a state she had been in. I glanced back at Catherine. She was still laying with her back to me. I closed the door and headed back to the landing. When I got there I saw Zanette looking out the front door. "Are you quite well, Zanette?"

She turned to face me and quickly closed it. She walked to the foot of the stairs as I descended. I took hold of her hand. "You should never go out at night on your own, my dear Zanette. It's not safe. It is only by God's grace that you were unharmed yesterday."

She gave no answer and still seemed somehow… altered. I pushed that from my mind and proceeded to escort her back to bed.

I was awake all night thinking about what had happened. I couldn't make sense of it. For hours I tossed and turned, unable to sleep. It seemed that mulling over the evening's events led to still more questions in my mind. Rather than settling the issue, I was left with some far more serious observations. Why did Zanette always eat alone?

In fact, why had I never seen a single morsel of food pass her lips? Why had I never seen her drink so much as a mouthful of water? Things that should have been obvious for a husband to know about his wife, I didn't seem to have answers for. Why?

I thought back to when I brought Catherine home. I knew Zanette was very unhappy about my deception. I could have understood her anger or sadness, had they been the emotions I witnessed. But there was something else that I saw, again, something in the eyes. With a growing feeling of trepidation, I realised that what I had seen seemed to be a flicker of some darker intent.

Zanette looked at Cathy so oddly. It was as if her anger was directed at Cathy rather than at me. Maybe the night was confusing me into seeing things that weren't there. Maybe it was jealousy that Zanette felt for Cathy? Zanette had been my only loved one for so long, and now with the baby on the way, this had brought us closer. I suddenly felt a deep remorse for my actions during what I then realised should have been a special, almost magical, time in our marriage. But surely Zanette wasn't jealous of a child? Yet she had made her feelings quite clear that evening, which I found unsettling and disproportionate, especially when she stormed out.

I thought back over our marriage and it seemed to me that for a while now she seemed different, as if changing bit by bit. Her moods were more frequent. I put it down to her being with child, but no – I remember this from before too. The way she looked at Catherine, even when she started talking to her, there was still an element there that I couldn't put my finger on, an edge to her voice, a slight curl of her lip sometimes...

I think that was when I began to fear a little for Catherine's safety around Zanette. I knew deep down that she wouldn't hurt her though. She couldn't possibly – that wasn't my Zanette. But why had Cathy been so scared of her tonight? It just didn't make sense. I resolved to speak with each of them separately to gain a better understanding.

By the time I had reached this decision, the sun was almost up. I decided to head to market. I had taken over any lifting that Zanette needed, and I was to buy a sack of four. I would get it done early before they awoke and therefore be back as early as possible to talk to them. My clothes were hanging over the end of the bed. I quietly slipped them on and tiptoed out of the room.

I brought my horse from the field and rode into town. I hoped I had not awoken Zanette. At that thought, I had another realisation. I had lain awake the whole night and yet it seemed to me that I had not heard Zanette sleeping. She had been as silent as the grave and hardly moved, but I had not noticed her breathing change to that of the sleeper or the dreamer. At that, I stopped myself. Was I thinking myself into a storm that was not there? Was I now seeking out ways to condemn her? I thought it would profit me better to put the matter into God's hands and to the back of my mind.

It was a lovely day, and I could feel the heat of the sun on my skin.

There was a slight breeze. It was on the chilly side. It wasn't long before I arrived at the marketplace in the centre of Halkirk. The people here were friendly and had always shown us kindness since our arrival from out of town. I had made some good friends here, albeit by myself.

Zanette didn't seem interested in getting to know the locals. While at the market I bumped into an old sailor buying vegetables and whisky. He was a kindly man in his fifties, by the name of Amis.

"Good morning Amis, how are you on this fine day?"

He turned and removed his cap. "Very well sir. A perfect day for sailing."

I smiled. "You sailing today then, Amis?"

He looked and shook his head. "No sir, perhaps tomorrow. We are awaiting our travellers but we are unsure when they will be arriving so we are making our preparations now."

"Hello Mrs McCloud. Just a sack of your finest flour, thank you."

She turned from serving a customer and smiled. "Of course, General Walker, anything for you!" She began to fill a sack.

"You best be careful me lad."

I looked at Amis. "Pardon?"

He placed his cap back on his head, pulled out his pipe and began to light it. "We have had people disappearing from the trails around these parts. There one day and gone the next. You best not be leaving your womenfolk and weans unprotected." He drew close to me to warn me further. "The very worst of it is too terrible to speak of in public." He stared into the middle distance with a look of foreboding. "We have come across one lady in the fields with her head clear blown awa'"

I was stunned. "My God, Amis. I did not know. I shall return quickly home. Was the man responsible caught?"

Amis looked at the woman eavesdropping into our conversation and she quickly turned away. "No. Some say she did it to herself. Some say it was a dark beast unknown to us. Very strange, if you're asking me. Buried in unconsecrated ground, she was. Upsetting for the family."

I nodded, not knowing what to think. "How awful."

Amis took a puff of his a pipe. "There have been tales floating around. The locals believe this to be what they call the striga up in these parts but I have heard on my travels that similar things have been happening in the north of England, and in London."

I prayed to myself that God would spare us more deaths.

"The striga? What's that?"

Amis tipped his pipe upside down and patted the bowl until the leavings inside fell to the floor. "Striga is an old time word for 'scream'. It seems people have heard screaming from different parts of the land, yet no bodies have been discovered so far. Those animals must have eaten every last morsel. Best keep watch over your family, sir. An' talking 'bout keeping watch – I must get back to the ship. I'm back on duty soon and the captain likes to be punctual. So I be off now sir. Take care, now."

I nodded to him. "And you my friend."

I collected my flour and was back on my horse ready to ride when all of a sudden I heard a woman's scream. It seemed to be coming from behind the warehouse near the port. I turned my horse and headed towards the cries. As I approached I saw the woman standing with her hands over her face, crying. I jumped down off my horse to find a second woman lying on the ground, extremely pale and thin. Her neck was black with bruising.

As I approached her, I noticed that her eyes were frozen open in horror, her mouth contorted into her last cry before expiring. Her face looked nothing so much as that of a woman of advanced years, yet she was young. I heard footsteps running around the building. A crowd began to gather, the port's watchman among them. My first instinct was to help the watchman find the rogue who had so terrified the very life out of this young woman. I wished I had carried my sword with me. Many's the time in twenty years I have been called upon to use it to defeat our country's foes and I could have been counted upon to defend the town as best we might. It now rested in its scabbard, in the parlour.

"Who did this?"

"Is she dead?"

"Did anyone see anything? Step back, everyone! Get back please!"

The crowd looked at the body in horror. Their fear was palpable. The girl's black neck was reminiscent of plague. People stepped back; some bustled quickly away. Fear arose in my chest. The killings were more frequent than I thought, and the beast was becoming bolder – enough to kill near a crowded market place. Suddenly afraid for Catherine, I remounted my horse and rode off in the direction of my house, hoping that Zanette was there to protect her.

He saw the cottage approaching ahead of him. Peaceful and surrounded by flowers, it was a wonderful sight to return to when I had been away. It soothed my heart and for a brief moment I thought no evil could occur here. This idyll was suddenly broken by a sharp scream. Catherine! I clipped my horse who, sensing my panic, galloped towards the house and reared up just outside. I jumped off, still clutching the flour.

I kicked open the door to find three people gathered around the stairs. There was at first a tall, slender woman with long, white hair at the bottom of the staircase. She quickly turned around to face me. Her eyes! I never saw eyes like that it in my life. They were bright crimson! I looked over her face to see two long sharp fangs on the top row of her teeth. There was a man further up the stairs. Our home was being invaded by attackers! It was then I noticed Zanette behind the other woman, kneeling down in front of – oh God – it was Catherine!

"Stop!" I screamed. "What are you doing?"

My eyes slid from Catherine's face. She was terrified but my gaze was drawn down to her neck, which was streaming with scarlet liquid. I looked at Zanette's mouth and saw it too was covered in blood. I was shaking inside with shock, not knowing how to comprehend what I was witnessing. I felt numb.

At that I dropped the flour, which slid from my hands, crashing to the floor in front of me, darting here and there into clouds. The first woman approached me with her mouth wide open, her fangs glistening and her eyes boring into my soul.

"Get back, demon!"

The woman stopped short and turned to face Zanette, who spoke to her as if she were human.

"Hold. He is not to be harmed!"

It was then that I realised that it was Zanette who commanded these attackers. My flesh ran cold at the dread thought. I looked at Zanette and then straight at Cathy, who was in the grip of the man. Her innocent little face was as pale as the moon with the shock, and looking so frightened at her neck and upper body covered in splashes and spreading pools of blood.

"Let her go, damn you!"

I was slowly edging my way towards the parlour, remembering my sword was just behind the doorframe. The man let go but not before he checked with Zanette. I could scarce believe that Zanette was the one behind all this – my own wife! What in God's name was going on? Who were these people and how could Zanette be doing this to my little girl?

I wanted to weep with pity at the sight but I held my mettle for the sake of Catherine. It would benefit her none to see me upset. She needed someone strong, someone who was going to protect her. I felt a deep pool of regret for dismissing her claims about Zanette the previous evening. I should have listened! But I could never have imagined such a turn of events, not even in a nightmare.

"Jon, this isn't what it looks like!"

I knew the minute I heard the words she was lying. I felt them pierce my heart. She began to move down the stairs towards me, never moving her gaze away from my eyes.

"Stay away from me Zanette! I don't know what you are you but you are not killing my daughter!"

I noticed her arm holding her stomach protectively. Our child slept within. At least, I had assumed our child lay within. Seeing my wife so transformed made my body shake, my mind was full of questions. I could not know what was contained within the walls of her belly. I didn't know what to believe anymore. This was not the woman I had fallen in love with and married. This was something else, another creature entirely: a base creature of darkness. My stomach lurched to recall the amount of time I had spent in her company, the nights I had unknowingly lay with a demon. I felt sick.

"Jon, please let me explain."

I continued to move slowly towards the parlour, staring at the malevolent trio, looking for the slightest sign of attack. "I won't say it again – let her go!"

Zanette nodded to the man holding Catherine and he released her. She ran to me quaking with fear, tears streaking her face. I held out my hand toward her. Catherine ran into me, hiding her face in my clothes. I immediately pulled her behind me, backing up into the parlour. Three pairs of red eyes were now fixed on us as I reached the doorframe. My hand felt around it for my sword: it was just inside. I pulled it from its scabbard and held it up in front of me like a shield. I had faced many fighting men in my career but the three creatures that faced me now shook me to my very core.

"Get out of my house!" I shouted. I could hear the fear in my voice.

Zanette stepped forward.

"Jon please listen." Her voice was soft and kind and for a moment I doubted my previous fears. But one look into those eyes and I knew I had been correct. She was lost to me now. What remained of my wife was some hideous shell of pretence. I looked straight into her eyes, warning her I was serious.

"I want nothing more to do with you – whatever you are! You are an abomination! Call your servants back or I swear I will be forced to defend myself."

Yet Zanette moved further towards me. I held the sword up and sliced the air front of her. It nearly caught the skin of her translucent neck. Now taking my threat seriously, she stood back. The woman with the white hair suddenly leapt forward to attack me. In a flash I raised the sword and with the barest flick of my wrist caught a vein. She grasped her throat, fruitlessly attempting to contain the dark streams of liquid leaping forth. Her eyes seemed to turn green and she fell to the floor, emitting a sputtering sound before falling silent. The blood gushed out from the open wound and formed a dark pool near my feet. I pushed Catherine still further out of harm's way, and stood back with her.

Zanette held a hand up to halt her henchman, never breaking gaze.

"Jon you need to understand I wasn't going to kill her. I was giving her a gift."

Anger tore through me. "A gift? A gift!" My eyes darted back and forth between both of them. "This is not a gift! This is the Devil's work. Creatures like you are not gifts! You are against God's will! I want nothing more to do with you or that… thing growing inside you!"

And then Zanette approached me, as I had seen her do many times before in our marriage. She would come to me and calm me when my work had aroused in me an irritable mood. She would soothe me and stroke my head, and make our little corner of the Earth well again... It all happened so fast. These were no longer the eyes of my loving wife; they were the eyes of darkness. I felt my whole body being wrenched in two that she was no longer there, and, before I knew what I was doing, I thrust the sword forward, and it disappeared into her stomach in a through-and-through.

Her eyes stretched wide, staring into mine with disbelief and she gasped. I let out a deep cry of pain at my own actions. Our eyes were no more than two inches apart. I held fast to my sword. She took the hilt of the sword into her hands and backed herself off the blade, groaning haltingly, breathlessly. Blood gathered and dripped from the glistening edge. Her movements became slow and childlike. Her eyes were filled with tears and looked down at her stomach and then up at me. She held her wound tightly and called out in short, frightened cries of pain. Blood rapidly emerged from between her fingers and was also now forcing its way down from her pale lips. Like a small child forgetting how to walk, she staggered forward no more than two steps, and dropped to the floor.

Her servant man took hold of her and began to pull her towards the door. At first I seemed to feel Zanette's pain when I saw the fear in my beloved's eyes as she realised the extent of her wound. This though was replaced by my love for Catherine. If I had not interrupted, the darkest forces I had ever known would have taken my little girl from me. Try as she might to pretend a show of affection, I knew that from the moment I introduced them, Zanette could not love my Catherine.

This bleeding ragdoll being dragged away in front of me was not the woman I thought I knew. Somehow that vision was gone. Instead this was some vile, writhing bloodsucker, human only in appearance. I knew I should feel no more shame for mortally wounding her. She tried to harm my daughter, an innocent child. She could not have become this monster overnight but over some considerable time. I believed Zanette must have lied to me from the beginning but, because of her beauty and her many other wicked charms, I had not been able to see it.

Although I had not witnessed the last breath escape from Zanette, I knew that in all likelihood she would be gravely wounded. Even if she somehow recovered, surely her injuries would mean that she would live the rest of her life as an invalid? And yet... Something inside made me wary of underestimating her. I did not like to leave a job unfinished.

My first priority however was to protect Catherine and make sure she was completely safe. Zanette would no longer be in our lives and especially not in Catherine's future. Her servant had remained unharmed. I would need to seek him out and destroy them both. I followed the evil pair outside, my sword in hand. I would have completed my task there and then, but Catherine had to come first.

"I shall allow you to leave while ensure my daughter is protected but as soon as she is safe, I will hunt you down like beasts. I promise you this – the next time we meet, you will breathe your last!"

I watched as tears streamed down Zanette's face as she was pulled towards the fields in front of the house. I watched until they reached the trees and were gone. I stared after them for a few silent minutes and closed the door; I locked it turning to see Catherine standing behind me. I ran to her and picked her up, holding her to me so tightly, my arms locked around her. I hugged my beloved child to me as if by doing so our flesh would join together and she would never be in danger again. I felt tears on my face, wet against her hair. Hurt and fear rose deep within me. Part of me didn't believe what had just happened, the extraordinary events of that day. I went over and over what had happened, scarcely believing it. I had nearly lost my child. Dear Lord, I nearly lost her. She was crying over my shoulder still shaking.

"Don't worry Cathy, sweetness. She's gone. I'll make sure no one hurts you again. As God is my witness, I promise you that. I'm so sorry for not believing you." My legs buckled and I started to slide down the door until we were sitting on the floor, bound together. I had thought myself to be the foremost warrior in the King's army. Yet this creature was the most formidable foe I had ever faced. I now understood. My own weakness, the love I felt for Zanette, had led me to be blind to her evil. Worst of all, the greatest gift in my life, was also its greatest vulnerability: Catherine.

That day I resolved to return Catherine to my cousin's in London for safety. It wasn't an easy journey. I had to explain to Catherine that what happened was to be kept between the two of us. I knew that if she told anyone they would not believe her. I did not wish for her to be looked at or treated differently. I would have done anything to protect my little girl from harm.

I thought back to my days as a carefree youth before I married. I was a soldier for hire, paid by the King. I fought for King James and my country, for my family and my village. Nothing though could have prepared me for the all-consuming need to protect my child. I look upon my life as being in two parts: before becoming a father and after becoming a father. It was Catherine I worked for now. She was everything. She came before village, country, even my monarch.

I eventually settled Catherine at Elizabeth's house, although it was a very long time before she would leave my side, even for an instant.

I would return to Halkirk but not before going to see some friends of mine from the Army. I knew I would need a well-trained band of soldiers to stand alongside me if I had to call on a greater force for combat. I have to admit it took all my powers of persuasion when I related my story of exactly what they would be up against. I daresay more than one thought that since I left my commission, my mind had become feeble.

But they offered to help when I told them that Cathy's life was in danger. No matter what they believed, they put it aside to stand with me in the fight I would need to win for the safety of my daughter and for all our families and children. Soon enough they would see the truth for themselves.

We journeyed north for several days. One day, we were glad to take our ease for a few hours at a tavern in Durham, in the north-east of England. It was a cold, wet day and we were glad of the shelter. We traversed the cobbled bridge that had seen many a market day and tied the horses under the arch of a tavern across the road on other side of the river.

A few tankards had been downed in the tavern, when I overheard a man talking about a special voyage that was going to take place off the northern coast of Scotland. It sounded not too far from Halkirk. I listened closely, hushing the men. The voyage would take a couple to an unpopulated island. I had not heard of the strange-sounding place: Fugloy. What I did recognise was the feeling in my insides telling me that Zanette had a part in this voyage.

We ate a good meal and rode off north as soon as possible, stopping only when necessary for food, drink and rest. It took a few days to reach the borders. The further we rode into Scotland the more tales of disappearance and deaths we encountered. In particular, the people of the region of Caithness had reported larger groups, a whole family included, suffering either death or an illness that had the appearance of the Black Death. People were afraid and had barricaded their doors. Some locals talked of wild beast attacks. A physician said he had discovered a pale, drawn corpse entirely drained of his blood: a young boy of around ten. Some used an ancient word, *hirudo* to describe the kind of beast: a bloodsucker. On hearing this, my men looked at one another, not saying a word. Any doubts they had had for the truth of my words or the health of my mind, they were beginning to put aside.

It was obvious to me that Zanette and her cronies had been far more active in the area than I had previously thought. She must have had something to do with these killings – the highest number of the dead on our whole journey appeared to be in our hometown. They had to be stopped no matter what the cost before they destroyed more lives, and I was the one to lead the attack.

We arrived in Halkirk a couple of days later and I rode straight to the centre of town and called a town meeting. I told people that I was organising a hunt and kill operation to finally track down these beasts. The town was buzzing with stories of the killings and talk about what the meeting would hold. Everyone gathered at the parish church.

"People of Halkirk, I have asked you here today to discuss an urgent and pressing matter. Recently, I have had the misfortune to discover a creature that goes against all of God's natural laws, preying on the weak and the vulnerable. You have all heard the rumours of bodies that have been found, drained of their blood in various locations across our beautiful country. I fear that it is not only Scotland that has been attacked. This creature I speak of is like nothing that has been encountered before. It appears human in appearance but is far from it.

"We need to destroy this entity before we suffer the loss of more of our loved ones. Look around you and see the faces of your wives, your children. Do you really want to live in fear of your families' safety? We need a plan of action to protect all those we hold dear by coming together and gaining support enough to track down and kill this being and stop it from harming anyone else. I am currently seeking strong, hardy men to join this noble mission. What say you?"

Silence filled the room, people looked at one another and whispered amongst themselves. Shock and fear could be seen spreading across some faces. Some husbands, however, looked at their wives and sat back in their chairs, as though what I had said was utterly ridiculous. Not one person stepped forward, nor did they speak. For a moment I felt like a fool. People began to drift away. I decided to take in some air and await their response.

As I was walking out, I saw a face I knew. It was Amis, the sailor I had met. He had been among the villagers. He had been the only one who believed what I said completely. He himself had told me the stories about the striga some time ago. I informed him of what I had discovered on my travels. Amis looked around the room.

"Let us talk outside."

We made our way out. We left people talking animatedly amongst themselves. We went to talk over by the church wall. This far from the public, it was obvious he did not wish to be overheard. I slowly approached him, looking over my shoulder.

"So you're looking for a female called Zanette, is that right?"

I looked at him and nodded. "Yes, do you know where she is?"

Amis pulled out his pipe and began to pack it full of tobacco, pressing down on the contents and then lighting it. "Not by the name of Zanette, no." He sucked in a deep breath through his pipe and let it out slowly.

"Then by what name?" I said, trying to calm myself.

"We recently travelled to an island called Fugloy with two passengers, by the name of Amelia and Lucas."

I stood waiting for more. "Yes?"

Amis looked at me and lent against the church wall. "I'm not saying it's them, yet it was passing strange – they carried no bags with them and no food, yet they did not come to the mess to eat. They kept themselves to themselves."

It was not much to go on. "Amis – could they be who we're looking for, or no?"

Amis stared me in the face and stood up straight. "I'd say it was worth a sea voyage, my friend." He paused and then walked on, around the corner.

If he was correct, we could set off almost immediately with his help. If he was mistaken, then we would have to keep looking until we were successful. But first I needed to find a ship to take us there. I looked around for Amis, but he had left.

I walked back into the church and gathered volunteers for my mission.

Our next step was to secure a ship and a crew to take us, and soon.

I made enquiries for days for a ship but no one would take us, even when I increased my price. People were afraid and wanted to stay close to their families. Men of the sea are superstitious and I heard many reasons why the mission would not put to sea. I was told it was too dangerous, that the shore could hardly be reached, even on a calm day, that the moon was not clear enough to navigate by, that sea serpents had been sighted...

At long last, we heard of a ship that was bound for the island. It was some distance from Halkirk though. It was setting sail from the north east of England in a couple of days. There was no way we would reach it by then.

Again we were held back by delay after delay. The only thing that we could do was to tell people the tales we had heard, and spread the word about a woman called Zanette, or Amelia and her servant, Lucas. We offered a reward for any trace of her whereabouts, any ship she might sail on or arrive on. The bounty was enough to attract a few contenders, former marksmen of the King's army, now eking out a living as hired militia. One way or another I would find her. I spent the days of delay training my volunteers in the art of fighting. We trained hard and long to develop many ways of killing Zanette and her accomplices.

The next time we met, I would be ready.

Chapter 5
Fugloy Island

Amelia

As promised, Callum, I mean Lucas, found a small, old dwelling surrounded by overgrown thorn branches and hardy bushes, survivors of the harsh weather. It wasn't much. It reminded me of my house back in France: a small stone-built cottage with only one room, a cooking area and sooty fireplace at the back. The roof had deteriorated a little and holes allowed the rain to fall through in places. For now though, this was my home.

Lucas started to clean the place up while I stood outside overlooking a small patch of grass and trees. Birds of all kinds filled the twilight air with their calls. I still couldn't believe how much my life had changed over the last couple of weeks. I looked down at my flat stomach and stroked it, for a moment thinking she or he was still slumbering in there. A tear rolled from my eye and once again I was flooded with images of what happened back in Halkirk.

I looked up at the sky, the rain drizzling on my face. I sucked in a deep breath of air and tried to calm myself. How could Jon have done this to me? It hurt so much I couldn't breathe.

"My queen, all is prepared."

I turned to find Lucas in the doorway. "I'll be right there."

I breathed deeply. I looked around this dark place that was going to be my home. I walked inside and sat next to the cold, empty fireplace on unsturdy old chair that felt as if it might give way with little warning. Few human comforts surrounded us. A feeling of desolation crept into my mind. I quickly dismissed it. This was my life now and I had to get used to it... somehow.

"Lucas, when is the ship due to arrive?"

Lucas was near the door, looking outside. "In the next day or two, my Queen."

I stood from the chair and walked towards him. "How many aboard the ship?"

"I gather there is about thirty to forty crew, my queen."

Interesting...I could have a small battalion in a matter of days. "Once they arrive, I want you to bring them to me, do you understand?"

"All of them? How am I to get all of them here?"

I placed my hand on the side of his face. "In whatever way you can, Lucas."

I walked to the back of the house where a small table and chair stood. I sat and gazed out of the small window close by. My heart started pounding and I could feel myself beginning to well up again. My child... I was going to be a mother and Jon took that away from me. I felt a rush of anger in my body. I could sense Lucas looking at me. He began to walk over. I put my hand up.

"Just leave me be."

He nodded and left. It had been a while since Lucas had left and I started to wonder where he was, when I heard creaking and banging coming from the roof. I went outside to see Lucas trying to fix the holes.

I sighed and re-entered the house where I sat back on the chair listening to world outside. It was dusk and the weather outside began to change.

The rain started pounding down on the cottage and despite Lucas' efforts, leaks sprang from many parts of the roof.

"I'll fix them by morning my queen."

In all honesty, my general malaise stopped me caring about such things. I was grateful, however, that Lucas was taking good care of me. We rested quietly that evening, each lost in thoughts of lives left behind, and possible futures. Neither of us felt the need to speak. Lucas lit the fire and we sat staring at it. It was the first time that day I had felt warmth.

I chose not to read his thoughts, so wasn't sure what he was thinking of. I could of course use my energy to listen, but with no way to feed, I knew that it would drain my strength. With nothing to sustain us at present I left him alone.

Morning came and it was a lovely day, cloudy but dry and with some glimpses of sunshine. Lucas didn't go outside so much during the day. I suppose, like me, he felt safer and more alive at night.

"My Queen, we should prepare for the arrival of the ship. If my calculations are correct they should be here a day or two at most." I went to the fireplace and picked up a burnt piece of wood. At the table, I began drawing on the top.

"This is what we shall do. Firstly, you will bring as many crew back here as possible. Before I turn more humans, I will need to build up strength by feeding. Secondly, I want you to bring me the captain. He will be a great asset to our colony and we will need him to bring more people over."

Lucas leant forward while I drew an outline of the island and roughly where we were situated. "I want a building, enough to house roughly one hundred people. I want separate chambers overlooking the ocean. It must be built close to the shoreline, high above the waters. How quickly can you erect this building?"

Lucas closed his eyes, working out the build in his mind. "If we use our strength collectively, I say it could be built within three to four months, my queen."

Three months. Hmm... "Very well. Have it completed as soon as possible."

It wouldn't be long until I had the Empire and Army I wanted.

A couple of days had passed and Lucas had gone to meet the ship. I had no idea what he had ordered but it filled me with great interest. Lucas was very resourceful and I trusted him to build my kingdom. That very day, I heard a march of people approaching from the other side of the island. I awaited the arrival of the men who would soon be under my control. I heard Lucas' voice from a distance.

"Thank you all for coming. Out of respect for your coming here to work, my lady would like to thank you personally before arranging your payment."

Payment? I had no money. I was momentarily puzzled by Lucas' promise to the men. It then occurred to me that his intention was to delay them with the promise of payment. I could then meet them individually and transform each of them.

I walked out of the house to see a gathering only a few yards away.

Lucas acknowledged me and then announced me to the men.

"Allow me to introduce my queen, Amelia."

I could see the men look to one another. "Queen?" some men murmured together.

Lucas turned to me and nodded. I stood feeling the energy rising within me, only slowly at first, but I felt stronger moment by moment. "Dear friends, thank you for coming to my island."

The men, unsure of what was happening, started talking amongst themselves. I could feel my energy almost to breaking point. "I wish you all a happy life within my coven."

"Coven? What dark hell is this?" one man screamed.

I released my will over the men in front of me. I instantly felt their hearts beating and, unexpectedly, the hearts of three women.

"Silence! I am Amelia, your queen! You will obey my every wish. Do you understand?"

The crowd stood still, quiet without moving and together they nodded. I could feel my energy weaken. I had to act quickly before they regained control of themselves.

"You will line up, and enter this house, one by one."

Every one of them, without question, moved into a single line in front of the cottage as I took up my seat inside. They entered one at a time. I drank.

Time and time again, I bit into my wrist to draw blood to spill into their wound. I was able to sustain my power with every mouthful. I transformed a score of them. I knew that more were aboard the ship including the captain, who would be so important to my cause. I needed the ship and someone to sail it.

I walked outside to find most of them on the floor convulsing and shaking. It took several minutes before all was quiet. One man remained. After all my work, I felt weak and needed to feed properly.

I approached him and tilted his head to one side. My fangs slid out, and down I went. My power over the men had waned and I struggled with my hold over the man in my grasp. As I drank though, he began to weaken, tears rolling down his horrified face. Suddenly his heart stopped beating. I had drunk every last bit of him. I was feeling refreshed and energised once again.

Facing my converts, I propelled my will out to cover them all. "Welcome to my family. You are all to start building our home. Lucas will show you the way and give you directions. Should anyone be foolish enough to break my will, you will answer to me. Do you understand?"

Everyone nodded and looked towards Lucas, who walked off leading the way to where the new home would be built. I watched them for a little while and decided to head to the ship and finish off what I required.

The journey didn't take me long as my strength was full and I could tap into the energy I required to get me there as quickly as possible, running a few miles within a matter of minutes. I reached the shore and on the beach was a small wooden boat, empty.

I climbed aboard and began to row myself across to the ship, anchored offshore. The waves were beginning to gather and the clouds overhead let out a roar of thunder. I reached the ship and was given a hand onboard from a crew member.

"Will you take me to see the captain?"

They looked from one to another and then down to the boat expecting to see some crew or at least that I had been escorted.

"Erm, this way my lady. He's in his chambers."

I followed the man to the wooden door.

"Right in there, miss, the door at the end."

I turned to the sailor and nodded.

"Thank you very much." I walked through the door and down a long dark passage. At the prow end was a double wooden door. I entered without knocking to find the captain bent over a table looking at his charts. He straightened up. He was a stocky man of over sixty with a face that the stormy seas had licked over many decades.

"Who the hell are you? Do you have no manners madam?"

I walked up to the table where there was a chair and sat down.

"By all means sit!"

I crossed my legs and placed my hands gently in my lap. "I take it you are captain of this vessel?"

He moved around the table and stood just at the side of me, his hand resting close to the sword attached to his belt. "What do you want?"

I looked up and stared into his eyes and smiled. "You, my good man." I allowed the energy to build within me and released it into the room. The captain dropped his hands and his gaze fell forward. He didn't blink or move. I could feel his heart beating, the blood flowing through his veins.

"Now listen to me. You are about to be given a gift. You will obey me and only me. Do you understand?"

The captain nodded mutely. "Very well. Come, kneel in front of me and bare your neck."

He moved slowly and did as I requested. My fangs slid down and I pulled him to me. My teeth sank into his flesh. The warm blood rushed through my veins and I pulled back to expose the wound. I raised my wrist and bit into it allowing a flow of blood to pour down my arm and drip into his wound.

His eyes shut and he fell backwards on to the floor. He started to shake and I could hear his heartbeat slowing down towards death. He convulsed, shaking hard, his fist clenched then after a few moments, all his tension slipped away and he lay flat and still.

I knelt beside him and watched the rest of his transformation. The wrinkles on his brown patched forehead and around his eyes began to disappear as his skin paled and tightened. His wild and wiry grey hair started to turn a silky brown. His stocky frame began to develop more contour. His eyes flew open, the colour of crimson.

"Now." I leaned in and took a fistful of his shirt, lifting him forward.

"Who am I?"

He slowly rose from the ground and bowed in front of me. "My queen."

I moved towards the door and, taking the handle, I said, "I have something for you to do, captain. Head back to the mainland and do whatever you can to bring one hundred people to my island. Do you understand?"

Again he bowed. "Yes my lady."

I thrust out my will to cover him and forced him down onto his knees.

"Sorry?"

He looked up, afraid he had offended me.

"My queen! Yes, my queen!"

"Very good. You leave tonight."

I walked out of the room and closed the door behind me. Back on deck the crew stared at me as I re-boarded the little boat. Behind me I heard the door open and the captain give orders to prepare to sail. The crew looked at one another and began their duties as ordered.

*

Over the next few weeks the ship came and went dropping off a great many people. I understood they had been told that a great seam of gold had been discovered here, so there were no shortage of volunteers. One by one these simpletons were turned.

I heard that there was a group baying for my blood. Calling us the *Hirudo* and *Upir*, meaning bloodsucker. I didn't want my colony called such ridiculous names; after much debating with Lucas we decided on Femme Fatale, or Vampire. This seemed to fit and I liked it a lot. I gathered all those who were turned in to a meeting place and I stood high upon some stones and looked out towards the crowd, most of them looking at me with big red eyes. Lucas stood in front of me. "Silence! Your queen is about to make a statement." He turned to me and nodded.

"Thank you, Lucas. You have all been given a gift, the gift of life. You will no longer be afraid of this world or the next. We will stand and take control of this world as our own. You will feed freely once we have conquered the rebels that are hunting me, your queen. This cannot and will not be. I proclaim that all who have tasted flesh and have my blood running through your veins will be from this moment known throughout the land as vampires!"

The crowd cheered.

"All bow to Her Royal Highness and the founder of all the undead! Queen Amelia!"

A loud roar filled the air.

"QUEEN AMELIA!"

Chapter 6
My Empire

Amelia

Almost three months had passed. Lucas kept his word. Our heightened strength and speed meant that in that time, he had produced a beautiful 100-roomed house a few hundred yards from the cliff edge. I often stood and watched them build, my colony of workers.

It would be our new home. Lucas showed me around the building, starting with the foyer. Deep, dark velvet reds, lush blacks and browns dressed the chairs, the soft furnishings and the stairway. In the centre of the room was a huge fireplace burning bright with wood retrieved from the surrounding woods.

He escorted me down the hall at the back of the foyer to two large doors. Gold filigree panels dressed the door. Lucas drew aside a piece of material to unveil a decorative shield that Lucas had produced for me. He told me that this was my crest and asked if I liked it. I must admit I did, my plans were coming together and I couldn't be happier.

Lucas directed me through the doors and down a long dark brick corridor lit by flaming sconces hanging from the wall. We came to another set of thick wooden doors, which Lucas opened for me. I walked through to find a huge room with high ceilings and stone walls on all sides. A stone walkway divided the room in two down the middle, and either side two huge pools flowed silently over the edges by the walls. Big golden lamps lit the way to the other end of the room, where nine hand-carved chairs were situated. One chair was placed at the centre. It was higher up with the most amazing golden crest above it.

"This, my queen, is your throne."

It was beautiful and I could tell a lot of hard work had gone into it, and indeed the rest of the room. I was stuck for words. I had never seen something so beautiful in my life. I couldn't help but smile.

"Lucas, it is beautiful. You have done a first rate job. Why are there four seats either side of the throne?

"My queen, these will be for your council."

I turned to face Lucas. "Council? Why do I need a council?"

Lucas walked forward towards the throne and sat in the seat to the left.

"My queen, a council will help you to build and manage your kingdom. You don't want enemies focusing on any weak spots you may have."

I could see his reason and in fact that it was a good idea to have people I could trust.

"Very well."

I approached the throne and was amazed how detailed it was. It was the only chair made of smooth stone, like marble. I ascended the first step, turned and sat down, placing my hands on the armrests. It was a strange feeling. I looked down at Lucas sitting there with his legs crossed, looking over the vast empty room.

"My queen, we are still building, but the house is ready to move into now."

I stood from my throne and walked back towards the doors. I turned to face him. "Shall we?"

Lucas stood up, smiled and walked towards me. "After you, my queen." He opened the door and we walked out.

It was exciting to see what was finished. All the rooms were dressed in red velvet with stone floors, huge fireplaces and flickering torches lighting the hallways. It was magical. I had finally got what I wanted, my seat of power, my castle, the cornerstone of my empire.

"My queen! Your chambers await."

He showed me through a set of double doors leading to a large room covered in the finest material and filled with gold hand-carved furniture.

In the middle was a large four-poster bed with engraving on the posts.

Draped round it was pure white cotton. It took my breath away.

Lucas showed me around my room. In front of a large window was a huge desk littered with fine ink quills and a large padded chair. On the other side of the room was a large double set of oak doors. I opened them and immediately felt the salt breeze over my face. They opened onto a large balcony overlooking the ocean beneath. It was outstanding.

I turned and walked back in the room.

"How many have we now?"

Lucas faced me. "Nearly 200 vampires and forty humans, my queen."

I walked over to the desk and sat behind it, placing my hands gently forward. "Once the humans have finished their duties, do we have anywhere to place them? We need a food source."

Lucas went to the desk, opened a drawer and pulled out a long scroll, the plans of the building. "Here, my queen. We have a secured cave towards the bottom of the cliff, directly linked to the main chambers. We will place them there until needed."

Suddenly our meeting was interrupted by a large bang as a man barged into the doors and they flew open, crashing into the walls. We span around to see him standing in the doorway, trying to catch his breath.

"How dare you burst in!" Lucas said walking towards the man with purpose.

"I'm sorry for intruding my lady, but we have a confrontation downstairs in the main room."

"Lucas! Allow the man to talk."

Lucas was already at the side of the man and about to place his hand around his throat before pulling back. "Go ahead, talk!"

The man, looking scared, took his gaze off Lucas and turned to me. "My lady, two of the men are disgruntled and trying to leave the building. Others are trying to halt their progress with force."

I turned to Lucas and waved at the man standing in the doorway. "Lucas – see to it. In fact, bring the two men to the main chambers. I think it's about time we put down some ground rules. We don't want the others causing disruption."

Lucas nodded and left the room.

So it's started already, I'm not even moved in yet and already there are rumblings of discord.

I made my way to the chamber and took my rightful place on the new throne. I felt exalted. I felt powerful and untouchable. Lucas walked in shortly afterwards with the two men, held securely by two vampires and then followed in by a dozen humans walking behind them. The two men were arguing and struggling to get free from the grasp of their restraints.

"Silence!"

The two men didn't pay any heed, and continued to argue. Lucas walked down towards me and took his seat by my side. The humans gathered at the back of the room looking towards one another.

Still the two continued their struggle and loud complaining. Silently I summoned my energy, releasing it into the room to cover the two men alone. They immediately stopped their bickering and looked forward. I stood up and walked to them. I felt their heartbeats and the blood flowing through them. I forced them onto their knees before ceasing my will, whereupon the two men looked up at me, silent and confused.

"Now. What seems to be the trouble?"

The men looked each other. The man on the right spoke first. "We want to leave."

I stared at him for a moment. "What is your name?"

"Brandon."

I looked to the other man. "And you?"

"Michael."

I turned and walked to my chair to sit back down. "So you wish to leave. I'm afraid that is quite impossible, gentleman. If you are unhappy in your duties, I'm sure I can make another use of you."

The one named Brandon stood. "We are leaving. You can't keep us here. We have done what you asked of us."

I didn't move. "I'm sure you have, but you must remain. You work for me now." I addressed the room on onlookers.

"Listen to me all of you. You will never leave this island and should you attempt it, you will be met with swift execution. You are in my land now."

I turned to Lucas. "Show them to the cave. All of them."

Lucas proceeded. Brandon reached down and pulled a knife from under his belt. "Stay back! I mean it!" He cast the blade from side to side threateningly.

I could see two vampires move forward. I placed my hand in the air, to which they stopped. I moved from my chair and approached him. "You wish to leave, Brandon. Very well."

I looked deep into his eyes. For a brief moment, triumph appeared in his eyes as if he had been victorious against me. He looked at the other humans, smugly. I exhaled, disappointed. I took his throat in my hands and pulled away the flesh. Huge amounts of blood flew up and out onto my arms. The man's body dropped to the floor, eyes wide open, still blinking. The rest of them gasped in shock; some screamed with fear.

"Does anybody else have any troubles they'd like to discuss?"

Nobody spoke. "You two." I pointed at the two vampires that had held them. "You are now my guards. Take the second man to the cave and make sure he cannot escape. Gather the others and place them all in the cave. Use force if necessary."

"Yes, my lady." The two vampires turned and guided the rest out of the room.

"Lucas, please dispose of that," I said, indicating the body lying on the floor.

"Of course." Lucas gathered two humans from the crowd and gave them instructions. I turned back to my throne.

Only after the room had cleared did a strange notion take a hold of me. I noticed the difference between how I felt now, and how I would have felt in the early days of my marriage. Perhaps one day I might again glimpse the young girl I once was, full of hope and love, in the days when my only desire was to be a good wife and a mother. Those feelings seemed such a long time ago now. I felt like the love that used to inhabit my heart had drained away through cruel treatment by others, through disappointment and through lack of use. The girl that I had been was no longer there. I felt cold and emotionless, as if I had lost my humanity.

I wondered if this was what I was supposed to be. I no longer felt warmth or compassion. It was as if the whole world was against me and I wouldn't allow it to hurt me anymore. I felt as if every part of me was looking at life in a different way. Humans destroyed all happiness that I had in the past and the more it happened, the weaker I felt. Happiness as a human was no longer my destiny. It was of some comfort to realise I need never experience those feelings of weakness and powerlessness again. But this did not make up for the fact that I was not to be the thing I had previously desired most: to be a mother. I quickly put the thought aside and returned to the present.

Whilst sitting there on my throne I couldn't help but think about Jonathan and his last words to me. Did he really hate me enough to come and destroy me? Was I really so repellent to him? This thought made me, for the first time, truly feel evil, and at the same time so very lonely.

Yet, I now had a kingdom. I would only grow stronger from here. I should have what I always wanted.

Chapter 7
Council

Amelia

Time seemed to pass so quickly that I barely took note of it. It had been almost ten years since the night I arrived in Dover. My castle was finished and we had grown in numbers. I now had the servants I had always wanted – some of our humans. There were four people on the Council now excluding Lucas, I always felt like he was my right arm. Things were beginning to come together.

I heard a rumour from the mainland that I was still being sought by Jonathan. Humans that were brought to the island would tell me about it. I found out that he was building a secret army to track us down and destroy everything I had built. But I was not going to allow him to take it all away. Lucas, my second in command wanted to travel back to the main land, hunt him down and destroy him and his army. I just couldn't bring myself to allow it. My foolish heart! Deep down I still loved him and the thought of killing him made my heart stop. I knew he didn't feel the same for me anymore. Although my own emotions were fading I still clung onto my love for him. I knew one day I would have to face him, but not yet.

The Council and I were gathered in the main chambers discussing our daily routine. We had two sisters on the council, Tanzeda and Borbala De Planis from France, by way of Eastern Europe, and Philippe from France. The sisters were quiet and polite which concealed a hunger for blood that I had never seen before in a vampire. They would discuss their votes together before answering. They both had long, dark, wavy hair and bright crimson eyes, which was odd. Their eyes never changed back to a normal colour.

They fed very often and treated humans like cattle. They never agreed with humans being treated as equals, as some of the other vampires wanted. The sisters were beautiful, as most vampires were when they changed. The sisters thought humans should know their place, and indeed would attack any vampire who disagreed with them.

Philippe was more outspoken and said whatever it was that came to mind. I had to admit that I had a very strong Council, making my life so much easier, and allowing them to cover in my absence. I was kept informed of all events though, and with my blood running through all their veins, I had a firm intuitive connection.

It was late afternoon when we gathered for a Council meeting. In turn a number of vampires and humans were allowed to plead their case. The sisters had little time for the humans but sat quietly and gave their answer at the end. First was a man called Zach, he had been put forth as the leader of the humans on our island. He stated the same request each and every time he addressed the Council. He wanted better living conditions, better food, more freedom. The answer was always the same from the Council.

"My queen," he began, "if you want better work quality out of the humans you should allow them more freedom. We feel like cattle amongst your kind and we fear who will be picked off next for food."

I would sit and listen to him but my mind constantly wandered, distracted by the past, hopeful but anticipating of future.

"My queen?"

I looked up sharply as Zach looked at me. "What say you?"

I looked around the chambers to the other Council members. All eyes were focused on me. I could hear the thoughts of the sisters becoming impatient with this man, and Philippe's thoughts too were a mass of annoyance. 'No' presented itself as their consensus.

"My dear man, after consideration we feel you are not listening to what we say. Time and time again you come to us and ask the same questions, and demand the same changes. You must know your place. You all must learn and accept your place! Your requests have been noted. Perhaps in the future, we can make a change, but for now, I will merely take what you have asked under advisement."

Zach stepped forward, "But my queen I need to go back with some sort of answer. They are waiting for me."

I placed my hands on either side of my throne and lent forward.

"I beg your pardon? How dare you challenge me! Do not test me Zach, you will have your answer in due course. Now leave us!"

Zach bowed then turned and left the chamber.

"We cannot allow this my queen, if you give them what they want it will never stop asking."

I turned to Philippe and sat back in my chair. "I understand what you are saying, but do not forget that they are our food supply and we do not want to create a hostile environment. I have too much on my mind at present, and we have too much to achieve. I believe we should allow one concession and give them better quarters."

The chamber filled with anger from everyone including Lucas.

"You cannot be serious, my queen."

I stood and walked down from my throne and over to the side of the pool, gazing into the shallow waters. I turned and looked at them still shouting and arguing. I felt my energy rise and released it into the room, I could feel my fangs descend.

"Silence!"

Everyone became quiet. I released my hold and saw them slowly coming back into focus.

"I respect your opinions, however Zach has a point. We need to look after our humans if we want to continue feeding from them and keep the peace."

Tanzeda stood and placed her hand on her hips.

"You don't know what you're doing. Philippe is right. If we give them what they want, it will not stop there. Soon we will be answering to them, is that what you want?"

I didn't have the energy to go into a full debate. "Tanzeda, you will not speak to me in such a manner. As for their request, allow Zach and the humans to have more comfortable quarters. Inform them that should they anger me in any way they will be confined back to the cave."

I turned and walked to the door. "Dismissed!"

I slowly walked out and back to my room. I opened the balcony doors and stepped outside. The sky was dark and it was raining. I looked down to see the waves crashing against the rocks underneath me. The breeze blew on my face and pushed my hair back.

I went inside to my desk. I opened the top drawer and took out a small wooden box. I sat down and placed the box on my lap. I slowly opened the lid and took out the locket that I had taken from my grandfather. I closed my hand around it, my eyes closed. My head flooded with regret. If there was only a way I could be the person he wanted me to be. I felt so lonely and empty. I missed him so much. This was the only object I had left from my past. I clung onto it as if it were made of emeralds. I opened my eyes to a knock. Lucas stepped inside and closed the door behind him.

"Are you unwell, my queen?"

I placed the locket back in the box and quickly placed it in the drawer. As I closed the drawer Lucas started walking over to me and sat himself down on the chair opposite me.

"My queen the ship has arrived with supplies."

I looked up at him. "Take care of it Lucas, I'm in no mood for this today."

Lucas stood and bowed and headed back to the door. He looked at me.

"Is there anything I can do for you?"

I stood from my chair and walked back to the balcony doors, without turning I said quietly, "Your duties Lucas!"

As he left, I returned to the cleansing air of the balcony.

I heard another light knock and in came one of the servants with a tray. On the tray was a silver jug and a glass. She was only a young girl with blonde hair and blue eyes, very small and slender. She reminded me of myself when I was younger. I turned and watched the girl place the drink down on my desk. I came inside and took a seat.

"What's your name child?"

She looked at me with fear in her eyes. "Eleanor, my queen."

I sat and watched her stand, nervously fiddling with her apron.

"What a lovely name Eleanor, please have a seat."

She looked up at me and started to cry. "I beg your pardon my queen I didn't mean to interrupt you."

I smiled at her and offered my hand pointing to the chair in front of me.

"You have not disturbed me Eleanor, please have a seat. I wish to talk to you a little."

The young girl bowed and took a seat. I sat back watching her, she looked at me through her wet eyes.

"Are you afraid of me, Eleanor?"

She nodded, her eyes wide in fear.

"Where is your family?"

She placed her hands over her eyes and wiped her face. "Dead my queen."

I stood and turned to look out of the window. "Did they die here?"

"No my queen. They were killed when our hovel burned down. I was the only one that survived."

I could feel my emotions building inside of me. I knew what it was like to have your loved ones taken away from you.

"I'm sorry to hear that Eleanor. I too had my family taken from me at a young age."

I turned and took my seat again, staring at the young girl. "You have been with me some time now, I believe?"

The girl looked up and nodded. "Yes my queen, approaching five years this spring."

For some reason I liked her. "I would like you to become my personal maid. You will have a room close by and listen only to me. Are you agreeable?"

The girl looked up but something in her eyes told me that she was afraid of what I was offering. "I–I don't want to d–die my queen."

I was a little shocked at that comment.

"Die! Why would you say such a thing? I do not wish to have you as my own blood supply. No harm will come to you under my ruling. Now answer me this, can you sew?"

The girl stared at me for a moment. "Yes my queen."

"Can you cook?"

Again the response was the same.

"Very well, you will cater to my needs. You have my promise that no harm shall come to you while you are under my protection. Gather your things and move into the chambers next door to me. I will inform everyone."

Eleanor stood and moved towards the door. "Thank you my queen."

I turned and stared out the window looking out at the raining pounding down on the balcony. For a few brief moments I was able to regain some of the warmth that fled my heart all those years ago. It disappeared in an instant with a sharp bang of my door. I turned to see an elderly man in my doorway.

"I want my gold!"

I slowly walked back to my desk and took my seat. Lucas was but a breath behind him. He grabbed the man by the throat and forced him to his knees. "You will pay for your outburst old man!"

I looked from Lucas to this man kneeling on my floor. "Lucas?"

He turned to look at me and I nodded to him. He let go of the old man who fell to the floor gasping, trying to get his breath.

"Now! Who are you? And what did you think you would gain by bursting into my chambers?"

The man looked up grabbing his throat and coughing. "I was promised gold to come here and now I find we are prisoners!' He pointed at Lucas. "I want what he promised me and then I'm leaving!"

I took a deep breath and sighed. "My dear man, you are not going anywhere. You are in my charge now. Normally I would have had your life for your impertinence. But I feel in a forgiving mood at present, so you will be confined to the cave until further notice."

"I will not, you cannot hold me here."

I could feel myself becoming less tolerant. "Don't test me old man, or you might not live through this outburst of yours."

The man slowly got to his feet and began to walk towards to me. Lucas was in front of him and, in a flash, took hold of his throat. He looked over his shoulder at me, awaiting my command.

"Lucas show this man to the cave, if he gives you any problems you know what to do."

Lucas nodded and forced the man back to the door. Lucas turned to me before leaving, the man struggling for breath in his grasp. "My queen we need to talk! Something has been brought to my attention. I think you should know. Allow me to take care of this man and I'll be right back."

"Can this not wait till later?"

"No my queen."

I waved at him and turned back to the window. "Very well."

I heard the door close and a scream coming from just outside. Lucas was never the patient type, I knew by that scream that Lucas had at least caused him some pain, but most likely had killed him. Lucas liked to control the humans around him, and he was very loyal to me. It didn't seem to matter that he was once a human. In fact, to me it seemed that he too was losing his humanity and compassion for the human race. I toyed with the thought that it must happen to everyone who joins our kind.

Moments later he returned. "Please come in Lucas. Apparently knocking is something that everyone has forgotten how to do. Please stop calling me my queen. Call me Amelia. It's bad enough with everyone calling me that. I should like to hear my actual name mentioned, sometimes."

Lucas walked over and sat down at my desk. "Amelia, I have some news. Back on the mainland it's rumoured that Jonathan is already on his search for you. It's only a matter of time before he finds us. May I suggest I take a small group of vampires back to the mainland and eradicate this at once?"

"Lucas, you know my intentions: at the moment I don't want any harm brought to Jon. However if you feel strongly, I will grant a few vampires leave to oversee his movements and report back to me. Nothing is to happen to him: do you understand?"

Lucas nodded and started to walk towards the door. "We shall leave with the ship."

I walked forward and placed my hands on my desk. "You are not to leave, Lucas. I need you here. You will send two others in your place."

"No." Lucas turned on his heels and stared right at me. "I will not allow that to happen. I would willingly take on this challenge. I will sort it out myself."

I could feel myself becoming agitated with him. "Lucas I will not repeat myself. Do as I ask. You're far too important to me to be risking your life. Should there be any problems, I shall re-evaluate the situation. One more thing, no harm is to come to Eleanor. I am taking her under my supervision."

Lucas looked confused. "Eleanor?"

I sat down. "Yes Eleanor, the human servant. She is now under my control and I don't want anything to happen to her."

Lucas nodded and turned towards the door. "I think you're making a huge mistake."

I stared at him. "Eleanor is mine. Do you understand?"

Lucas turned and walked towards me. "I'm not talking about the human, I'm talking about Jonathan. You should allow me to go."

I stood up and walked around the desk and placed myself in front of him. "Don't overstep your mark, Lucas. I will not tolerate it."

Lucas frowned and walked out the door, slamming it behind him.

I don't know what's got into him. Why would he risk everything? He must know that Jon will be able to identify him. If he doesn't do as he is asked I may be forced to make him listen. Jon will kill him on sight. He saw what happened to Jane. Jonathan is quick and brave. The last thing I want is for him to find me.

There was a knock at the door. Eleanor entered quietly. "I have placed my things in the room next door like you asked. Is there anything else I can do for you, my queen?"

I walked around the desk and stood once again in front of the window.

"You can alert the Council members that I wish to see them in the chamber at once."

"Yes, my queen." I heard the door open and shut.

I really must sort out this problem. I can't have Lucas risking everything. I must set some ground rules. Starting with the Council.

I walked in and proceeded to my throne. Everyone was there including Lucas, sulking in his chair. He didn't even look up when I entered the room.

"Ah, I see you are all here, good. I wish to make some things absolutely clear. I know that some of you wish my plans to change in regard to the small problem on the mainland..."

"Small problem? Are you forgetting who it is that is pursuing us?"

I placed myself in front of Lucas, my energy rising within. "Listen to me Lucas. You are not in charge and you never will be. I can tolerate only so much Lucas, don't test me. I grow tired of your constant arguments." I walked back to my throne and sat.

"Right, we have a small problem with a group back on the mainland. At present they do not know where we are. To keep the peace we will not be attacking first. Lucas is to send a couple of guards to keep an eye on them and report back to us frequently. If there is any reason for concern then we will discuss action to be taken then and not before. Do I make myself clear?" Everyone in the room agreed.

"Very well, Lucas, attend to your business. The rest of you, to your duties!" I walked out. I walked to the main lounge and sat near the big stone fireplace. Dark, red velvet curtains on either side of the windows shuddered in the draft as I swept past. I sat staring at the open fire, thinking. Mainly of Jonathan.

Chapter 8
The Army

Jonathan Walker

Six years had passed since the night I found out about Amelia. Catherine was still safe living with Elizabeth in London. I arrived back in Halkirk to gather people to join my alliance. I trained them in battle and purchased swords, knives and even crossbows, an old-fashioned weapon but some of the older men preferred them. We trained hard in the fields near my home. We worked long and hard to raise the fighting standard as befits an attack on a dangerous foe.

There were twelve men in my group and we all focussed on protecting our families as our main aim. It kept us strong. We would fight each other to see who could gain control of their opponent. I was pleased by their progress. From this group, I sent the two strongest men out in search of information on the whereabouts of Amelia and the man she was travelling with. The men were gone for months at a time, spreading the information I taught them. I was propelled onwards by a constant burning need to track down Zanette and prevent further deaths. I vowed I would find her even if it took the rest of my life. I had to.

I received news on a possible location for Amelia. It seemed to confirm the place that Amis had told me six years ago, the location of an island north-east of Scotland. It was called Fugloy Island, one of the Faroes Islands. I wasn't sure how to get there but I would find a way. I had yet to find the sailing passage, but providing a good amount of coins would bring someone forwards, in time.

I received news that a ship was coming into port down in London. This ship was coming from Fugloy Island and would return there in the next couple of weeks, having gathered supplies. That was the very ship I had been seeking. We would go down to London and clear a passage to Fugloy. If Zanette was on that island, we would find her.

I gathered the men and told them my plan. The years of waiting and training had built them into impatient soldiers and they raised a cheer to finally be given their mission.

We gathered our belongings and rode to London. We had to make good time to ensure we did not miss the ship. After that, a simple payment should buy our berths, although my insides were again telling me that given the strange circumstances of our quest, all might not be straightforward.

We arrived in London the day the ship was due to depart. As we approached the ship, we were met by a young man in a captain's uniform. There was something familiar about him, but also odd. It was if I was looking at an older man but with the body of a young one. There was something familiar in the way he moved but I could not quite pinpoint what it was. I approached him.

"Good afternoon."

The captain looked at me and lit up a pipe. "What do you want?"

He didn't seem friendly. In fact he seemed quite hostile. "We are looking for a job and place to lay our heads."

The captain stared at me. "Heads? How many are there of you?"

I looked into his eyes and a chill ran down my spine: there lay the tiniest flicker of red. I could have been mistaken; it could have been the light.

It was a beautiful day and the sun was high, not a cloud in sight.

"A dozen altogether. Do you need men?"

The captain turned to look towards his ship, and then back to me. "I have no use for you, but I do know someone who is looking for miners. Over on Fugloy Island, there is a man looking for experienced men to dig and find gold. He will give you a job and a place to lay your head."

My spirits rose: we would be sailing to the island directly. "There are jobs and passage for all of us?"

The captain grunted "Aye" and strode up the gangplank to his ship. "I set sail in one hour. If you're not aboard by then I shall not wait for you."

He took hold of a rope and began to coil it. "You will board and you will be quiet. Any trouble from you or your men and you will be swimming the rest of the way. Do I make myself clear, boy?"

"Perfectly," I replied. *Boy*? The man must have been younger than me by at least ten years. Yet his voice sounded older. I put it to the back of my mind: we had gained passage to Fugloy Island. I returned to the alley where the men were waiting and told them the news.

"Remember, don't say a word about our mission. On the ship and the island, we must appear to be just like the others until the time is right."

Everyone nodded, took up their bundles, and we made our way aboard the ship. The captain was talking to another man onboard the deck. He stopped once he spotted us approaching. "Down there." He pointed towards a door that led to the galley.

The barque was in a dire condition: the wood inside was slimy with moss and mould, rotten floorboards surrounded us and the smell of decay hung in the stagnant air. It made my stomach retch. From my days on the battlefield, I recalled exactly what the stench was and a grim sense of foreboding travelled its way through my body. I knew the smell from that day at the cottage when I had banished Zanette. It was the smell of fluids of the body and rotting flesh. There was very little light in the galley. Filled with trepidation, we lit a couple of rusted lanterns that we found lying on the floor.

As the wick took the flame and grew strong, light hit the walls, and to a man, we all reacted in horror. Blood had been sprayed over the walls in fine mists and in larger washes. What looked like claw marks had dug into the timbers of the walls, ceiling and floor. We gazed open mouthed, taking in the grim sight. Wood had been dented and splintered where it had been kicked. A closer look revealed the claw marks had been made by both adult fingers, and fingers that were far too small to make much more of an impact than small scratches at waist height. My heart grew heavy as I realised what this meant. Many people, both young and old, had been on board this ship and for some reason were desperate to escape. By now we were all feeling extremely uneasy.

"You there."

I looked up to see the captain on the stairs, putting down a bucket of water and looking down at me.

"My name is John."

He didn't look amused. "I care not for your name. While you are on board my ship you will earn your passage." He threw down wet mops and cloths. "You will swab this room clean and remain below as we sail.

"You will be allowed on deck only in the evenings and you will eat and sleep down here. Is that understood?"

Everyone nodded. The captain made to leave.

"There's a pleasant man," one of the men said under his breath darkly, trying to raise our spirits.

The captain overheard him, marched back down the stairs and up to his face.

"You cross me and you'll be put overboard and keelhauled! I won't tolerate insubordination on my ship!" He stormed out, slamming the door behind him. I turned to the men.

"We must wash away this horror. We cannot risk losing any of our number to the captain's whim. We must hold fast to our swords until we reach our destination. Together we are strong. We must all reach the island."

It was approaching night-time and much of the stench remained. I was keen for us to take in fresh air and, as the general, it should be me who went first. I decided to check the lay of the deck, and that it was safe for us to visit. The rest of the men stayed in the galley, very subdued but unable to sleep.

The moon was high in the night sky, dancing in and out of the thin clouds and she afforded me clear views of the ship and the surface of the sea. The deck was empty: not a soul was about. It was eerily quiet; seafarers might have mistaken ours as a ghost ship. The only sounds were the creaking of the ship and the flapping of the sails as the vessel moved gently up and down on the undulating waves. It was a fairly still night. I toured the deck, taking in its layout. Part of my role as an officer had been to use such knowledge in case of battle.

Finally, I walked over to the side of the ship and rested against the wooden railing. I gazed out at the sea, although I could see little on the horizon. Looking down at the water, I became lost in thought. I wondered how deep these seas were, what lay at the bottom and how many souls had been lost to Neptune over the years. Would we be the next to join him?

"You're going to Fugloy Island I take it?"

I turned to see a man in a filthy top and ragged dark navy trousers. He was possessed of a face that had been carved by the sea, and deep furrows traced his forehead and eyes. Over the years, the winds had eroded his hair back over his head, yet a beard still protected his chin.

"Yes. We're going to try and make a living."

The man looked out across the vast ocean. "You're wasting your time, sir."

I turned to face him. "Why do you say that?"

He glanced over his shoulder and around the boat.

"I hear all kinds of stories about that place. People will go ashore, never to be seen again."

"If you're afraid of the voyage then why do it?"

"My family needs the money. This pays well. I keep my head down and do my duties. But be on your guard – this is not a place I would be from choice."

A sudden creak from behind us set the sailor's face tense. We turned to see the door closing to the captain's quarters.

"I'm in for it now."

"Why?" I asked.

"He knows." Fear covered his face and he quickly left.

Knows what? I wanted to find out more but it was too late: he'd gone. I went below deck to get my head down. I lay there slowly rocking back and forward with the movement from the ship, until, a long time later, I must have drifted off to an uneasy sleep.

Over the next few days the voyage kept to the same routine: no one spoke, except my men amongst ourselves. There was still a strange atmosphere on board. As the days passed, I kept a lookout for the man I'd met that night, but I never saw him again. I finally asked the captain about him but he merely shrugged and turned away.

I knew we were getting close to the island: birds were flying overhead.

The smell of the salt water and the refreshing breeze up on deck was invigorating. It was extremely cold, though. The clouds had darkened the sky and flecks of rain were starting to fall. The captain approached me.

"We are nearly there. Gather your men and your belongings. We will drop anchor within the hour."

The smile on his face didn't inspire confidence. It was the type of smile that hid something, as if he knew of some dark surprise that was planned for us. Little did he realise that we knew what was ahead. I just hoped that we survived whatever awaited us on this, bleak isle.

We arrived nearby and anchored offshore. We would be put on a boat over to the island. We were to be met by someone on the coast who would take care of us, since there was no one else on board the ship to do so. I was surprised to find out that we were expected.

I had visions of Zanette standing on the coast awaiting our arrival and pictured the look on her face when she saw me. I saw it again and again. I saw myself condemning her kind as against nature. I knew God would help us to stop her. God, too, would forgive her. But it would be my life's work to strike her down. My resolution was absolute. I would put an end to this killer like I had done any foe of the King. She was as contagious as the black disease of my childhood and was spreading her plague to others.

I knew of at least one follower of hers that was still alive. Callum was the name she had called him that last day I saw her. I would need to find and kill him too. I reasoned they would be together. With both dead, it would be over and I could return to my life in England. I trusted in God to keep me safe, and held my daughter in my mind as the driving force of my mission. I missed Cathy desperately but I would soon be with her again. I would move back to London, gain a home and live in peace. Now though I had to put such thoughts out of my head.

It took a while to reach the coast. The sea was unforgiving and would sweep us back with every stroke of the oars. Everyone had to pitch in to help row and steer. It was hard work fighting the great grey waves. We finally put ashore, exhausted. As expected, someone was on the coast awaiting our arrival. A tall, stocky man with short hair and a black suit stood patiently on the shore, barely moving. He had deep, dark eyes and an odd demeanour, not dissimilar to the captain. Again there seemed a contradiction in that he appeared to behave like an older person, yet looked younger than I. He kept his words to a minimum, but they were spoken in the voice of a younger man. We dragged our belongings off the boat and onto the beach.

"Follow me."

We did as he asked. His gruff brevity was slightly unnerving. He gave us no introduction and hardly spoke more. When we asked questions we were only given a nod or a grunt. The only thing he did say was that it was a couple of hours' trek and to keep up. We kept our heads down and followed him.

Evening was approaching and the rain was beating down on us, soaking us completely. Thunder filled the air. The wind was strong and we fought it every step. We could only just make out the man that was our guide away in front. He did not appear to struggle in the wild conditions. After a couple of hours I could see in the distance a large new-built house. It was the biggest building I had ever seen and was situated back from the edge of a cliff. Lamps flickered away in the windows. The house got bigger and more impressive the closer we came. This was not what I was expecting at all.

I figured that the owner of the gold mine must live here. I wondered where Zanette might be. We trudged onwards, our feet soaked in cold, wet mud. I will admit my only thought then was to get the men inside, and get warm.

Chapter 9
The New Recruits

Amelia

"My queen, the shipment has arrived and with it twelve humans. Do you want me to place them in the cave until you wish to address them?"

"Yes Lucas, we must keep watch over them. I will see to them in due course but for now, I place them in your charge."

Lucas left the main chamber. I continued with the business at hand, discussing a problem we had encountered. Philippe strode over to me and continued after the interruption.

"My queen we must find a way to store blood. The vampires are feeding regularly and we do not have the resources to continue feeding everybody. We have a limited supply of humans and our coven is three times the amount of humans. We need to bring more humans to the island if we are to survive and not starve."

I tapped my fingernails on the side of my throne and looked at Philippe.

"I'm aware of the situation Philippe. We are doing what we can without bringing attention to ourselves. Do not forget we are still only a small coven and must remain inconspicuous until we have greater resources. It will have to be a supply that is within this building, a collecting point of some sort. We will disperse and take a week to consider options. We shall meet again next week to discuss it. For now we have enough to keep our supply going. I will leave it to you Philippe to ensure a daily ration is enforced."

Philippe walked to the edge of a pool and stood in contemplation for a moment before turning to the sisters. "What say you? Do you agree with this?" They looked at each other and nodded. Tanzeda approached Philippe. She took his hand and raised it to her mouth. She lightly kissed his hand.

"You worry too much, Philippe. The Queen has already said she will look into it. You mustn't worry so."

I looked at Tanzeda and Philippe, surprised to find that there appeared to be more to their relationship than being fellow Council members. I had never seen her do that before.

"Do either of you have anything you would like to tell me?" Both looked at me and shook their heads.

"No my queen. I would like to reassure Philippe that all shall be well." They exchanged a brief glance and then returned to their seats. I was not convinced and felt there was something unspoken between the pair.

I supposed it was not of great importance if their relationship was closer than it appeared. Certainly I had not seen evidence of it, but still I felt a little uneasy. I thought I knew everything about all of my subjects: our shared blood made it easy to hear their thoughts. I pondered the idea of introducing a regulation against members of Council becoming personally involved. I could not have disobedience and I could not have any distraction from the completion of my plans.

Borbala stood with a question about the caves that spread underground beneath the main building. We had mentioned using them for storage of food and equipment. "I believe the workers have finished the lower levels of the house. What are your thoughts for the use of these levels, my queen? We have received no exact plans."

"As you know, we have designed them for storage. However, we may need to reinforce them and use them as holding pens for humans or prisoners."

Borbala smiled. "Very good, my queen. They will be most useful, I think."

I looked around the room towards the others. "Are there any other areas to attend to?"

No one spoke. "Very well, you are dismissed. Philippe? See that no one gets more blood supply than necessary."

All stood as I left the chamber. Philippe left to attend to his duty immediately.

That afternoon I heard that the humans had been placed in the cave as requested. I spent most of my time in my chambers, mainly outside on the balcony watching the waves crash against the rocks below.

Occasionally, Eleanor would come in and deliver my supply of blood. It seemed more appropriate to my status to drink out of a glass than drawing it from the neck myself, although my preference was for the original way. The blood was always cold when drinking out of a glass.

It didn't give me the same satisfaction. Sometimes I would go and indulge myself on a human; I often craved the act, but ignored my desires.

I watched Eleanor clean my room. She was light on her feet and she would do all her tasks with such devotion that I almost forgot that, in reality, she was a prisoner here. We would chat a little from time to time. She would tell me about her past and we would swap histories. I knew that the Council would not approve of such friendliness with a servant. Lucas had muttered one day that I was playing with my food. It felt cold to dismiss our friendship like this. I liked Eleanor, perhaps more than I cared to admit to the others. I still felt the old feelings about being a mother and did not seem to be able to eradicate them from my heart. I tried to be strong but I could not bear the thought of turning into some stone-hearted ruthless leader. I hated the thought that it might already be too late.

I was well on the way to having everything that I had always wanted. Yet I had become diverted by a growing idea. I did not seem to be enjoying this new life as much as I thought. To think: six years ago I had a husband, a loving home and even a baby on the way and, apart from having to feed occasionally, life was perfect. Now look at me – I am a Vampire Queen on my own island, with a huge stately dwelling. I have grown a large coven and have servants. And yet I yearned for more.

I was not born into the life of a ruler. I was unused to such opulence. I imagined I would take to this life with ease, yet I seemed unable to control my emotions. One moment it would feel like I was losing my humanity and the next I would pray for its return. My mind felt quite distracted by it. Another part of me enjoyed feeling more powerful than I ever had in my life before, the ruling and the freedom. It was liberating to be able to do and say what I wanted with few arguments. Maybe I would be a great ruler and someday I might be content with who and what I am.

Two raps on the door interrupted my searching questions. "Yes?"

It was Lucas. "Amelia, everything you have requested has been carried out. The humans are locked in the cave. Is there anything I can get you?"

I was still on the balcony with my back to the salt air watching Lucas walk in. I placed my hands on the railing. "No, not at the moment…"

Lucas turned to leave. "Actually – yes there is one thing you can do. I want Tanzeda and Philippe watched. I want to know if there is anything romantic between them. I am not happy with Council members being too friendly with one another. In fact, let that be known. Whilst in my home and within my coven any love entanglements are to meet with my approval."

Lucas' eyes widened; he appeared taken aback. Evidently he wasn't expecting me to say such a thing. "As you wish," he said, and closed the door behind him as he left.

Eleanor was still in my room cleaning. She would gently pick things up to dust and then reposition them. She had a gift of making the place look attractive and cared for. I noticed that since moving into the room next door, she seemed more relaxed. She was striking, her blonde hair bounced as she worked. For a brief moment I thought she would make a wonderful addition to my coven. But as the Council stated, we don't have the resources to change any more humans at present. I was going to ask Eleanor if she would like to join our family. I hadn't given others a choice, so in one way I was being unfair, but then Eleanor meant more to me. I decided to put the matter aside for another day.

"My queen, do you wish me to dress you for this evening?"

I snapped out of my daydreaming. "This evening? Yes of course. Go ahead."

She left the room and stepped into an adjoining smaller area in which I kept my clothes. She began to look through my eveningwear.

"I like this one, my queen: you would look rather elegant." She pulled out a dark blue satin dress with a white net scarf and navy blue shoes to match.

"Yes that will be fine, thank you."

Eleanor came and placed the outfit carefully on the bed. "Should I attend to your hair first, my queen?"

A quick look into the mirror at my hair hanging loosely down around my shoulders made me confirm. "Please do, Eleanor."

I went and sat in my chair in front of the mirror. Eleanor came over and began gently brushing it. It was soothing and my worries about enjoying the life I had created slipped away. I didn't even notice the smell of her blood until she leaned over to place the brush down on my dressing table. A warm waft of sweet-smelling youth flooded my nose. I could feel my fangs starting to push down on my lower teeth. I tried not to breathe but the scent was so inviting. As she reached down again her neck became very close and I noticed her suddenly stare at me in the mirror. I turned to look. She had noticed my eyes burning bright crimson and my lowered fangs. I turned away from the mirror and her view.

"Fetch me my drink!"

Eleanor quickly ran for the jug. Nervous, she reached for it too quickly. It slipped from her hand, spilling blood all over the floor followed by a crash of the jug.

"Oh no! I am so very sorry my queen! I'll clean it up at once!"

She shot a look at the dressing table looking to gauge my reaction, but I was no longer there. By now, I was but a foot away from her. She gasped, backing up against the desk that now held the empty jug. I slowly moved towards her, my eyes fixed on hers. I could hear the sound of her heart beating faster and faster. The shortage of blood meant I had never felt so hungry.

Before I knew it, I had her by the throat and was lifting her up off the floor. I moved in close, my breath caressing her neck, saliva dripping from my fangs. I was just about to pierce the skin when I caught sight of her eyes. They were streaming with tears. She was frozen in terror and could not speak. I blinked, snapping out of my trance, and let go of her immediately. Her body slumped forward and she held her neck and crawled away.

I moved back. "Get out," I said quietly, not looking at her.

I heard her scramble to her feet and run out of the door. I stood leaning against the dressing table, breathing heavily. I looked up into the mirror and for the first time noticed how terrifying my blood-red eyes and sharp teeth looked. I was utterly shocked. I had never gazed upon myself in the glass like this. My skin that once had been flushed and healthy was a translucent pale, almost blue, colour. Beads of sweat had appeared at my forehead and the whole picture seemed to possess a quaking, jagged quality, like some wild thing I had heard of in the tales of my childhood. I was a monster.

I dropped onto the chair and examined my likeness as the moments passed by. My eyes were already starting to turn back to their bright blue and my fangs started to withdraw. I rested there, trying to compose myself. There was a knock at the door. I had to overcome my instinct to hide. "Yes, what is it?"

One of the guards stepped a foot in the door and bowed. "Pardon me my queen, but you wished to see the humans that arrived today."

I had forgotten. I resigned myself to carry out this duty. Alone once more, I dressed myself in the gown that Eleanor had laid out for me and slipped on the shoes. My heart felt heavy. I would apologise to Eleanor later when she had calmed down.

I followed the guard to the cave. It was a long walk, down narrow stone corridors lit by the small fires burning in the holders. We reached the cave. I peered in to see four or five men lying on the floor.

"Open the bars," I commanded. The guard took out his key and proceed to open the bar doors. I stood there looking around the cave at the sleeping men. "I thought there were twelve men here."

The guard stepped forward and lowered his voice. "They are working on the land my queen, collecting firewood."

I nodded and turned to walk out when I heard a voice behind me. "What do you want from us?"

I turned and saw a man in his fifties, although he could have been older.

"You will find out soon enough." I swept out, leaving his shouts to grow quieter behind me as I left. "When the other men return from their work, bring all twelve to the main chamber. I believe the Council may want to meet these men. We might have a great use for them."

The guard nodded and followed me to the main council chamber.

"One more thing: make sure that you take reinforcements with you when you collect the dozen."

"Yes my queen," said the guard. He walked me to my throne and then left.

I was the first to arrive. It was a peaceful room and the only sounds were of the water trickling from the pools and the crackling fire that lit the room. It was beautiful.

Lucas was the second member to arrive. "Good evening Amelia." He made for his chair, at my side.

"Good Evening Lucas. Have you had a productive afternoon?"

"Yes. I have taken the liberty of making use of the men that arrived today. I have locked them back in the cave for the time being."

"Excellent. I too have come up with a plan to help us with the blood shortage."

At that the sisters arrived, walking in with Philippe. Before I could move on to the business at hand, I was interrupted. Philippe's face was irate. He stormed towards me thrusting his chin in the air.

"Is this true? That we must ask your permission if we wish to court?"

I nodded calmly.

"What gives you the right to control who we see?"

I stood from my throne and walked down the two steps to face him. I felt my energy rising. This was not the first time Philippe had defiantly questioned my word.

"Philippe you will understand your place here. If you wish to leave the coven, then I'm sure we can come to some arrangement. However in this house you will obey my rules. Is that in any way unclear?" Philippe came closer to me. His eyes were flaming red, his fangs had emerged and his hands were clenched into fists.

"How dare you! Who do you think you are, talking to me in such a manner? Without me, your so-called coven would fall to pieces!"

"Do not threaten me Philippe. I am not in the mood to deal with your outbursts today."

He marched over to the sisters and placed his arm around Tanzeda's waist. "You cannot and will not stop me from having affairs with whomever I wish!"

I moved calmly towards him and smiled. "My dear Philippe, you are in no position to demand what I can and cannot do. For your insolence, I'm stripping you of your title. You are no longer welcome as a Council member."

He seemed neither surprised nor disappointed. In fact, he seemed rather pleased with himself. "Very well, I will continue this at my own leisure. Come Tanzeda. She has made herself quite clear. We are free to leave."

Tanzeda didn't move. She no longer met Philippe's gaze but stared at me, anxiously. "What about me, my queen? Am I too stripped of my title?"

I smiled. "Of course not." She seemed relieved. "Philippe, I think you misunderstood what I said. I never said you could leave. I said we could arrange something for you."

Philippe turned and watched me for a moment. "Exactly what are you going to do? Force me never to see her again?"

I smiled and walked calmly back to my throne. "Not quite." I toyed with him. I sat down carefully and placed my hands on my knees.

"Well, when you have thought about that, my queen, please *do* let me know. I'll be gathering my things!" He began to storm out of the chamber, glancing over his shoulder at Tanzeda, who remained immobile.

"Are you coming?"

Tanzeda looked at me, then to him. "I'm sorry Philippe but I cannot. I'm happy here. I'm sorry." She walked towards me, bowed and took her seat next to her sister, Borbala.

"You are going to let her rule you, is that it? Her kingdom is going to fall and burn, I can assure you!"

With that he resumed his march towards the door. I released my energy and aimed it at him. He ceased his march and within moments was unable even to move his head.

"I don't take threats lightly, Philippe. I am tired of your moods. I no longer think your future is with us. Guards!"

Four guards hurried in.

"Take him to the caves. He will burn for his insolence at sunrise."

Tanzeda rose in shock from her chair. "My lady – no! Please – I beg of you. Will you not consider a banishment instead?" Borbala placed a protective hand on her sister's arm.

I fixed my gaze on her. "Unless you wish to share his fate, I suggest you quiet down."

She retook her seat, looking silently at Philippe, tears forming at her eyes. Borbala took her sister's hands in hers. "Shh, dear sister."

I looked up to see the guards dragging Philippe away.

"Unhand me, you fools!" he barked angrily, but his pleading eyes never once left the gaze of Tanzeda.

The doors slammed shut.

"I believe I will have to pick my council more carefully in future. I will not be made to look a fool. Starting tomorrow we will have new rules in place and punishments for breaking them. I will not be disobeyed.

"And now, unless we are to hear yet more insolence, I should like to get on with the more pressing business of continuing to be able to feed ourselves! Lucas? I have thought about the shortage of blood and I have decided that, along with the rationing plan, a large storage area is also required. It should be kept cool and should be of a large size in order to store all of the human blood we drain. I suggest one of the underground caves. You shall take on this task. You must ensure the pool is covered and guarded at all times.

"Yes, Amelia."

"Thank you. It is good to hear somebody who is keen to hold on to his head! Dismissed." I left the chamber. The door slammed behind me, echoing a report off the walls.

The humans that arrived that morning would have to wait until the next day to know their fate. I passed the guard outside my chamber. "No one is to disturb me tonight, do you understand?"

"Yes my queen."

I locked the door behind me and headed to the balcony for some air, wanting to consider the evening's events further. My eyes took in the night sky and I watched the moon rise and, over the next few hours, followed its journey from left to right. I had had enough insubordination. I could not rule effectively if I could not rely on my followers' complete obedience. I would put rules in place to force them to listen. I was still taken by surprise by Philippe's behaviour. How dare he? Clearly, if one of my closest advisors could stage this protest, I had a lot of work to do. I sighed at the thought of the size of the many tasks ahead.

For now though, I would rest and think. I would begin again tomorrow.

Chapter 10
The Burning Escape

Jonathan Walker

We reached the house soaked to the bone. Our guide didn't seem fazed by it. We approached the big thick wooden doors at the front of the house and walked in. It was a large, grey stone building of a size that one might associate with aristocracy, such were its dimensions.

I halted upon entry as I was met by the most opulent interior. Inside it was luxuriously decorated with the finest tapestries and materials from the best merchants I had noticed on trips to London. We were quickly escorted into a large stone-floored room with stairs leading from the left to a huge inside balcony that overlooked the entire room. I had never seen such extravagance.

On the far side of the room was a vast fireplace with wooden logs burning, spitting and crackling. The light was subdued and calm. Candles were dotted around the room, their flames straining against the draught from the open doors. People stared at us from dark corners, where small groups gathered at carved wooden tables inlaid with contrasting marquetry. At the back of the room was another set of double doors covered in iron with two men posted outside. Our escort finally spoke.

"Leave your things here. They will be bought to your quarters."

Without saying another word he waved for us to follow him. Through the double doors at the back we turned left through a small passage. It was dark with the odd flickering of light from the fire torches standing proud of the walls. The tunnel wound on and on. We seemed to be descending below the house. We finally stopped at some bars. I peered through them, but could only make out a dark cave.

"You can sleep in here tonight until the lady of the house sees you."

"Pardon? You want us to sleep in there?"

The guide just nodded.

We peered into the cave dubiously. "We still don't know your name."

The guide exhaled sharply. "If you want to work here you will do as you are asked. The lady of the manor will come down to see you shortly."

I walked in to see if there was any light ahead. The others followed me. I span around at the sound of clinking metal as the guide locked us in.

"What do you think you are doing? We are not prisoners!"

The guide grunted and walked away down the passage and disappeared. Something wasn't right here. His final look towards us had seemed to be that of an animal sizing up his kill, rather than welcoming new workers. He was very odd. The cave was damp and cold and dark. The only light came from the passage and even that wasn't enough to properly make anything out in the dimness.

"Charles?" I called.

"Over here, John."

As my eyes grew more used to the dark, I began to make out a shadow leaning against the wall. "Did you bring any tools or weapons with you?" I could just make out his figure walking towards me.

"No – I left them in my bag upstairs."

So we had no weapons, no tools and no way out. We were trapped.

"Charles, why did you not think ahead?"

"I was awaiting your orders, John."

I held on to the bars and rested my forehead between two of them, to see if I could see anyone else similarly imprisoned. "We will just have to wait for the lady of the house to come down. I was under the impression that we would be working for a man. The captain did say that, didn't he?"

No one answered.

A short while passed before we saw anybody. I heard footsteps coming down the passage. Two men stood to one side of the bars talking to a third man I could not see.

"What about these men?" I heard one say to the other. I saw a shadow peer round the bars and lean back again. "For now we require wood, take half of them and go."

Again I heard footsteps walking off into the distance. One of the two men unlocked the door.

"Hello gentleman my name is Angus and this is Duncan. We apologise for leaving you down here unattended. I'm afraid we had to attend to other matters. We heard you have come to mine for gold, is that right?"

I stepped forward, looking at the two men smiling at me. "Yes that's right. We were given no welcome."

The two men looked at each other and smiled. "You must forgive our friend Fingal, he is in desperate need of some manners."

Angus offered his hand. I stepped closer and shook it along with Duncan's.

"I'm sorry to say this gentleman but we no longer require miners. But we do need craftsman and lumberjacks. As you can tell, we go through a lot of firewood in this house."

This sounded better than being stuck in another cave digging for small pieces of gold.

"That sounds fine. About half of us can handle an axe and the others are good general handymen."

"Very well. Until you meet with the lady of the house, you will have to stay in here. It will only be a couple of days and then I'm sure she will find you better quarters to sleep in. For now we require your assistance in bringing in some logs for the fires. After that you will be brought food and water."

I nodded. "Thank you." I turned around and stared at the men in the dim light. "Charles, Owen and Andrew come with me. The rest of you will stay here."

"Very well gentlemen if you would be kind enough to follow me I will show you where we go for the logs and also equip you with the necessary tools."

We followed Duncan back up the narrow passageway. I heard the bar doors close behind me and lock. It was a very odd system indeed that we would be kept locked up. It was not right. I had a crawling feeling in my guts. *Just remember why you're here,* I thought to myself.

As we walked through the atrium I saw our belongings still gathered on the floor below the stairs. Our every move was being observed too closely for comfort. Eyes fixed on us as we left the building. The weather was still the same. Rain pounded down on the ground and the whistling wind snapped at my face. It was freezing now. I bundled my jacket up to my chin and followed the two men across open land to a small wooded area. They didn't seem affected by the weather and strolled forth as if they were walking on a sunny day. Something was definitely out of kilter here, and it was up to me to find out what that was.

We arrived at the woods and were handed axes and rope.

"Collect as much as you can and tie them up. We will take them back to the house and place them in one of the caves to dry out."

I almost couldn't hear with the wind whirling around us. We set to work, chopping down trees and tying up the logs. Every time I looked up, the two men were talking. Their contribution might have completed the job sooner. It was vexing. The way they conversed though was unnerving, with lowered voices and intense stares. The rain quickly soaked through all our clothing. Grit from the ground abraded our cold, wet hands and the wind whipped our faces raw with the freezing rain. I could hardly see as the droplets fell into my eyes. It was a long shift before one of the overseers called time.

We gathered what logs we had and lashed it together with rope. Branches whipped back and forth, out of control, catching our skin and drawing blood. I arranged the men into pairs to begin the long, slow task of hauling the wood back to the big house. It was heavy work. Rain lashed down and formed small rivulets on the path, flooding our sodden shoes. We dragged the dense, soaking timbers falteringly behind us, the wind forcing us this side and that, the mud clinging onto our feet as they sank into the ground. More than once our faces met the mud as our footing slid away. Our overseers helped to carry the wood back yet required no assistance on their heavy loads. Their path seemed somehow easier.

It was a long trudge. I felt like my legs were going to give way but then I saw the house appear in the distance. I could make it out a little clearer by this time, as the rain had eased. Darkness was falling. I noticed that the house was new, so the owners had not been here long. This made me wonder about the new owner, the lady of the house. I knew it was imperative to cooperate as we needed somewhere to sleep while we hunted for Zanette and her companion, who we suspected were living somewhere on the island. We didn't have time to waste but we had no indication where to start our search. She could be anywhere.

We reached the house and piled up our day's work of logs out in front. They would have to be stored somewhere to dry before being thrown on the fires. I assumed our orders would come the next day. We trudged heavily inside to get warm, peeling off our limp and dripping jackets. We approached the fireplace, so grateful to feel heat again. It was much needed. The room was empty, not a person in sight and we slumped onto chairs around the fire. We sat in numb silence, entranced by the flames.

Duncan walked past us, his open arms full of wet moss-covered logs. Considering he had just hauled a large cache himself, he seemed remarkably fresh. He disappeared down the narrow passage way.

"Once you have got warm and dry, would you kindly follow me back to the cave please? The lady of the house will not be pleased to find you dripping all over her new furniture."

I nodded towards Angus. "My hands are numb yet."

Angus nodded and waited patiently for us to shake the chill off. "Once you are settled in the cave tonight I will send down food."

The thought of food raised all our spirits. I was so hungry by this time and could tell the others were as well. We managed to dry off a little. Duncan reappeared quickly and went over to speak to Angus. They whispered to each other and then turned to us.

"If you would like to follow me, I'll show you back to the cave. We will send down the servants with food shortly for you."

We turned and followed Duncan back towards the narrow hallway when the double doors at the back of the room flew open and in came to two other men dragging a third. He was shouting and screaming.

"Let go of me at once!"

I started forward, ready to defend or to fight as necessary, but Duncan placed his arm in front of me to stop my progress. We watched as the men dragged him towards the narrow corridor. As he passed us he looked straight into my eyes. There was something familiar there. They were slightly tinted, almost reddish in colour, although that could have been the glare from the fire. He angrily continued to shout his protests as he was dragged down the corridor.

"The Queen is quite mad! Don't you understand…?" His voice trailed off. "She will have…"

I watched after him, and caught a glimpse of a long corridor with burning torches on the walls leading to another set of doors, but then the doors closest to me fell closed.

Queen?

I turned to Duncan. He looked from me to Angus and did not break his gaze as he explained. "Pay no attention to him. I'm afraid he is not well. If you would follow me. Please stay close: once the sun has gone it gets as dark as pitch in here."

I couldn't help but feel suspicious as I reflected on recent events. We followed Duncan down the corridor. And our reward for a long day of back-breaking work? A dark, damp cave.

We weren't there long before we heard someone shouting. "Guards!"

Charles turned to me while I was trying to find a dry patch to lie down. "He called for guards. I was correct – we are prisoners here!"

I lay down on the cold, hard floor yet it was a relief to rest. I replied "We must not jump to conclusions, Charles, we only saw him briefly upstairs while he was raving. Let me tell you: he did not look well."

Charles didn't seem convinced and continued to listen to the man screaming and shouting. "Someone is coming Jon."

Suddenly alert, I hauled my body up off the ground to where Charles was standing and we both listened carefully to the soft footsteps approaching. I tried to peer around the bars but couldn't see anything. I noticed a light gradually coming into focus.

It was a young girl of about nineteen, with a sweet face. She was holding a tray upon which were a candle, a jug, some bread and what looked and smelt like meat.

"Good evening gentlemen. I have brought food and water for you." She summoned a guard to open the gate. She stepped inside and placed the large tray on the ground.

"When we will be able to leave this cave?"

The girl turned to face me nervously. She didn't say a word, just bobbed a curtsy, and walked out.

"Mistress? Mistress! Have the courtesy to reply!"

The guard wore a world-weary expression and locked the door. He too kept mute and returned to his post. Just as the light was about to disappear entirely, she put her head around the corner.

"The Queen will see you tomorrow, after the execution."

Then she disappeared again before I could say another word. I turned to Charles. "An execution?" I said. "Surely she doesn't mean one of us?"

"Perhaps it's the man we saw being dragged out," said Charles.

I turned and stared through the bars, hardly able to make out any shape. James' voice then chipped in. "Now that was a beautiful young wench. Shame she didn't stay long."

Same old James. He always had an eye for the women.

"James – keep your mind off the servant will you? This could be serious. She said someone is getting executed tomorrow."

James came forward and stood next to Charles who was leaning on the bars. "I'm not talking about the servant I'm talking about the lady of the house."

"You saw her?"

James nodded. "She came down not long after you left this morning."

I looked around the cave in an attempt to make out the other men. "And you are only now telling me of this?"

"I didn't think it important."

I sighed and began to walk around the cave. "Wait. What did she mean when she said Queen?"

Nobody replied. Charles made a suggestion. "Perhaps we should ask someone."

I turned and laughed. "Of course why did I not think of that? Charles – if she has already been down here and we are not to be welcomed by our host, then perhaps you were right. We are prisoners after all."

"We therefore need an escape plan. Did any of you notice another way out of here?"

Silence reigned. "Very well. We heard that the man who was dragged down here was going to be executed tomorrow so I'm assuming we will be gathered to watch. That's when we will make our escape."

I heard Charles sigh. "But we don't have any weapons or tools. We don't have anything. And where would we go?"

I thought for a few moments. "Our bags are still upstairs. If we can get to them tomorrow then we can take what we need."

"What makes you think that they will still be there?" said Charles walking over to me.

"They were still there upon our return from work. It is likely they have been overlooked under the stairway. First we need to find out who this so-called Queen is."

I walked over to the bars and shouted. "Anyone there. You there! I demand to see the lady of the house!"

But no one came. All I could hear were the shouts of the man in the next cave.

"You there – what's your name?"

No reply.

"I said – what is your name?" I heard movement.

"How dare you speak to me?"

"We just want to know what you know." For a moment he was quiet and then,

"You don't need to know. You won't live long enough to do anything about it."

"What do you mean?"

"Nothing. Stop talking to me. If they hear you, you will be executed before me, I can assure you."

He didn't say anything more after that. I tried calling again but no reply came after that.

As I had thought, all was not well in this house, and on the island itself since we arrived, and dark deeds were taking place. Perhaps the Holy Church had not been able to reach this isle, and it had fallen to the Devil and his minions.

It became imperative that we should find a way out. If that man was telling the truth, we may have landed ourselves in a demonic pit. Even if this man's mind had fallen into folly, his treatment had been harsh. And we too had been treated very poorly since we arrived. I could not forget our priority. We had a job to do and if we did not escape, we would never find Zanette and if that were to happen, who knows how many people would lose their lives?

I made an announcement to the men. "Here is the scheme. Tomorrow we must ambush the guard or servant who comes with food and run for the way out. We can always return to the island to seek Zanette at a later point, but first we need to get as far away as possible from this house, if not the island, otherwise our plans will be ruined."

We spent the next few hours solidifying the plan. We sat and ate the food and water but it was only fit for dogs. We agreed that tomorrow's execution would be the perfect distraction to make our escape. And, with God's grace we would succeed.

Chapter 11
Eleanor's Choice

Amelia

Morning came after a night sitting on the balcony watching the clouds pass by. My door opened and in walked Eleanor. She didn't seem her usual self and was evidently still on edge due to my recent behaviour. I watched as she placed a jug and a glass on my desk and begin her duties. I sat and poured myself a glass. I watched as the thick, red liquid filled my glass. I placed the jug down gently and stared at the goblet of blood in my hands. Apart from a slight hunger, I felt nothing towards it. It was not the same drinking it cold but I had resigned myself to get used to it. I sipped it while watching Eleanor clean. Her eyes were constantly checking my whereabouts. Her worried eyes fixed on the glass as I drank from it.

"Eleanor I wish to talk to you; sit, I pray."

I watched as she remade the bed I never slept in. Every night she turned down the sheets and every morning she made the bed again, changing the sheets every so often. It was futile, but I did not stop her. I liked her being with me. She cautiously walked over and took a seat. She was rooted to the spot and stared at me holding onto the edge of the chair.

"I wish to apologise for scaring you yesterday; it was not my intention."

She looked up into my eyes. "Thank you, my queen." There was a long pause. She made to return to work.

"Wait – please. I wish to talk to you."

"Have I done something wrong, my queen?"

I stood and walked around the desk and leaned on the side looking down into her eyes.

"Not at all. I wish to speak to you regarding a position here with me and the other Council members. You see, you remind me in so many ways of myself when I was younger. I care a great deal for you. Would you like to join me and my kind?"

Eleanor looked shocked and swallowed her gasp.

"I'm not sure my queen, may I take some time to think about this?"

"Yes. I will grant you some time but I would like your answer by noon tomorrow."

"Yes, my queen."

"No one is to know about this offer, Eleanor. Should they find out, I will be forced to retract it. Is that understood?"

"Yes, my queen."

She left and I was once more alone in an empty room. I walked over to my dressing table and sat staring into the mirror. *I hope I have done the right thing.*

A few moments later a knock came at the door and in walked Lucas.

"Amelia are you sure you want to go ahead with this?"

I looked at him, a little confused. "Ahead with what?"

"With the execution of Philippe? Is it absolutely necessary?"

I stood and walked over to Lucas and placed my hands on his shoulders.

"Lucas, if I don't follow through with my actions it will only mean weakness. I don't want anybody else thinking they can get away with defying my orders. From the very start Philippe contradicted me and followed his own path. He was never loyal to me. He only thought of himself, not the bigger picture of what we aim to achieve here. Although I turned him, I cannot control him. There must be no weaknesses in our coven. You said this yourself, Lucas. So Philippe must pay for his behaviour with his life. I think we will burn him. What think you?"

Lucas nodded agreeably. "As you wish. I'll prepare a pyre with logs and have Philippe shackled until it is time."

I watched as Lucas walked out the door. Am I doing the right thing? I can't afford to have others follow in his footsteps. It may be a harsh lesson for everyone but it is one they must learn. I suddenly caught my reflection in the mirror and was struck yet again by my own actions.

What have I turned into? I felt like I was losing every part of my true self. My human self. Which was my true self now? I was never like this. What was it that had changed in me that I have turned into this? If it wasn't for the glimmer of humanity still flowing through my veins, I'm not sure what I would have become. I wondered desolately if there was even a way back to the way I was, or if I was to be like this for eternity. Do I allow it to consume me or do I fight as long as I can to keep it from overtaking the last part of me? I felt disrupted lately, but why?

Over the last few days, I was sensing something different, something in the wind maybe or the moon…? My thoughts would not focus on any other subject but went round and round repeatedly in my mind.

My body warns me of danger and yet I cannot see. I'm hungry but I rarely feed. I'm tired but cannot sleep. I live in a house with over 200 vampires and forty humans. I can feel their thoughts and desires. I am surrounded by people who are just like me and I have never felt more alone. Perhaps this life is not for me. Perhaps Jon was right that I am against the laws of nature... And what if I never feel love again? The very thought of this filled me with cold despair. If I ended my life I would save myself such agony...

I sat alone in my chambers looking back over my life. I relived memories of my childhood, of growing up and living with Grandmama and Grandpapa, of my marriage to Jon. Somewhere in me, I can still feel him as a part of me. My heart still pounded when I thought about him. I remember the way he smelt, as if he were still standing beside me, and that familiar aroma of musk was the only thing between us. When I thought about the unborn child that was taken away from me at the hands of the man I loved, it brought tears to my eyes, as if no time had passed. I felt angry again and so very sad, it was difficult to breathe.

My child, my sweet innocent child should be running around playing in the fields, discovering the flowers and the animals, making shapes out of the clouds, paddling in the stream... My life was not supposed to be like this! Why could I not have lived a normal existence, as others do? Been a wife and a mother? Instead I have fled to an island in the middle of nowhere. Now, I only lead half a life. What if one day Jon finds me and carries out his threat? Why does he hate me so much? If that day came, would I be able to defend myself? Would I be able to defend everything that I had built over the years? Would I want to?

The tears flowed too easily. I was no cold-hearted beast if I felt this way. I had to gather my strength. I could not carry on thinking in this way and remain strong for my followers. I paced around my room looking for some distraction. I hadn't fed in almost two weeks. My jug was replaced but never emptied. I felt weaker than ever and more and more often my emotions were being forced to the surface.

"My queen," I turned to see Lucas peer around my door. "I did knock."

I gathered myself and walked over to meet him at the door. "Yes Lucas what is it?"

"It's time for the Council meeting."

I almost forgot. Time passes so quickly when you don't need to sleep.

"Very well Lucas, I shall join you shortly."

I heard his footsteps fade. I had to face my subjects. I reapplied my brave face. I walked to the side of my bed and rang the bell for Eleanor. I sat silently on the edge of the bed and waited, staring out of the windows. I felt weak and, for the first time in a very long time, so much more tired than I should.

After Eleanor had finished getting me ready, I made my way down to the council chambers. The guards outside stood erect on my approach and opened the doors. I found the sisters and Lucas already seated. They stood and bowed as I entered. I walked down the aisle to my throne and took my seat. Lucas stood and walked in front of us all.

"My queen, Tanzeda and Borbala, I wish to discuss what we are to do with the twelve men in the cave. They have been there now for a few days and Zach, who appears to speak for the humans, is asking for a decision. I personally think we should harvest their blood to sustain us until we have a better group of humans."

"Lucas I'm not sure that would be wise, however, as our supplies are running low, I think a vote is a necessity." I too stood. "All those in favour, say *Aye*."

I, and the rest of the Council, spoke in unison. "Aye."

"Very well Lucas. See to it that all twelve of the new arrivals are drained and stored but ensure that they are kept in the cave at all times."

Lucas nodded and sat back down.

"Does anyone have any other items they would like to discuss?" Tanzeda stood and walked awkwardly to the front, looking down at her feet. She seemed to be working out what to say.

"Tanzeda? You wish to speak?"

"Yes my queen. I wish to know what is to become of Philippe."

I looked from Lucas to Borbala. "Let me make myself perfectly clear. Philippe was a Council leader until he chose to defy my orders. His actions make it apparent that he has forgotten where his loyalties ought to lie. You would all do well to remember that I made you and therefore I can end your lives just as quickly. Everyone should know their place. If not, those who wish to follow in his footsteps shall take the consequences. I will not be made a fool of, is this understood?"

Tanzeda bowed but didn't speak. The others responded, "Yes, my queen."

"He will be put to death this evening. I have decided that it shall be by fire. If it occurs to anyone to attempt to free him, do not forget that you cannot hide your thoughts and feelings from me." I caught Tanzeda looking at me from the corner of her eyes but she once again looked down when I threw my glare at her.

"Anything else?" After a moment's silence, I began to make my way out of the room, calling behind me, "Dismissed!" As I approached the doors, they were opened by the guards.

"One more thing, my queen." I turned to address Lucas.

"Yes?"

"I had a thought. Would it be wise to allow the twelve men in the cave to witness the burning this evening in order to demonstrate your authority?"

I thought about it for a moment and realised it was a good idea. "Very well Lucas. Do as you see fit. But I place them in your charge so you must ensure they do not escape."

Lucas bowed and I turned and walked out.

I decided to go for a walk outside, hoping the air would clear my thoughts. As I walked through the large room I noticed vampires seated in every corner. They all stood when they saw me and bobbed and bowed. It was a testament to my power and I should have felt proud, but instead I felt ashamed. How could I lead when I didn't know how to feel? I couldn't make up my mind. I indicated to the guards following me to stay back. I felt like I needed time on my own and left the house.

I must have walked for miles. A fresh breeze caught my face. I approached the edge of a cliff and stared out towards the sea, the wind whipping at my hair. I felt trapped in a life of misery. I felt so alone with no one to turn to. It was a strange territory to be in. I wasn't accustomed to this. How was I supposed to carry on with no support? I was still young and yet I had gone through so much. How was I to continue?

I looked down to the sea below, crashing on the pointed rocks. Weak flesh would not survive being dashed against them. I wondered how many sailors had been lost on these shores. Ships were rarely able to land closer than a mile away due to the thousands of treacherous rocks hidden beneath the water.

As I gazed, my eyes came to rest on the nests of hundreds of white and black birds nesting on the side of the cliff. I noticed how different they appeared to the birds back at home, having brightly coloured beaks. I thought how difficult life must be for them. How many eggs must they lose each year to the weather, dashing their hopes for the future? And yet each year they returned to start again.

The thought of those birds stayed with me. Each year they begin again. They are not caught up in the past. They are not weighed down by the deaths all around them. They choose this most dangerous place to raise a family. They must have such strength to overcome the sad accidents that must happen. They don't just survive: they thrive. I breathed in the salty air knowing it would cleanse me from the inside and raise my spirits. I took still more deep breaths, each one making me feel stronger, clearer and filling me with purpose. I learned a lot from those birds that day.

On my return to the house, I saw Lucas standing outside, waiting for me. He was eager to talk to me. "My queen – I was worried about you. I have had the guards looking for you. Where have you been?"

I stopped and sighed. It seemed as though I was watched all the time.

"Lucas I'm quite well. You shouldn't worry so. I am able to go out without the need to inform you or anyone else for that matter."

"I was merely concerned for your safety, Amelia."

Has it come to this now – that I need to inform every one of my whereabouts? Was this the truth of being a ruler? I felt more like a servant being told where I could go, when, and with whom. What was wrong with taking some time for myself? I had to put a stop to this.

"Lucas, I should remind you that I am Queen and I do not need to explain my actions or do anything if I don't see fit. I am aware of your loyalty to me and it is treasured, but do not forget who and what I am."

Lucas lowered his head and looked ashamed at my reproach. "My queen I am truly sorry, I meant no disrespect. I just worry about you. I shall not do it again. Forgive me." Lucas turned to leave.

"Wait Lucas. I do appreciate your concern, but I am in no danger on this island. Should the time arise when my life is in danger then, by all means, worry, but until then I would appreciate some space."

Lucas nodded.

"One more thing Lucas, I have told you repeatedly to call me by my name. I do not extend the invitation to others."

Lucas again nodded. "I beg your pardon, Amelia." He turned and walked back inside with a smile on his face. I knew he worried about me. I also know that he cares for me in a way that I don't think I could ever return. He has been loyal to me since the night he was turned without even a second thought about his wife, whose life I took. I followed Lucas into the house.

I was greeted by an army of guards. They looked ready to set off. I directed my question towards the guard in front. "What on earth is this? Explain yourself!"

"My queen, we were gathered to search for you. At last you have returned to us."

I found myself feeling angry inside when instead I should have felt like I was protected, wanted, perhaps even loved. Unfortunately, it had the opposite effect by making me feel even more caged than it did before.

"Your search is not needed. As you can ascertain, I am quite well and in no need of your services gentlemen. Get back to your duties!"

I watched as the guards fell out and return to their stations.

"Amelia, the logs are ready in the main cave."

I looked at Lucas and realised he was referring to the burning of Philippe. "Can we accommodate such a blaze inside the building?"

Lucas nodded. "Yes. It is an open cave looking out towards the sea. Only half is enclosed: the rest is wide open. Should he try to flee, he will be met by jagged rocks that will tear his body apart. There is no escape."

"Prepare him. The burning starts at sundown." I nodded at Lucas and returned to my quarters to change. I was met at the top of the stairs by Eleanor with her head down, standing quietly.

"Eleanor? Are you well my child?"

She lifted her head "Yes my queen. You wanted an answer from me regarding your offer yesterday."

"Ah yes, follow me to my chambers and we can discuss this in private." I walked past her and into my chambers. I heard her heartbeat as she followed. It was pounding heavily.

"Close the door, Eleanor." I walked over to my desk and sat. She closed the door but barely stepped further into the room.

"Please have a seat Eleanor." I sensed her feelings of caution as she took a seat. She was playing with her fingers and, although she was seated, her body was tense, as if ready to take flight at a moment's notice.

"I believe you have answer for me."

She nodded, fidgeting. "May I ask you a question, my queen?"

I nodded, looking gently at her.

"If I say no to your offer, would you be angry?"

A few moments passed while I mulled over this option. It was hard to tell her of the stark realities of this situation. Would I tell her that she might become another source of food for us? That her life could well be in danger from the others, and that I might not be able to protect her forever? It was a decision that could tear someone in half. I was asking her to choose between the life of the hunted and the life of the killer.

"Eleanor, you must understand my child, that my kind is driven by our compulsion to feed. This ultimately cannot be controlled. As you're aware, we have a very special diet, with a limited supply on this island. I must be honest with you: I will not be able to hold the others off for very long without sacrificing some of my kind. At present I'm unwilling to do so. Your answer will seal your fate here with us. Yes, of course, it is a difficult decision, but one that you must make for the sake of your own survival. If not, I will be forced to make that decision for you based on the outcome of the Council. As you know, they do not respect human life.

"However I'm willing to protect you in whatever way I can. I'm sorry to be so blunt, Eleanor, but you deserve the truth, and this is the true picture of our lives here. I am unable to give you any more time on the matter."

Silence filled the room. Eleanor's cheeks burned with emotion.

"What is your answer, child?"

She looked up into my eyes and a shining teardrop fell from her chin. Her lips quivered as she tried to speak. She was shaking. "I don't want to die."

"Is that your answer?"

She blinked back tears and took a deep breath. "Will it hurt?"

I placed my hand on top of hers and spoke gently to her. "For a moment it will, but you will recover quickly."

I watched as she moved her hands back and forward over her knees.

"Oh ma'am... it doesn't seem as though I have a choice."

I could feel heart pounding and she blinked away the tears.

"I'm afraid our choices in this life are limited my dear. I'm offering you a new way of life, a secure future in my home. The choice, however, is yours to make." I watched her for a moment; she did not move. I gathered my energy and pushed it towards her, listening for her thoughts. She was quite confused and veering from hope to despair. Her thoughts flashed images of loved ones and of memories past. There were many pictures of playing on a beach and giggling, carrying a small poppet everywhere with her... The fear of death seemed to take up the larger part of her mind.

"I will need an answer now, Eleanor. So what is it going to be?"

Her wide eyes stared into mine and she swallowed hard. "I believe I don't have any option other than to say yes."

"Is that your answer? You wish to join us?"

Eleanor looked out of the window and turned back to me.

"Yes. May I know when my queen? I would prefer to make preparations before my transition."

"I'm afraid I cannot allow that Eleanor. You have made your decision and I cannot afford for the others to find out what I have offered you.

"They will be pleased that I allowed you time to think about my offer."

"Then when?"

I stood and walked around the side of the desk. I could summon my energy at will, although I was still weakened by not having fed for some time. I could hear the blood flowing through her veins, its insistent beat drumming against my ears. Her stomach rumbled with a lurching fear. I held my energy over her and forced her to sit still. She looked like a statue, so beautiful and young. I walked behind her and tilted her head to one side. I stroked the soft skin over her prominent vein. She visibly shivered.

I felt my fangs descend and drip with saliva. The burning sensation in my dry, dry throat drew me to her neck immediately. My teeth pierced her thin membrane and slid into her vein, my lips enclosing the crime. Immediately I felt the rush of warm blood entering my parched body. I closed my eyes and was carried away by the sweetest sensation of this long-awaited feed. I hungrily devoured her, mouthful after mouthful flooding my system with glowing, pulsating power. It felt like my whole being was lighting up with vibrant life after a long, miserly winter of darkness. I felt like I was being taken out of myself, that I was so much more than human. I felt limitless, lost in a sparkling sea of possibilities...

It felt like I was a long way away when something pulled me back into reality and I realised, with a sharp intake of breath that Eleanor's heartbeat was no longer pounding. I quickly released her neck listening intently for that beat, praying I had not gone too far. I gazed at her neck, willing a beat to appear.

At long last I heard the faintest thud. It was followed by a long interval of silence, but it meant she lived still. Another beat and then another confirmed she would survive. I exhaled in relief. I quickly ripped my wrist open with my teeth and exposed the vein therein. My seething blood crept down my hand as I held it over her neck and allowed it to enter her wound.

Nothing happened straight away and so I watched. In a quick movement, she thrust herself back against the chair and collapsed to the ground. She was convulsing and a fine foam appeared at her mouth. Her eyes were wide open in fear. Tears poured from her eyes and she bore witness to this unearthly transformation. Just as suddenly, she came to a sudden stop. She was entirely still, staring ahead in surprise, like a statue.

I heard no heartbeat, no breath, nothing. I leaned over and gathered her slight frame into my arms and took her to my bed, where I laid her down. I arranged the covers around her. I stroked the hair away from her face. I held her small hand in mine and waited.

She had been amazing, stronger than she thought she could be. I felt so close to her. She could have been my daughter. At that moment, I could have fallen into a trap of anger and despair thinking about the loss of my own child, but instead I began to wonder if I could become a kind of mother to Eleanor.

Gazing out at the evening sky, I hoped I had done the right thing by offering this to her. I knew she didn't want this. It was really me that wanted this to keep her near me, to ensure her survival. I hoped one day she would truly understand that I wanted to keep her safe.

After drinking her blood for so long I knew her body would take a while to repair the damage I had caused. It had made me feel strong again, however. I noticed that my emotions were reduced to the smallest whispers in my head. I felt my drive return and the concern for the survival of our kind again took precedence.

I felt like I was powerful once more, restored to my full strength. I was back, and there was only one item on my list for that day:

Philippe.

Chapter 12
The Burning

Amelia

I summoned Lucas to take me to the cave where Philippe was being held. Had I been too hasty with the death sentence? I resolved to go and speak with him. Then again, it would not do any harm to put the fear of God in to him and indeed everyone else. They had to understand that I was in command and my word was law. I wondered if spending time in the cave had brought him round to my way of thinking.

Lucas and I approached the cave doors accompanied by four guards. I peered through the bars to see Philippe shackled to the cave wall. He looked lifeless. His head was hanging down and he looked dishevelled. I waved to the guard to open the doors and stepped inside. Philippe slowly raised his head.

"Philippe, you understand why you have been brought down here don't you? I cannot and will not allow anyone to speak as you did. I have decided that burning you is unnecessary. You will be punished but, because I can be merciful, I wish to commute your sentence to a lesser punishment."

Philippe bared his teeth at me and snapped, "Do with me as you wish. But I warn you that once I am out of these shackles I plan to bring you down. You have treated me as though I was one of those filthy humans. You are a disgrace to our throne and I will make sure everyone knows how evil you truly are. It's only a matter of time before someone brings you down."

I could scarce believe how bitter he had become after only a few days in the cave. I suspected his hatred of me had been building for some considerable time before it was out in the open. I could sense how badly he wanted to hurt me and I knew he would do so at the first opportunity.

"Philippe you understand that threats like that are taken extremely seriously. You could have taken a lesser punishment and been released in a few days. However after this latest outburst it is obvious I was correct in my initial punishment: you will burn. I will not spend my time forcing you to do my bidding, knowing that once released your only plan is to attack me."

"Get out!" he shouted huskily.

"As you wish. Philippe, you will be burned at sundown this evening. Perhaps your attitude might improve in the next life."

I felt his eyes boring into my back as we left the cave.

As we walked, Lucas briefed me on the plan for the evening's execution. Slowly, I became aware of a familiar aroma in the air. I stopped at the cave we were passing and peered inside. In the dark confines of the cave I could barely make out the shapes of men. Some were sleeping and others simply stared blankly at me. In the flaming torchlight that the guards were holding, my eyes could see a little way into the cave.

"Are these the men you were talking about, Lucas?"

"Yes, they came with the last shipment."

I turned back to them still smelling the air. The aroma was strong and it reminded me so much of Jon. He couldn't be in there, surely? My heartbeat grew stronger at the thought of the possibility of him being there. I drank in a deep breath of the scent of him, reminiscing about the idyllic time when we were first together.

"My queen?" Lucas returned to where I had stopped.

"Sorry Lucas, I was distracted. What did you say?" I dismissed my foolish idea. My mind was playing tricks I was sure. But where was that scent coming from?

"Amelia, we must attend to the other matters upstairs."

"Of course."

I followed him up the passage, glancing back over my shoulder one final time. It wasn't possible. It must be that another of the new arrivals smelled just like him. A familiar ache in my heart appeared, yet my head was filled with desire to see him again even though I knew he didn't want anything more to do with me. It was folly to think like this: Jon wanted me dead. I followed Lucas to the lounge, still in my own thoughts and not paying attention to what he was saying. As we entered, he stopped our progress.

"Guards: leave us." They left and Lucas pulled me to one side.

"What do you think you are doing, handling me like this, Lucas?"

Lucas nodded and leaned in closer. For a moment I thought he was going to kiss me. The way he looked into my eyes and held me so tight with both of his hands. "Amelia, is it true you have turned another?"

Looking into his eyes I was unable to respond straight away. He shook me a little, waiting for an answer. "Amelia?"

"I beg your pardon? How dare you question me? My actions are no concern of yours unless I choose to share them!"

"I thought such decisions were supposed to be brought to the Council for agreement first. You know the situation we are in. We can barely feed ourselves now without another mouth to feed. What on earth were you thinking?"

"Just who do you think you are? What I do has nothing to do with you or anybody else for that matter. I've sentenced one already who thought he could control me and I will not tolerate it, even from you Lucas!"

"Amelia I'm concerned. The news has spread throughout the house that you favour your maidservant, Eleanor. Is it true she has been turned?"

I glared at him and strode into the lounge where everybody was gathered. They ceased their conversations and turned and stood to face me as I walked over to the fireplace. I could sense every single person in the room.

"Listen to me all of you. I have been made aware of a rumour being spread. To put an end to this petty gossip, I can confirm that, yes – Eleanor is now one of us. In future you will keep such trivial thoughts to yourself. Do not forget that I am your queen and answer to nobody. Do I make myself clear?"

People bowed their heads and consented, "Yes my queen."

I noticed Lucas heading for the main council chambers, the door closing behind him. I was suddenly very aware of all eyes being on me.

"Carry on with your business!"

Conversations slowly began again as people retook their seats. I headed back to my room to see how Eleanor was getting on. I entered the room and was surprised to see her standing by the window. Her long blonde hair was now as white as snow. She turned and smiled at me. Her smooth, pale face glowed and her eyes were a dark red. She seemed more composed than I had known her to be previously. She knelt down.

"My queen."

I walked over to her and placed a hand on her head. Stroking the top of her hair I slowly moved my fingers to lift her chin.

"Eleanor, please stand. As you can tell I'm very fond of you. I see you as a daughter."

"My queen I am unsure how to act. I feel so confused and my emotions are swirling around inside me."

"Yes, they will for a while. If you are feeling like this you must be hungry. You will find that your emotions fade once you have fed. Go to my jug and pour yourself a glass. You will feel much better, I promise." She walked to the desk and started to pour a glass. She watched as the glass filled with cool, thick, red liquid. She stopped and placed the glass down on the desk. "I don't think I can."

"Eleanor, you need to feed or you will grow weak. The last thing you want is your emotions taking control of you. I too know that feeling.

"Close your eyes… Now, imagine being able to hunt down and feed from an actual person. Imagine their neck. See a prominent vein. Feel your teeth descend. Now drink."

Her breathing became deeper and more frequent. I watched as she stared at the glass. She brought into her lips and closed her eyes. She started to sip. Her eyes flew open and turned a burning red, bright and glowing. She gulped down the blood from the glass, picked up the jug and began to drink from it. The glass fell to the floor and smashed as she became totally focussed on the jug, noisily devouring its contents. Finally she lowered the jug and gasped for air, a red trail falling from her lips.

"Better?"

She nodded, panting. Her eyes and fangs made her look dangerous, yet elegant at the same time. I took her hand.

"You look amazing Eleanor. You will make a great addition to our home." I turned as a knock came at the door.

"Yes?"

It was Lucas. He closed the door behind him. "This must be Eleanor, our new recruit."

"Was there something you wanted, Lucas?"

He looked from her to me.

"Yes. Everything is ready as requested. Everyone is waiting down in the cave along with the other Council members."

"And Philippe?"

"Shackled to the post."

"I'll join you shortly. Thank you Lucas." Lucas nodded and left. I turned to Eleanor.

"You may stay in your chambers if you wish."

Eleanor nodded and walked to the door. "Thank you my queen. I think I should take some time to adjust."

"Of course. I will be along later to see you."

Eleanor curtseyed and quietly left my room.

I went to my wardrobe to get ready for the evening. I pulled out a long, silk dress, the colour of jet, and shoes to match. I pinned my hair up into a swirling mass of curls on my head and gently applied some rouge. I walked over to the drawer of my desk and pulled out the box inside. I opened it and took out my locket, tying it at the back of my neck. I looked in the mirror and sighed. I looked beautiful.

I took a few moments to compose myself and then headed for the cave, escorted by the guards from outside my room. As I arrived I was met by Lucas waiting just outside the iron bars.

"Good evening Amelia. Your throne is prepared and everyone is waiting for you."

I followed him in. He announced my arrival. "Everyone: silence please. The Queen."

As I walked in, everyone bowed and the crowd parted. I walked through and took my seat which had been placed facing Philippe, who was shackled to a post.

The cave was vast and I could hear the sea through its huge entrance overlooking the ocean. We were high above the water and the post that held Philippe had been erected near to the ledge outside the cave's mouth. He was surrounded on all sides by kindling and logs, piled up high.

By my left were Tanzeda and Borbala. Borbala was comforting her sister as she watched Philippe stare at her from the post. On my right was Lucas, sitting back comfortably with his legs crossed and a blank expression on his face. I could tell he didn't want to be here. He had made it clear on a couple of occasions that he thought I had overreacted.

The crowd was behind me and to either side of the throne facing Philippe. The guards walked in and stood either side of Philippe and myself. I looked around the room and waited for silence.

I nodded to Lucas to begin the proceedings. He looked at me and bowed his head. He slowly rose from his seat and walked down to Philippe. He turned his back on him and faced the crowd. He took a deep breath and looked at his paramour, Tanzeda who was crying into her sister's arms.

"On this day Philippe has been charged with threatening our Queen and defying her orders. She has made it clear what will happen to those who question her authority. She does not take such threats lightly, and the punishment for this crime is death." Lucas turned and faced Philippe.

"Philippe you have been found guilty by your queen and your peers. Do you have any last words?"

Philippe looked from Tanzeda to Lucas.

"She is not nor will she ever be my queen. She does not rule me. She will fall and fall soon!"

The watching crowds reacted with discord at anyone challenging their queen so rudely. Lucas turned away from Philippe and nodded to the guard standing nearby holding a lighted torch. Lucas walked back to his seat and watched the guard go over and light the logs around Philippe's feet. The dry tinder sucked up the flames lustily and the fire spread quickly. Philippe made no reaction immediately but stared out in front, his chin raised in insolent defiance.

Tanzeda cried out and tried to free herself from her sister but Borbala held on tightly to her, bringing her to her knees and wrapping her arms around her to try and shield her from what she was about to witness. I watched them on the floor of the cave. Tanzeda was shaking with fear and misery. I could feel everything inside her. The love and passion she had for him. She ached for him and she was deeply distressed.

"Borbala – control your sister. As a Council member she must lead by example."

I turned to see Lucas sitting forward, his head turned to them. He looked at me and sat back in his seat. Borbala lifted her sister from the floor and placed her back in the chair still holding on to her.

I watched as the flames surrounded Philippe and began to climb up his legs. He could no longer keep quiet and began to moan in pain. The flames burned at his clothes to his skin underneath. His cries grew louder. I watched his face as he tried not to cry out but failed. The smouldering fire grew higher and wider. The rising smoke, filled the sky above and was swiftly moved by the winds. I turned to look at Tanzeda who was nestled in her sister's arms.

I turned to hear a crack coming from the blaze in front of me. The post holding Philippe looked unsteady and was starting to tip.

Lucas stood immediately and yelled to the guards. "Get more wood! Stoke the fire! Support the post!"

At this, Philippe seized his advantage and made his break for freedom. He pushed the post and it fell backwards landing close to the cliff edge. He looked up one last time at Tanzeda and pushed himself off the edge. The guards were too late. He had fallen into the sea.

Lucas and I ran to edge and looked down to see parts of Philippe's clothes on the rocks below.

"Luckily it seems as though in the end he has chosen to take his own life. You there! You let him escape!"

The guards looked at one another in embarrassed silence. I pointed at a guard close by. "Ensure this does not happen again. And send a band of men to find his body."

I walked past them to the entrance of the cave. "Find him by sunrise or you will be next!"

I slammed the doors open and stormed away to my chambers. *Could these imbeciles do nothing right? What on earth is next? What more could go wrong?*

Lucas followed me and knocked on my door. "What?" I demanded.

Lucas walked in. "I have sent a team to search for his body. I will make a full investigation into how this could have happened, my queen."

"I know what went wrong Lucas. This task was left to someone who is unable to fix a post securely – and indeed a criminal! I am extremely displeased about this. You will find him and bring him back to me or I swear you will be next!"

"Yes Amelia. I will see to it personally."

I was so angry it felt as though I could explode. "In future, you will refer to me as your queen. I have been far too lenient with you and it is showing through your mistakes. Now – get out!"

Lucas bowed and left my chambers. I could hear him screaming at the guards in the corridor. I went to the balcony to breathe the cool air and settle my temper.

I knew Lucas wasn't really that bad but at that moment I could have torn even my closest allies to pieces. I was furious. Were they mocking me? I vowed to make sure that such a mistake could not happen again. Those fools. Something had to be done about their idiocy, and soon.

Chapter 13
Trapped

Jonathan Walker

I awoke to the smell of smoke. I got up and looked around the cave that had become our holding cell. I called out urgently for Charles who was still asleep.

"Charles – Charles? Can you smell that?"

Charles sat up rubbing his eyes, "What, sorry? Smell what?"

I walked over to the bars to hear a voice shouting. I couldn't make out what was being said except that it was a woman's voice. I could smell smoke. But this smell was unusual… With a lurching horror I recognised it, and it filled me with dread.

During the last of the plague years I witnessed several friends and neighbours of our village contract the disease and be delivered to the Good Lord within days. There were so many. Scores. Far too many to bury. Our priest, Father George, had held a Mass for all the dead. The stronger men of the village had laid the dead out in rows. Women and children had collected kindling and gathered it all together to place upon the dead. We prayed for their immortal souls and set the pyre alight. It was still burning several days later. That was the first and only time I have smelled bodies burning. Until now. It made me sick to my stomach. Charles came over and stood next to me holding the bars in front of him.

"What on earth is that terrible smell?"

"That is the smell of burning flesh. Someone is on fire, Charles," I said quietly.

Charles turned around and went back to lie on the floor. I couldn't understand his casual reaction. "Are you not just a little curious about that?"

Charles made himself comfortable on the floor. "Not really. I saw enough of that business against the Spanish." He turned over and went back to sleep. No one else was awake.

The silence was broken by a heavy door swinging open and hitting the wall with such a force it awoke the others. I strained to see what was happening but couldn't see anybody. Someone was approaching. Whoever it was, was walking quickly. I could hear shouting in the distance: a man's angry voice. There was more movement and a torch was lighting up the passageway. I could hear more people moving now, and one set of footsteps in particular storming towards us.

Suddenly a woman appeared. She was all in black and her skirts flew around her like low clouds as she marched. My heart stopped as I took in the sight. Everything seemed to slow down. But ...no – it couldn't possibly be... Could it? Coming sharply to my senses, I felt my heart again, pounding forcefully against my chest. I dived against the wall at the sight of her. I was not mistaken: it was Zanette.

Zanette had stormed past the cell so quickly she had not noticed me. I was stunned. The woman I had sought all these years, was in fact in this very building. How did I not see her before? In truth I had forgotten how beautiful she was. Yet now she seemed different somehow, darker. She no longer had a slight look of naivety that I remembered in the young woman I married, and to whom I was still married.

I blinked and shook my head attempting to clear my thoughts. My mission was to kill her and her companion. I had no idea how many lives she had ended: countless people. She wasn't human and the thought of our married life together in the past revolted my stomach. I couldn't believe she was here the whole time, right above our heads.

It suddenly struck me that she must be aware that I was there on her island. She must do. Charles was right, we were prisoners. This was no accommodation cell.

We still had found no opportunity to escape and, after seeing Zanette, it became an even higher priority, especially if she was indeed aware of my presence. If she knew I was here she would certainly try to kill me before I had a chance to kill her first. I turned to face the others who were now awake from the noise.

"Listen everyone. The one we have been looking for is here. She has been here this whole time. We need to escape, and quickly. We are being kept here against our will. We haven't been killed, so it must be that we are being kept alive for some other reason. We are not being fed properly so it is obvious they do not wish us to be at full strength. What they want of us I do not dare to consider. We must not stay long enough to find out. As you all know I have seen what she is capable of. We must act now before it's too late."

Charles got up and approached me. "What? You mean Zanette is here?"

"Yes Charles – she walked past our cave a few moments ago."

"Are you quite sure?"

"I know her only too well, Charles. It was her. She walked past."

"Then we must redouble our efforts to escape. We can't just walk out. We are trapped but there must be a way…"

"We must somehow trick the guards into unlocking these doors, and then we need only make a run for it."

"That much seems obvious, John."

"Charles this is serious. If we don't get out we might not get the opportunity before we are put to death."

Charles paced around the cave in thought. "I have it! Here is what we do. We wait until the guards come for us and then we make our move."

"What makes you think they will?" I asked.

"If she knew for certain that you were here, she would already have taken action against us. Yet she has not. I am not convinced that she knows for definite. John – it's been days and we have yet to have the audience we were promised. We have not received a decent amount of food. If you were correct, surely we would have had a visit by now?"

He did have a point. Only I had seen her. Yet she had not stopped to address me. Obtaining visible proof for the rest of the men could prove deadly. The only way to prove it would be to request that audience and somehow escape on the way.

I stood near the bars shouting for the guards but to no avail. It was obvious that something else was happening upstairs with all the shouting and sounds of running. The guards were not at their posts, but running back and forth in confusion, as if something unexpected had happened. I could hear people talking as they ran past our cave. From what I could ascertain, they were looking for someone. I continued to shout for the guards if they past. Finally one answered me, approaching the iron bars where I stood but still checking up and down the passage.

"What?"

"I want to see the lady of the house!"

He looked at me and laughed. "Is that right? Well, prepare for a long wait, peasant." He turned to walk off. I reached through and grabbed his arm.

"I demand to see her, now!"

He brought the hilt of his sword down on my fingers. "Take your filthy hands off me before I break your arm!" My hand snapped back in pain.

"You won't be in there much longer anyway," he scoffed as he walked away.

I wondered what he meant by that as I heard him laughing with his partner in the distance. I turned back to see Charles staring at me from the ground.

"Just give it up John. They aren't going to unlock the doors."

I knew he was right. They had other priorities. I sat back down against the rock wall and fell back into devising the escape plan. I became aware of soft footsteps approaching, not those of the shod guards, but small, soft and barefoot. I peered out into the darkness and could make out the shape of a young girl coming from the cave, following the path of the guards, looking for something with a torch. I could see her now. It was the same girl that had earlier brought the food. I needed to talk gently so as not to frighten her.

"Excuse me, mistress," I whispered.

She stopped and answered me, timidly. "Yes, sir?" She glanced around her to make sure no one had caught her in this act.

"Mistress, would you do me the kindness of bringing me a little light? It's so dark in here and we can't see anything."

"I'm not supposed to talk to prisoners."

Charles was right. "Please, look kindly upon our request. We have not eaten since yesterday and are feeling tired and weak. We would just like a light to warm our fingers and lift our hearts."

She made no answer, but walked on. I had to think of another plan. Moments later though, she came back with a bright torch and handed it to me through the bars. "Please tell nobody how you got this."

Before I could answer, she ran off down the passage. I turned to Charles.

"I need everyone to strip off some clothes."

They all sat up and looked at me and at each other.

"Quickly men! There isn't much time!"

"Sorry, old chap?" Charles said getting off the ground.

"We must burn some of our clothes. If am right, the guards will have to come and put it out. They need us alive, remember. When they open the bars, we can overpower them and make our escape."

"What if they don't?" one of the men said. "What then? Do we just sit in here and smoke ourselves to death?"

"If we don't try now we may end up dying in a much worse way. We must not just sit here and wait to be killed. We are fighting men. We must at least try."

Charles got up and looked around the cave. "You heard him, men." He removed his cloak and shirt and threw them into the centre of the cave.

"I hope this works, Jon."

"Remember we must look defenceless when they come."

Others began to add items of clothing to the pile. Some of our clothing was damp from the cave and would not light, but others lit up easily. The damp items gave off a useful amount of smoke. It would add to the general atmosphere of confusion and, as it began to fill the cave, we could use it to hide. The fire took a hold of the clothes and grew strong but it would not burn for very long.

The cave began to fill with smoke and the heat coming from it was very welcome. The men lay down on the ground to avoid the smoke as it rose and filled the cave and drifted out along the passageways. Charles started coughing along with a few others. I too felt as though I couldn't breathe. Nobody was responding.

But then our plan began to work. Two guards running down the passage stopped and quickly ran for the keys. They noticed the twelve of us lying on the ground and assumed the worst.

"Bring water!"

I heard the doors unlock and fly open. A guard ran in with a bucket of water and threw it on the fire. "Clear the cave of smoke or it'll be our heads!"

In the thick smoke, he was unaware that the door had fallen open and that the other guard had gone to get more water. We silently crawled on the floor to the open door, then scrambled to our feet.

"Stop!"

We had been heard!

Charles now holding the lit torch swung it and hit the guard on the head. He fell to his knees, holding his head dizzily, and coughing. It gave us enough time to make the escape. We heard footsteps coming down the passage that we were heading down. We ran into the nearest cave and backed up to the wall so no one could see us in the smoky shadows. I heard someone shout at the guard.

"Where are they? You fool! You let them escape. The Queen is going to be furious. Find them and quick!"

We waited until the sound of their footsteps faded. We walked up the passage towards the main room. I held my hand behind me to signal the others to wait while I checked it was safe to go ahead. The room was clear of people, so we slowly proceeded to the door. All was calm in the chamber with only the sounds of the wind outside and the crackling of the fire.

We reached the door and I waved everyone out. I was about to follow when I heard something from the balcony overlooking the room. I looked up to see Zanette standing with her hands resting on the banister. I believe our eyes met for a moment and what felt like an electrical force shot between us. I hurriedly blinked and withdrew, closing the door behind me. Had she recognised me?

We went outside into the cold, whipping wind. The rain lashed our naked torsos. But we had life and we had freedom so we pressed ahead. We headed towards the coast, checking all the while that no one had followed us. It was dark and visibility was poor. Every now and then, a dagger of lightning would cleave the sky and light our way. What we were going to do once we had made it to the coast, I had no idea. There had only been the one ship for months that had brought us here in the first place. We were stuck on an island with no way off.

We eventually made it to the coast. Everyone was tired but we had encountered no other buildings within which we could shelter. We walked along the shore and eventually found a small cave at the sea's edge of the sand. We ran inside, panting and regaining our breath. We would shelter here the night and renew our efforts tomorrow. For safety, we made our way to the back of the cave, away from the possibility of being seen in the main entrance.

At that point I didn't tell my men that I had seen Zanette a second time. They had seemed sceptical when I raised it before and now we had more pressing matters to attend to, it didn't seem important. I think deep down none of them really believed the story I had told them about wild human–like creatures that drank blood. It sounded too fantastical to be believed. I knew they were here because I was paying them. They all knew what to expect in a straightforward battle: many had been to fight the French and the Spanish, but no one could truly prepare for what we faced. Not really.

We settled that night and rested until we could make a plan of our next step. We couldn't leave so the only question now was what happens next? I knew we had to kill Zanette but she was surrounded with people.

How had she managed to raise this settlement? Perhaps her companion, Callum was wealthy and secured a home here. So many questions flooded my mind. Was Zanette the lady of the house? Had the guards been talking about her? It had been over six years since last I saw her and she had not changed at all yet I felt older and less energetic. I had been an older husband to her and now it was taking its toll on me.

If I was going to stop her from hurting the people in the house, I had to act soon. They wouldn't necessarily know what they were living with. The question that commanded most of my thoughts though was, would I be able to end the life of my wife? Could I go through with killing the woman who could have been a mother to Catherine? I had been able to make an attempt on her life once before, but that had been provoked when I thought my life and the life of Catherine was in mortal danger. I had a sudden frightful thought: what had happened to the child? Was Zanette raising my child? Is it possible the baby had survived? Surely not. Was I about to kill the mother of my child?

I struggled to sleep all night and my mind would not quieten. I was tired, hungry and now it seemed like we were stuck on this island. There had to be something that could be done. I used the long, cold darkness of that harsh night to think of a plan to free ourselves and all the others who were in danger.

Chapter 14
The New Council Member

Amelia

I was still furious when Eleanor came in. She was carrying a jug and glass and placed it on the desk. She seemed more relaxed with her new life. I watched as she carried out her duties with grace. For the first time I forgot all about my troubles and everything that had happened that evening. Eleanor had that calming effect on me when she was in the room. She always made me feel brighter.

"Eleanor I would like it if you would become part of the Council. I believe you would be a great asset to me."

Eleanor looked up, stunned. "I don't know what to say, my queen. I'm honoured."

"That settles it then. I will inform the others of the decision. You will have to take an oath."

I could see she was surprised by my offer.

"An oath?"

"Yes Eleanor. You will be asked to pledge a blood oath to me and to the rest of the Council. It is a very important part of the ceremony."

Eleanor thought for a moment. "It would be such an honour, my queen. It has been some time since I felt part of a family. I appreciate everything you have done for me. I will not let you down, I promise."

I smiled and walked over to my desk and poured my drink. The taste was just bearable.

I advised Eleanor that I was to attend the Council meeting and for her to accompany me at midnight. She seemed nervous, no matter how I tried to calm her fears. I watched as she moved around the room tidying and dusting, plumping up the pillows of a bed I never slept in.

I turned sharply to the sound of thunder outside my window. I walked out on to the balcony and watched the ocean furiously lashing at the rocks below. The wind rushed past me and the dark skies glowered overhead. I could see glimpses of the moon rising and being covered by clouds as they rushed by. It was enchanting.

Every now and then I could smell a faint aroma on the wind and by now I knew exactly who it was. The scent had spun me back in time to memories of living with my husband. It was Jon's scent, and unforgettable. The scent had been carried on the wind. It was faint but unmistakable. I reasoned that he must be hiding near the coast and looking out for a ship. I was certain that if I could smell him, my hunters too would make easy work of tracking him down.

Their first task, though, was to discover the whereabouts of Philippe. Nobody had been able to confirm if he had survived his fall onto the rocks. It seemed unlikely, yet no body had been seen dashed upon the rocks and nothing had washed up on shore. I was sure I could feel his energy still and my instincts told me to be wary.

"My queen! Lucas is here to see you."

I turned to see Eleanor opening the doors to admit Lucas.

"Lucas, have you news on Philippe's body?"

"Not yet my queen. I have everyone possible looking for him."

I felt sorry that I had passed harsh words towards Lucas. I knew that he would never have treated me in such a way. "Lucas, have a seat."

"I wish to apologise for my rudeness earlier. As you know I am fond of you and I do realise that you have been there when I needed you most. Please accept my apology. You may still call me Amelia." I watched as he studied my face. I could see his eyes gloss but he never allowed his tears to flow.

"No need for apologies, Amelia. You are our ruler and I admire your control and strength. I live to serve you. I am honoured by your affection and the trust you place in me." He stood and bowed.

"I'll see you tonight, Amelia." He smiled and walked out. I must admit I did feel calmer. I longed for a time when I could always be in control of my emotions rather than have them control me. I was sure the others could detect my inner turmoil and saw it as weakness. I still felt the need to enforce the rules I had created: otherwise what was the point of having them? I wanted my subjects to know that I would not be defied without consequences. I did not want to look like a fool. And yet somehow, all of these matters did not seem as urgent as they had done earlier.

After thinking it over a while longer, I strolled down to the council chambers with Eleanor. We chatted a little on the way. She was quite anxious as she wasn't sure what to expect. We entered the chamber and the Council members arose and bobbed and bowed. I took my place on the throne.

"First I would like to say that we have a new addition to the Council. Allow me to introduce Eleanor."

I waved at Eleanor who was standing at the back of the room. I watched as she slowly walked forward, looking from me to the others.

Borbala rose angrily. "With all due respect my queen, should we not vote on important decisions such as these?"

"Borbala I appreciate your loyalty to me. But do not mistake who is in charge here. In light of recent events, a seat on the Council has become available. I have elected Eleanor to take this seat. She will undergo the oath as procedure but I will not be overruled on this matter. Do I make myself clear?"

Borbala didn't respond, simply nodding her head curtly and sitting. I turned to Eleanor and indicated the chair left vacant by Philippe.

"Lucas, as my advisor you may began the oath."

Lucas walked over to Eleanor and held out his hand. "May I?"

She looked at me for guidance. I nodded. She placed her hand in Lucas's and stood.

"Eleanor what is your last name?"

"It's Beckindale, my lord."

"Eleanor Beckindale, you have been chosen to join the Council and serve your queen, Amelia, in all aspects of her kingdom. In order for you to fully pledge your loyalty a blood oath is due. This involves her majesty and the rest of the Council partaking of some of your blood, which will be drawn from your wrist. Do you understand?"

Eleanor nodded. Lucas brought her by the hand to kneel in front of me. I arose as Lucas drew back her sleeve. I looked into her eyes and smiled. My teeth came forth and I sank them into her wrist. A flash of images of Eleanor's life flooded into my head, from when she was a young girl up to the present. I detached and returned to my seat.

Lucas then proceeded to drink from her wrist. I watched as Eleanor looked away. I knew it shouldn't hurt her to any great extent, but as she was so new to this life, she would still have such lingering reactions from her human past. Lucas then escorted her to Borbala and Tanzeda who drank in turn. I then brought her back to Lucas for the remaining part of the oath.

"Eleanor you have pledged your allegiance to your queen and to the Council. Now repeat after me: 'I Eleanor Beckindale, give my life and blood to serve the Queen and Council with true respect and loyalty.'"

"I Eleanor Beckindale give my life and blood to serve the Queen and Council with true respect and loyalty."

"I will do my utmost to protect and serve with my soul or I will be removed from the oath by fire."

She looked up at me. I nodded for her continue.

"I will do my utmost to protect and serve with my soul. Or I will be removed from the oath by…" She hesitated for moment before she continued, "…fire."

"Eleanor, take your seat. You have pledged your oath by blood and promise. Welcome to the order."

Everyone stood and clapped as she took her seat. I too stood and watched as she let out a sigh of relief. Everyone sat and waited to begin.

"Now, with the ceremony over, let us return to the business at hand. I wish to know what news we have on Philippe's whereabouts and the men that escaped." I turned to Lucas, who stood.

"I have assigned two troops of guards to search for both parties, my queen. I am still waiting for their findings on both accounts."

"Lucas you are to concentrate on finding Philippe's body only. I will instruct another to locate the whereabouts of the others."

Lucas nodded and returned to his seat. I turned to Tanzeda. "Tanzeda. You will find the others who have escaped. Do what you will with them but I want the one called Jon back alive. Is that understood?"

"Yes, my queen. I will see to it personally."

"Very well. Do we know when the ship is to return with supplies?"

Borbala stood. "I believe the captain should have just arrived in London today and therefore should be setting sail in the next couple of days."

I nodded. "Is there anything else?"

"Yes, my queen. The leader of the humans, Zach, wishes to approach the Council with some concerns."

I looked at Lucas with a sigh. "Show him in."

Lucas waved to the guard at the back of the room who opened the door.

Zach walked in and came to the front. He bowed and began to speak. "My queen, the others and I are deeply distressed and fearful for our lives. We heard of the burning and wish to know if we are safe from the same fate?"

Watching him closely, I didn't speak. Silence filled the room and I could see all were awaiting my answer. "Is that everything Zach?"

He nodded.

"Then you may leave."

"But…?" He watched my face and backed slowly away to the rear of the room. "What am I to tell the others my queen?"

"You may tell them what you please, Zach. I have no intention of replying to this impudent question. You will refresh their memories as to who is in charge here. If they wish to discuss this matter personally, I'm sure the Council and I would adore it. However, you will tell them also that, if they do so, it may indeed be their final act." Zach looked at me wide-eyed in fear and quickly left.

"Who does he think he is? Are we not generous in our treatment of them? If need be, I'm prepared to revoke our kind offer and place them back in the caves!"

The Council was in agreement. I did have a grudging admiration for someone who would stand up to authority in the most dangerous circumstances. Zach seemed a nice man but his loyalties were evidently to the humans and this was highly irritating.

After the meeting had finished, I walked back to my room. Somehow I felt safer there than anywhere else. I spent a lot of time in my chambers. It was the only place I could sit and think, and feel that most elusive of feelings in my life: like I was home. I had everything I needed in my room and with guards placed outside of my door I felt safe and calm. I sat looking out of the window at the calm waters.

I spent time reflecting on my history. How quickly my time on earth thus far had passed; how much had happened. I held the locket around my neck and stared out of the window in contemplation. I was twenty-seven years old yet I felt like I had lived several lives in those short years. I watched the moon's reflection on the calm sea, as she danced in and out of the silver clouds.

The locket was all I had left of my old life, the only remnant that had survived from my entire family. I vowed to myself that I would never take it off. I was brought out of my thoughts by a knock on my door, and in walked Lucas. He walked over to me and I felt his hand on my shoulder.

"Amelia... Might I ask..." he hesitated, "How are you? You have been very different lately."

I looked up to him and saw his eyes sparkling in light from the candles around the room. I sighed looking up at the heavens.

"All is well. I believe I am different because I am not feeding correctly Lucas. You know how hunger plays with our emotions."

I didn't realise I had placed my hand on top of his. I turned to see him looking at my hand. He lifted my hand in his and kissed the back of it, placing it gently back down on my shoulder. I pulled it away and turned away from him.

I heard the doors open, "Good night my queen," he said and left me to face the night alone.

What had just happened? I didn't see Lucas in that way. At least I didn't think I did. I couldn't think about it. It was neither the time nor the place. With everything so disrupted, I didn't want to think about it. He has always been there for me and almost never questioned my orders. He had been loyal and trustworthy. But somehow the images of his wife flooded into my head. The way he seemed distraught by what happened to her and then suddenly, after I had turned him, he acted as if she had never existed and from then on had followed me.

The more I thought about it the more distracting it became. Perhaps he hadn't been terribly happy with her. I didn't want to ask him about it. He had always acted like a new life had begun there and then, as if he had been reborn into a life where his past didn't seem to be important to him anymore. I wondered if that was what happened to each of our converts? I could still remember my history, my life before I turned.

Surely they did too?

My mind was filled with questions. My mind was always filled with questions though. I had always been curious and spent a lot of time reflecting, depending on my mood. I spent the rest of that night thinking, but trying not to focus too much on the escapees. Why had they run away from me? I provided a good life. Why did Zach and the other humans want to leave too? Why did everyone leave me?

I watched the moon trace her path across the sky, leaving the earth to fall away in the opposite direction.

Chapter 15
Philippe's Return

Amelia

Morning came and again I watched the sunrise illuminating the calm sea beneath clear blue skies. Occasionally a white, fluffy cloud would pass by. I had finished the jug of blood, which Eleanor had placed by my chair. I was still holding a half-full glass when Eleanor entered the room.

"Morning my queen!"

"Oh good morning Eleanor." I drained my glass.

"Is there anything I can get you this morning?"

"No thank you. Have a maidservant prepare my clothes."

She paused. "But I am here to do that, my queen."

I stood facing her, taking her hands in mine. "Eleanor, you are a Council member now, not my servant."

She walked towards me and sighed. "If it's all the same to you I would like to continue with my duties. I feel more relaxed when I'm busy."

I did not wish to argue with her. "As you wish," I smiled. I watched as she walked to the adjoining dressing room and picked out my clothes and shoes. I walked and sat down at my dressing table. She laid out the items on the bed and came over to begin combing my hair. I looked into the mirror staring blankly for a while.

"Are you well, my queen? You don't seem yourself."

"Quite well, Eleanor, thank you. Please – continue."

"I'm just concerned for you."

I watched her through the mirror as she brushed my hair. This time she left it down and placed a black silk ribbon around my hair at the back and pinned it into place. She dabbed black eye shadow around my eyes and soft pink cream on my lips. I looked young, and the way she dressed me made me feel beautiful.

"Is there anything else I can get for you my queen?"

I stared into the mirror watching my reflection without turning. I waved absently behind me. "No thank you."

Eleanor left the room. She had dressed me in black today, a long, flowing dress with short sleeves and a black silk shawl that draped over my shoulders was pinned to my dress. It was beautiful and fitted my body perfectly. It took me a while to realise that Lucas had entered the room and was looking on from the door.

"Lucas?" I jumped.

"I beg your pardon; I don't think you heard my knock."

"Evidently not. What is it?"

Lucas walked closer to me leaving the doors open behind him. "Amelia, I'm not sure how to put this. I believe Philippe may well be alive."

I looked around the room before focusing back on Lucas. "What makes you think he survived?"

"We found a couple of bodies towards the edge of the coast, on the far side of the island. It appears he has picked off a couple of our escapees."

"Was John among them?" I asked, too quickly.

"We have searched the entire island with no trace of him so far. We know he can't leave the island, however, he is covering his tracks well. Our search continues."

"He was not one of the bodies found?"

"Definitely not, Amelia."

For some reason I felt relieved. He was on this island to kill me and yet I was relieved to know he was alive somewhere. I could be jeopardising the entire coven, thinking this way.

"Amelia are you well?"

I snapped back into focus and saw Lucas looking at me with a confused and worried look on his face.

"Yes Lucas. I am quite well. I was merely thinking about our next move." I couldn't tell him the truth: he wouldn't understand.

"Amelia, you do realise that once Philippe has regained enough strength, he will undoubtedly come to take his revenge upon you."

I was not afraid of Philippe. I made him and had the power to control him. "He would be very foolish indeed to come back here and try to kill me, Lucas. He will not get that close."

"Amelia, with all due respect, you have appeared a little distracted lately, as if you are lost in a daydream, if you will. It will only take a moment for him to seize the opportunity to get close enough to cause you harm."

"Lucas you worry too much. If you are concerned for my safety, have some extra guards place outside of my room."

Lucas smiled. I knew he was waiting for me to say that. He bowed and left. I know that he will have had guards waiting on the landing already. He was so loyal to me. As I was watched the doors close, I became aware of an odd sensation: a feeling that crawled up my back and made me shudder. I heard a sound behind me and spun around to see Philippe standing in the balcony doors.

"Perhaps we could chat, Amelia. I see you don't follow your own rules."

"I beg your pardon?"

He was standing in the doorway wearing a dirty white shirt that he had obviously removed from one of the bodies he had drained. He held a sword in his left hand. I noticed that he was no longer burnt and in fact looked quite recovered and healthy. "Lucas and yourself. I don't remember ever being asked to call you Amelia."

"And you may not start now, Philippe." I turned my face towards the door to shout for the guards.

"I wouldn't do that if I were you, Amelia. You don't want anything happening to… who was it you were talking about? John? He's a strapping fine fellow, isn't he? It's a shame I may have to kill him."

I looked at him and my face fell. "You have John?"

He smirked and looked at the floor before focusing on my eyes again. I felt my energy rise within me. *First I'll read his mind and then I'll make sure he doesn't survive the next fire.*

"Yes my dear. Bound and gagged. What I struggle to comprehend is that this man was supposed to be the love of your life although he is here to kill you, now. I have had my share of failed romances, but none of my passions has wanted to murder me," he smirked. "I have not had the chance to taste him yet, but I am sure I will have plenty of time."

"You will not get off this island, Philippe!"

My energy was taking its time building. I hadn't had nearly enough blood since yesterday because of the shortage, just one glass today so far. I still felt my energy was far weaker than it should be.

"On the contrary. You will organise my travel to wherever I want. Or you will not see John again. I might even turn him. What do you think of that?"

"You don't know how!"

"Perhaps not but I shall enjoy the attempt. John may not survive it! However, first I have a score to settle with you."

Stepping forward he wielded his sword out in front. My energy was still not high enough to release. I had to buy more time. I saw the jug on my desk; I had to get to it. Philippe saw me looking at the jug and smirked, swiping it away with his sword.

"What? No weapon?" The jug flew off the desk and crashed to the floor releasing a spray of blood from the trickle that remained. But I did not want the jug as a weapon, only an alarm. The doors flew open and in ran three guards. Philippe made a dash for the balcony. I released what energy I had and surrounded him. He stopped.

"Take him to the cave and make sure he cannot escape this time."

I watched as the guards went over. As they approached him, I released my hold on Philippe – but it was a little too soon. He turned quickly and plunged his sword into the nearest attacking guard. The others stepped back as we watched him fall to the floor.

Philippe held out his sword warning us not to come any closer. "Next time, my so-called Queen. You won't always have your guards to protect you and, when that day comes, I'll be there!"

"You will never get the opportunity Philippe, do not forget who made you!"

He moved backwards to the balcony, keeping his eyes on us as he did.

"Adieu ma petite reine!" he blew me a kiss, flung himself off the balcony and disappeared below.

"I want that man's head on a spike! Take the guard to the blood pool and then launch a hunt for Philippe!"

The guards walked over and collected the limp body of the guard, dragging him behind them as they went.

"Lucas!" I shouted. He ran in.

"What happened?"

"Philippe is indeed alive. Find him!"

Lucas looked from me to the guards dragging the body out. "I'm terribly sorry Amelia. He should never have got that close. I will see to it personally that he is found."

"Use all our resources to find him. I want that man dead at all costs."

Lucas quickly ran out of the room shouting for the guards. I followed the guard being dragged to the pool underneath the council chambers. It was the cave that we had used to store blood in a dug-out pit. They placed the guard gently in and stood back. The wounded guard floated for a while and then slipped beneath the liquid. The guards looked at me dumbly, like dogs that think their master has hidden a treat. From the centre of the pool a ripple came to the surface. The guards as one looked back at the pool whose surface was now being disrupted with more and larger ripples before a whole rush of bubbles hit the air and disappeared amid a fountain of blood, beneath which the guard appeared bent over.

He undulated back and forth like a snake before straightening up and tipping his head back in a roar of life that reverberated off the walls of the cave, his entire body coated in blood as if he had been flayed, his fangs down.

He noisily took in a great gulp of air, his head thrown back, a wide-open mouth uppermost of his body. He breathed laboured breaths over and over until finally his chest came to be calm. He opened his eyes and looked around, taking in his surroundings, as if he had returned home from a distant land. Eventually he took a step forward, and trudged unsteadily out of the pool.

"Thank you for saving me, my queen."

I nodded. "Clean yourself up and find Philippe."

"Yes my queen, at once."

"Now. Leave me."

I watched as they left the cave. I was alone with a giant pool of blood. I needed to feed, such was the weakness inside me. I would immerse myself and be reborn stronger and more powerful. Now the pool was finished, I could come here regularly to feed and renew my power. I undid my brooch and my dress fell to the floor.

I stepped into the pool and was immediately transfixed by the feeling. I solemnly walked to the centre and dipped beneath the surface. As I surfaced, my teeth had emerged and I drew in mouthful after mouthful of the nourishing liquid of life. I spread my arms and drew handfuls of blood towards my face. I let myself fall gracefully backwards into the embrace of the viscous drink, thick rivulets rushing past my neck.

I swam and spun, taking in mouthfuls. I tipped back my head and dripped the blood from my fingers into my mouth. I lay at the side, lapping it up with my tongue. It was like a dance and I gave myself to the experience. I felt my energy increasing with every intake, darting through my body like the power of lightning.

When I had finally had my fill, I stepped out and cleaned myself in a nearby water pool. I piled my hair up high and tight in the form of a crown on my head and redressed.

I walked to the main room to find it empty. I could feel every vampire on the island. I expected to feel Philippe out there too, yet his energy was closer. I tuned in fully, and then I knew where Philippe was. He was here in this very house.

I could feel the guards and the other vampires in hunting packs all over the island. I looked around the room. The silence was eerily unsettling yet I had the upper hand: I could feel exactly where he was and followed my instincts. I walked to the council chamber's doors. Opening them I walked down the passageway that led to main chambers. He wouldn't get away from us this time. *Let's see how quick he is*, I thought. I walked down and threw open the doors. There, sitting on my throne, was Philippe.

"What took you so long?"

"Philippe you have made it quite clear that you don't wish to obey me, yet with numerous chances to escape you still come back here. I should be flattered. Do you really think this coup will be a success?"

"There has only ever been one thing I wanted, and that's your throne."

"You do realise that will never happen Philippe." He sat crossed-legged, his sword drawn in one hand, and his dagger in the other, tapping his leg. "What makes you think you would even have a chance?"

"Well, my dear, I do have a few tricks up my sleeve."

Because I felt so much stronger than before, I was able to tap into my energy quickly. I focused on him, building my energy inside. He, though, could sense what I was doing.

"Not so fast Amelia. You try anything and you will never see Jon again."

"Don't threaten me Philippe. My men are all over the island and will discover him soon enough."

"What about your favourite, Eleanor?"

I stared at him, bristling with anger as I strode. "Where is she?"

"She's safe. For now."

"You touch a hair on her head and I'll draw and quarter you myself!" My energy was high within me, and ready to be released. Philippe jumped down from the throne and walked towards me. His long, black hair was a tousled mess around his shoulders.

"So, we finally see who comes out of this alive."

"If you think you have the skills to end this, Philippe, let us see."

He grunted and ran towards me, with teeth clenched. I watched as he raised his dagger over his shoulder and flung it forward towards me. I turned my head to one side and raised my arm in defence. Suddenly I felt my energy flow around me, up my body and down my arm. It flew out of me like ripples on the water and slammed straight into Philippe, throwing him backwards over my throne onto the stone wall behind it. I felt an intense pain hit my arm as the dagger plunged itself into my skin and a trickle of blood began to fall from the wound.

It was only then that I noticed the distance from where Philippe had started to where he had landed. Had I caused this? I brought my hand to my face and looked at it. I was amazed.

"How...?"

I felt the blade move in my arm as my body forced it out. It fell to the ground, the noise echoing around the chamber. I watched as the wound healed itself. I felt the energy snap back within me. I looked at Philippe who seemed to be coming round to wakefulness on the floor. He turned his head to look at me with a stunned expression on his face.

"Very good Amelia. I didn't realise that you were able to do that."

At that moment, I felt a sharp point thrust into the back of my neck. A smell filled my nose, a scent I hadn't been close to in several years. I didn't need to turn around.

"John?"

"You have been very busy building a home I see."

I felt his breath on my neck as he leaned forward and I found myself closing my eyes and savouring the moment, drinking him in. "Zanette I am sorry, but I cannot and will not allow you to continue with this."

My energy flew out around me in defence but I had a feeling that it wouldn't affect him. Why, I didn't know. I had tried it once before, unsuccessfully, long ago.

"You're in league with Philippe?"

"Not quite. You have almost saved me the bother of killing him later. I told you before, I cannot allow you to live. You are against God's will." I felt the pressure of the blade in my neck increase. "You kill our child and now you're going to kill me is that it?" I said.

"I wasn't aiming for the baby I was aiming for your heart, Zanette."

"Then you must have the worst aim in all of Christendom. And my name is Amelia."

"I care not."

Philippe was still somewhat dazed, lying on the floor, looking at me.

"May God forgive you, Amelia."

I felt the blade starting to push into my flesh before I heard a loud thud and the dagger came to a halt. I heard John fall to the floor behind me. I turned quickly to see Lucas standing there with a log in his hands, breathing heavily.

"I'm sorry I'm late."

I looked down to see Jon laid on the floor, out cold. I breathed a sigh of relief and turned back to Philippe.

"See him to the caves and ensure he is tightly bound."

"Yes, my queen."

I heard Lucas shout for the guards who came rushing over to Philippe.

They collected him roughly and hauled him out of the chamber.

"And John?"

I turned and looked down at him. He had been about to kill me. Finally my sympathy had run out. I had hoped that there would be some part of his heart that still loved me, however small, and that he would spare my life. I now understood that there could be no such feeling there.

With a heavy heart, I said, "Bind him and take him to the cave also."

Lucas nodded and bent over, grabbed him by the neck and threw him towards the guards near the door.

"See to it that he cannot move or escape or you will suffer the consequences."

The guards nodded.

"Have you recovered, Amelia?"

"Yes thank you Lucas." I turned towards my throne and sat, recovering. We spoke no words for several moments, taking in the events. I couldn't help but think what might have happened if Lucas hadn't arrived in time.

Eventually he said, "Shall we burn John as well?"

I looked up and stared into his eyes for a moment.

"No. I have other plans for him."

Lucas nodded and retreated out of the room. I was left alone. I watched as the doors closed, and sighed.

I gazed out of a window at the trees blowing gently in the breeze. The sun was out and I had a clear view of the horizon over the far sea. Gulls hovered and played at the cliffs.

Am I to have no happiness? I thought. *No child, no husband, no home, no family… What is left for me? And what of Jon? What must be done about him?*

I watched the undulating sea, and for as long as it took a gull to fly from one side of the bay to the other, I mulled it over as I breathed in the salt air.

There was only one answer…

Chapter 16
The Truce

Jonathan Walker

Morning arrived early in the cave and the men stirred reluctantly.

I was already awake, and relieved the watch so he could get a couple of hours' sleep before we had to set off.

The sea was a lot calmer this morning and the bad weather had ceased for now. The cave was inhospitably damp, cold and dark but better to be here than in that house. I didn't tell the others I had seen Zanette again. I remember her as Zanette and even with a change of name, she would always be that to me. But this was not the main thing on my mind. The people in the house were in terrible danger. I was sure they didn't know her true nature.

It was strange being in the house with so much happening all around us. Everyone seemed to refer to her as the lady of house but how had that arisen? It could not be her house; I knew she had not the funds to build it. Throughout the night I could hear people shouting to each other. I knew they were looking for us. We left seaweed and other detritus from the beach in the mouth of the cave so that it looked as if no one had disturbed it. We kept quiet and huddled in the back of the cave. The search parties passed by and even brought their torches in to look, but each time we evaded discovery.

The men were hungry. We could not do the work ahead of us on an empty stomach. So after discussing it, a few of the men went out looking for different types of food. Some went to fish with basic spears that we had made, some went to hunt for game, some gathered seaweed or looked for fruits or other edible food. On this island we had seen no tavern, no other buildings in fact, aside from the house.

We sat and waited for their return, whittling rudimentary weapons from sticks and gathering logs and rocks. Hours had passed and every now and again two of us would walk back to the mouth of the cave to see if there was any sign of them. It was approaching midmorning and we still hadn't heard anything. I decided to send a team of two men to look for them.

When I thought I would not be seen, I went to the water's edge to wash and refresh myself. I turned to see a figure approaching from the rocks. I quickly ran back inside but I was aware that I had been seen. I warned the others that remained inside, that we had been seen and to prepare. We gathered rocks and our sharpened sticks and hid out in the darkness of the cave, alert, waiting. Charles was next to me asking questions.

"For God's sake be quiet, man. If it is but one man, we may have a chance but if it is many, we will need our wits about us and all the strength we can muster."

Time seemed to progress incredibly slowly as we waited, paused for action, our hands holding our weapons, ready to throw upon my command. Then a figure appeared, standing outside of the cave. We watched to see what he would do but he did not move, a black silhouette in the cave's mouth, the sea lapping behind him. He merely gazed into the darkness of the interior.

"Do you think he knows we are here?" Charles whispered.

A reply came from several yards away, outside of the cave and made us start in unison. "I'm afraid so gentlemen. The smell of blood that flows through your veins fills this cave and the beating of your hearts is quite amplified."

How could he have heard that whisper, let alone our heartbeats? Was he a conjuror? Or a witch? The figure walked slowly in. I felt the rock, ready in my hand.

"Don't fret man. I am not here to harm you. You have no need of that lump of rock in your hand."

I heard a gasp as the men reacted to this magic. How could he have known we had rocks ready to throw? As leader, it was down to me to address him. "What do you want?"

"I'm here to give you the opportunity to carry out your mission, Jonathan."

How did he know my name? I stepped forward out of the shade. As I got closer I could see what this man looked like. He was a tall, slender man with dark hair, ruffled around his shoulders. Fresh blood stained his mouth: *he must be like Zanette.*

"What are you?" I looked at him with a growing feeling of wariness.

"My dear boy, you would think you would know your enemies rather much better than this. You are trying to kill all of those like me, apparently. However you do not seem to have got very far."

"I will not ask you again. Who and what are you?"

The man looked around the cave and smiled.

"You might as well come out of the shadows. You cannot hide from me."

"My name is Philippe and I am at your service." He bowed elegantly as befits an aristocratic Frenchman and walked towards a large stone near the cave's wall to sit.

"I was a Council member at the Manor, until that filthy, bloodsucking ruler decided to try and take my life... twice. I assume she is the one you seek?"

The men slowly emerged and stood near me, still holding their logs and rocks that they had found. "Go on," I said.

"I believe you were married to Amelia?"

"Zanette? Yes. It feels like a lifetime ago. What of it?"

"I think you will find her type has grown in numbers since she landed here nearly seven years ago."

"You're telling me that you're infected too?"

"If you mean did she turn me, then yes."

"Turn you?"

"Yes. She is a very powerful upir."

"Pardon? What in heaven's name is an upir?"

"Vampire, you silly man. Have you not done your research? She is the first of our kind and therefore very powerful. I also assume you are the ones that escaped?"

"Yes but we are going back."

"My dear fellow, do you really think you can just walk back in? You were lucky to get out at all. However I can help you do that. I was one of many who helped build that house."

"And why should I trust you? What makes you think I would join you to kill your kind?"

"Because without me you will never get close enough to put those weak skills of yours into practice."

"I'll show you weak, you murdering..." I turned to see Charles step forward holding a log. Philippe merely smiled, amused.

"Now, now."

"How about I wipe that grin off your face?"

"You may try but you will fail."

Charles held up the log. "I have had enough of this."

"Wait, Charles," I said, placing my hand on Charles's shoulder.

"What do you want out of this, Philippe?"

"My house back. I'll help you take care of Amelia and the others and then you will never see me again. I will simply disappear."

"So you can infect others? I think not."

"Unfortunately, I don't hold the power or knowledge to do that. So you can rest assured that I will be the only living upir on earth."

"If we help you with this, what makes you think we would leave you on this island alive?"

"Because without my help, her domain will grow and grow until there are too many for you to handle. I'm sure that you will try and kill me but that's a risk I'm willing to take. I have just one condition. I want you to leave Tanzeda alone. We will quite happily live our lives out here."

"Who?"

"Tanzeda is a vampire and Council member. Your so-called wife had forbidden our love and attempted to put me to death by burning me at the stake. How kind."

"Ah, so you're doing this for love, is that it?"

"Exactly."

I was surprised that creatures like Philippe and his kind could feel love. I must admit, if he were telling the truth then his help would be a considerable advantage. I could always deal with him later. I turned to Charles. "He makes a good case, Charles. We could use his help to get back inside...." I turned back to Philippe. "…But if this is a trap, I'll make sure your death will be our final aim. Understand?"

"Yes, Jonathan, you have made yourself quite clear." He stood and started to walk out of the cave.

"Where are you going?"

He looked over his shoulder at me. "To see an old friend and gather your supplies. I'll be back soon."

"Do you want us to follow? We will have to wait until the others return."

"No need. I'll be back shortly." He paused at the caves mouth. "I, um, wouldn't count on the others coming back."

"Why not?"

"I'm sorry to say that… I had to feed."

Charles ran at him, log in hand, ready to attack. "You murdering dog!"

With a strength that was more than human, Philippe knocked him back across the cave.

"Watch your manners, boy," he spat darkly, and left.

I helped Charles off the floor.

"Let go. How can you work with him after what he has done and what he is?"

"We have little choice, Charles. Besides I never promised to let him live, did I? Right now, we are totally outnumbered. They are in command of God knows how many of those creatures. We need him to get inside.

"First we take care of what we came for, then we take care of him."

Charles shrugged and straightened his clothes. We both just stood there looking out towards the opening of the cave. There was nothing for it but to work together. War commands uneasy bedfellows sometimes. I knew he only wanted us for reinforcements but we needed him to gain access. If he was right about Amelia, we needed weapons and by the sounds of it, lots of them.

I was preparing for the greatest battle of my life, more perilous than any I had known on the battlefields of Europe. I sat aside from the men and thought about my future, free of this threat, about protecting Catherine and about growing old.

True to his word, Philippe returned carrying bags. As he walked into the cave he flung them towards our feet. "Prepare yourselves well. It is time."

We looked down at the bags he had thrown to us. They were indeed the ones that we had arrived on the island with but had left behind at the house.

"We leave at once."

"Wait a minute. What's the plan?"

"The plan, dear boy, is for you to follow me. We will enter the house via the caves underneath. There is a passageway that leads all the way to the main chamber of the house. It will be empty. There, Amelia will meet us."

"How can you be sure of that?"

"Because Amelia and the Council members take a blood oath. This enables Amelia to have a far stronger connection to us. She will undoubtedly feel my presence as we enter the house. In fact she may well know of my location now, that's why it is imperative that we leave at once. So arm yourselves."

I turned to see Charles looking at Philippe with pure distain.

"You must save your anger for the battle ahead, boy!" Philippe exclaimed.

"If he calls me boy one more time, I swear I'll knock his head clean off!" Charles replied.

A little laughter came from Philippe as he made his way out of the cave.

"Brace yourselves, men," I said, "the sooner we do this, the sooner we can go home to our families, the ones we fight to protect."

Out of the twelve men, only I, Charles and three others remained. Philippe had shortened our ranks considerably. And I wrestled with the notion that it was on purpose in order to keep our numbers manageable.

He needed us but probably knew that we weren't going to leave him on the island without fight. Five would be preferable to twelve in his eyes but, to our eyes, five meant the vicious murder of seven of our brothers.

We armed ourselves and grimly followed Philippe out of the cave, each searching our minds for ways to both succeed in our mission, and end the life of this vicious murderer we had been forced to work alongside. Staring at his back as he led, I know that we could have hacked him to pieces with our combined might, but that pleasure would have to wait.

Staying close to the shoreline, we walked to the far side of the cliff where the house was situated. Philippe turned and ducked, waving at us to keep down. Birds were nesting all around us, not just on the cliffs, but hidden in the tufts of wild grasses and thorn bushes all around us. Any sudden movement by us could startle them and give away our location. We slowly passed the cliff until we reached the cave Philippe was talking about. What he failed to mention was that this cave was half submerged under the water and the passageway that led inside was very narrow.

"How far is that passage?" I said to Philippe who was looking around us checking we were not being observed.

"About 200 yards in."

Charles climbed round me. "Are you taken by folly? We will never make it!"

"A strapping young man like you?" Philippe replied, wryly, "I'm sure you could. But you will not be going. Only Jon and I will go. The rest of you: approach the front doors of the house and wait in hiding for my signal. There is plenty of cover."

Charles appealed to me. "We would be like sitting ducks, John. I don't like this."

Philippe turned to Charles.

"Listen, I don't have time for this. Go to the house and hide well. There will be no guards there as they are all out looking for me. You will be quite safe for now."

Before anyone else could argue he jumped into the small passageway and began to swim. I followed into the deep pool at its head and the shock of the freezing water hit me like needles on my skin. I took a deep breath and dived under. The disturbed water made it hard to see my way. I felt like the sides of the passage were getting closer. I ploughed on, determined to get through it. All I kept in my mind was Catherine. I had to return to her. I had to protect her. I couldn't see Philippe anywhere ahead. My chest started to ache as the cold made it harder to intake enough gasps of air as I pulled myself along the passage.

Finally a hand grabbed my shoulder and pulled me up. "This way."

I lurched for air and my lungs burned under the duress. He had pulled me up into a small cave. I watched as he disappeared up a linking passageway branching off to the left. I remembered that Philippe was carrying both a sword and a dagger. My only weapon was my dagger.

Suddenly mistrustful of the situation, I realised that I needed to have my only weapon at hand. I dragged myself out of the small pool and stripped my jacket off. I took my dagger and placed it in my boot. I had left my other weapons with the men. I hoped I would not be called upon to use force until we met up again. I imagined the men had now reached the front of the house and were hiding and waiting for Philippe's signal.

I stumbled up the second passageway. The streams made it slippery and I lost my footing, splashing head first into the icy water and banging my head. Spluttering, I hauled my heavy body onto my barked knees again and forced myself onwards. The tunnel spiralled upwards and each step was a loaded effort.

At last, I managed to get to the top. It opened out onto to a large area lit by fire on the walls. I could hear the wind whirling around me as it rushed past me and into the open area. On the far side I saw some steps. I figured they must lead to the main chamber Philippe had mentioned. I quietly ran up the steps keeping my back to the wall and often looking behind me as I went.

I reached a wall at the top of the stairs and it seemed like a dead end until I noticed light coming from underneath it. I gently pushed on the wall and it slid slightly forward of its position. I squeezed by, allowing the wall to close on itself. It brought me out behind a pillar. I looked around this to see two very large pools of water with a walkway in the middle, leading to a cluster of chairs. Philippe was sitting on the middle one which was set higher than the others. It was a beautifully handcrafted stone chair.

Suddenly the doors to the room flew open and in strode Zanette. I hid behind the pillar, dripping, peeking around its edge. It was a little hard to hear over the running water that was near me. I watched while they talked. She slowly walked forward towards him. I kept my eye on the door to make sure no one else was with her.

I watched as Philippe stood and walked forward. She must have said something to him as he bared his teeth and flung his dagger towards her. She lifted her arm and, from nowhere, a wave-like power bolted from her hand, sending Philippe flying over to the back, crashing into the wall.

I saw the dagger lodge in the flesh of her arm. She looked towards it. As I looked on, amazed, the blade reversed itself out of her flesh through no earthly agency. Something invisible was pushing the blade out yet she was not holding it. At that moment I knew: she was possessed of a demon. She must be killed with all speed.

I silently crept forward taking my dagger from my boot. I reached the door and looked through it to check no one was there. I walked up behind her and held the dagger to the back of her neck.

"Very good, Zanette. I didn't realise that you were able to do that."

"Jon?" she said.

"You have been very busy building a home, I see."

"You will not get away with this," she replied.

I moved closer to her and spoke gently in her ear. "Zanette I am sorry but I cannot and will not allow you to continue with this." I suddenly felt something wash over me, a strange energy I had not felt before. Had I been bewitched by this demon? I found that all the hairs on my neck were standing on end.

"You're in league with Philippe?" She seemed surprised.

"Not quite. You saved me the bother of killing him later. I told you before I cannot allow you to continue. It's against God's will."

"You kill our child and now you're going to kill me, is that it?"

The thought of what she accused me of made my stomach turn. "I wasn't aiming for the baby I was aiming for your heart, Zanette."

"In that case you have the worst aim in all of Christendom."

"Killing the evil inside you was a bonus, Zanette. I couldn't allow that thing to live!"

"I am now Amelia, damn you!"

"I think I shall continue to call you Zanette. A wise man recently told me it is Greek for 'long teeth'. Only God can forgive you for your heinous deeds."

At that moment, I felt a blinding pain in my head. I gasped and everything went dark…

Chapter 17
My Decision

Amelia

Lucas went to gather the rest of the house and informed them of the events of the day. Jon and Philippe had both been taken away. Three more men were found hiding outside and joined John in the cave. I couldn't believe Jon was really going to kill me after all these years, after all we had meant to each other. I knew he was angry at me for what happened with Catherine but to find him in league with Philippe in a plot to end my life took me completely by surprise. I thanked the heavens that Lucas was on hand to stop him.

It was a long hard decision making process to determine what I must do about John. I still had that familiar tug in my heart but his murderous intent had left me with few options. My decision as to what to do about Philippe, on the other hand, was simple. He would be returned to the stake to burn and this time I would make sure he couldn't escape. His threats against Eleanor were untrue. She had not been captured but had entered the chamber in time to see both men being dragged out. John was unconscious. Philippe was awake, but wounded.

Only I remained in the chamber, trying to make a decision about John. I sat there for ages looking at the empty chamber trying to think of some way to change John's mind and keep him alive, but without success. There was really only one answer; he had to die. I was most reluctant but it had to be done: he had made his choice. My love for John was still there even after everything he had done to me. But I was more fearful for my own life: if John were to be released, he would undoubtedly come after me again.

Eleanor approached me half running with small, swift steps. Sadness gripped her face.

"My queen, you are safe now?" I could see tears in her eyes.

"Yes, sweetness, I'm fine. If you don't mind, I would rather be alone for the moment."

"Yes, of course. I'm sorry to interrupt, it's just that Lucas is wanting to know what we are to do with the men captured today."

I breathed in deeply and slowly released it. The other men I was less concerned about.

"Tell him to drain the others of their blood, but to leave John to me. He is not to be touched without my word."

"Yes my queen. I will pass the message on immediately."

"Thank you, Eleanor," I said kindly and she bowed and left.

I stared into space and time passed by. Eventually a feeling of resolution came over me. I would go through with it. First Philippe would burn. Then I would attend to Jon. I shouted for the guard standing outside the chamber doors.

"Yes my queen?"

"Summon Lucas."

"Yes my queen, at once."

I watched as he closed the door.

I really hated Philippe. I should have known there was something wrong with him when he was turned. I should have realised, but I was forever giving him another chance. He constantly contradicted me, arguing with me over everything. He was always trying to gain support from the sisters to overrule my decisions in order to deprive me of feeding until I was weak.

I should have stopped him sooner. I was also angry with myself for letting this get out of control. But that would not happen again. I now knew it was imperative that I, above and before anyone else, had to feed and make sure I maintained my strength and power. All those under my rule would be able to feel this energy running through their veins too.

"Amelia you wanted to see me?"

"Lucas…Yes, I want you to prepare the fire for Philippe. I want him burned by midnight. Ensure he cannot escape this time and make sure he is bound securely to rock this time."

"Of course, Amelia. I will see to it."

"And Lucas – have extra guards surrounding him just in case. I don't want a repeat."

"As you wish, Amelia."

The sooner Philippe was put to death, the sooner I could relax. Jon, on the other hand, will live to fear me, and by my hand he will die. It was only right. We are still married after all. It will be like granting me my freedom again.

Moments later, the mortal screams of the men in the caves echoed throughout the chamber. I smiled as I realised the guards must be enjoying their work a little too much. My guards though were performing a valuable service in keeping our blood pool well supplied. They should have felt honoured. The screams came to an end. And now, they felt nothing.

I received word that everything was prepared for the burning of Philippe. I couldn't wait any longer. I wanted him out of my life once and for all. I again summoned Lucas.

"Make sure Lucas that no one from the house is there except for the guards. I am taking no chances with this. It will be a private burning. Intimate, really."

"Yes Amelia."

The evening was approaching fast and I was very much looking forward to watching Philippe burn. The longer the day went on the more my bloodlust grew. I summoned Eleanor to the chambers and advised her that I wished to look my best for the event, and to prepare my outfit. She excitedly scurried out of the room, seeming more eager about the burning than I did.

In my chambers Eleanor had laid out my gown and began dressing me. This time she had chosen very well: a long, white silk dress, that she had made less than a month ago from silk we had shipped from London. She was a gifted seamstress. It draped around me and fitted my body perfectly. She placed my hair in tight curls and pinned them up with added jewels. In the mirror, I looked and felt divine.

I turned to a knock at my door. A guard bowed and advised me that everything was in order and was awaiting my arrival. I told him I would be there shortly. I looked at Eleanor who was standing behind me.

"I believe it's time. Go and inform Lucas I'm on my way."

"Of course, my queen."

I wanted a few moments alone. As Eleanor left, I walked out onto the balcony. The weather outside had once again become thundery and snow was falling, unusual for the time of year. The wind was calm. I watched the snow fall, gently drifting down over the sea. I could hear the crashing of the waves from the rocks below.

I took a deep breath. *This is it*, I thought, *it's time*. For the briefest moment I wondered if I was doing the right thing but this was immediately replaced by images of Philippe's deceit and betrayal. I recovered myself. I knew it had to be done. I went into my dressing table drawer and found my locket to place it around my neck. I looked in the mirror one last time before I left the room.

My escort guards were outside waiting for me. Lucas had arranged that no one was to leave me alone after the incident with Philippe and John down in the Council chambers. I walked down with my head held high, two guards in front and two behind. I felt regal and strong. I glided down to the cave.

I was met by the sight of Philippe tied to a stone post at the edge of the open cave. Guards were stationed behind him in case of another escape attempt. Lucas met me at the gate doors and walked me to my throne. As requested no one had been allowed in except Council members and guards.

Tanzeda wasn't there. Although she should have been, I understood and allowed it. Borbala, on the other hand, was present and sitting next to Eleanor, watching Philippe all the time, their eyes fixed on his face. I watched as Lucas took his seat by my right side and without saying a word waved to the nearest guard holding a lit torch to proceed. Philippe was gagged and couldn't speak although his moans were loud as he struggled to break free.

The guard lit the fire and we witnessed the smoke beginning to rise. It took a few moments for the flames to reach his legs but, once they had caught fire, it was if divine intervention was powering the flames. Philippe could not stop coughing amidst the smoke and his shouts were becoming drier and huskier. I could hear the crackling of the fire and the suddenly turbulent ocean beneath him crashing against the rocks below. He jumped and writhed to free himself as his clothing was eaten by his hungry foe. His skin darkened from white to red, and then to black. All watched as the flames rapidly increased and approached his chest, the heat consuming his hair in seconds.

Philippe then made a sound I had never heard before, a long, unholy bellow with the last of his voice, his whole being going into the production of it. His head dropped to his chest. Then, he fell silent, his movements slowed until there were only twitches from his arm or a finger and it was not clear if there was the smallest possibility that Philippe might be somewhere within, or whether it was the living fire who now controlled his body.

The fire now spoke for both of them, hissing and spitting its deadly message. Philippe was being gradually flayed, his skin peeled away, small patches floating off on heat currents, up and up into the night sky. It reached his contorted and immobile face and caught fire. Not a whisper was to be heard as all present stared mutely ahead. The only sounds were the cackles of the god of fire as he consumed his sacrifice.

By the end, Philippe was nothing more than burning bones tied at the wrists with iron chains.

The smoke filled the air outside, drifting gently along in cold winds. The fire, deprived of fuel, began to ebb away, its task complete. There was nothing left of Philippe but ashes and partial bones that fell to the base of the stone post he had been tied to. The chains fell to the floor with a clank, which seemed to break the spell that had enchanted the room into silence.

The threat of Philippe was never going to return. I took a deep breath and stood. I looked around the room and didn't say a word. I nodded and made way for the door. It had been a solemn experience. I was relieved that the whole business was over with. He was a betrayer and a liar. He got exactly what he deserved.

*

I made my way to see John in his cave. He too was bound, his arms raised above his head, chained to the wall on the far side of the cave; his head hung down. I instructed the guard to open the door and walked in.

"John?"

He slowly looked up. He had been beaten up. Both eyes had been blacked and were swollen. A large bruise covered the left-hand side of his face. Dried blood caked his mouth.

"You will never get away with this Zanette," he slurred, his voice barely audible. I noticed several of his teeth were missing.

"My name is Amelia."

"Your name is Death," he spluttered. "Don't care what you call yourself... All those lives you ruined..."

"I have given them a new way of life, John. They are happy."

"They're not happy, witch! They're ruled by you and must obey. Not the same."

I looked over my shoulder to the guards behind me.

"Leave me."

The guards bowed and walked outside the cell.

"John why did you come here? You could have lived out your life back on the mainland. You must realise I cannot allow you to leave now, after your attempt on my life."

"Life?" he cackled. "Infecting others? Feeding on humans? Only the Devil's spawn could call this a life."

"I'm sorry you feel like that John."

"What are you going to do with me? Burn me too?"

"No John, I'm not going to burn you. I'm going to feed on you."

"I hope my blood kills you!"

"You have left me with no choice."

"Then get on with it. Do whatever it is you think you need to do. But killing me will not stop this war. Don't you think I have thought about that?"

"I will deal with whatever comes, John. You are no threat now. I will not allow anyone to threaten me or my kind anymore."

"Get out, demon seed!"

I stared at him for a moment unused to taking orders from anyone. I walked away. Just before I left I looked over my shoulder towards him.

"I may even turn you yet, John."

"Go to Hell!" he croaked. "I will never follow you or your way of life."

I smiled. "You won't have a choice, my dear." I left the cell and the guards locked it behind me.

Was I really considering turning him? It was a thought. But something inside told me that if I did, I would end up in the same situation as I had done with Philippe. I couldn't allow that to happen.

It was clear that John no longer cared for me. He was so consumed with fear and anger that when he looked at me all I could see was pure hatred. Deep down inside of me, I still felt that little something for him, and it seemed that no matter what happened I would always have that. But I had a new life now. I would have to remember the good times we had together and forget the rest after he was gone. I would not sacrifice myself for someone who looked at me with pure disdain. I had a choice to make: would I burn him or drain him? The Council would insist on burning, but I was not sure I could watch him burn alive.

Back in my chambers, I laid down on the bed. There were many things running around my mind. As I lay there, I could hear the guards outside my door whispering to one another, apparently concerned about my health and strength. The wind had got up and I could hear the sea crashing against the rocks. I heard sharp distress calls of birds who had lost their mates in the storm.

As I lay still and tried to think, the sounds of the house were getting louder. The footsteps of the many who resided here were walking about. I felt every single one of them inside myself. I realised that this was the feeling of connection that I had been searching for. This is what I wanted. I was part of a huge family that I had made for myself. So why did I still feel alone?

I felt weak at that moment so I asked one of the guards to request that Eleanor bring my drink. Moments later Eleanor walked in carrying a jug and glass on a silver tray. She placed it gently on my desk, poured me a glass and brought it over to my nightstand. She did not speak, seeming to sense that my thoughts were troubling me. She quietly withdrew.

At last I reached a decision. I finally decided what I was going to do about Jon.

I arose and sat on the edge of my bed, slowly sipping the cold blood. It flowed into my fangs and from there, around my body. I felt instantly better. I took a deep breath and pushed myself off the bed, returning the glass on my dressing table. I gave myself one last glance in the mirror to check my appearance and walked to the doors.

The guards were surprised to see me. They followed me down to main lounge where everyone was gathered. My subjects were sitting, drinking and talking amongst themselves. If I am to be an effective ruler, I thought, I would need to understand my kind. For the years we have lived here and indeed since they were turned, I had never really socialised with them, always keeping myself separated, and aloof. But it was now time for this to change. As I reached the last step, everyone turned and looked at me and bowed or curtsied. I walked over to the fireplace and sat down on a large armchair. Two others were sitting near me. Silence fell over the crowd. They were all listening intently, to find out what I would say.

"Good evening," I said softly. The two vampires looked at each other in confusion and then back at me.

"Good evening, your highness."

"I would like to ask you both some questions. Firstly your names?"

"My name is Florence and this is Edward, your highness."

"It's a pleasure to meet you both. How are you finding your home here?"

"Well… I have to say that we are pleased to be in the company of such a beautiful queen. I feel free here." Florence was a small woman with dark hair and green eyes. She sat elegantly on the armchair opposite me.

"And you?" I said, looking towards Edward, a tall blond man with a moustache, deep blue eyes and the youth that nearly all my converts possessed.

"The same, my queen."

"Wonderful."

"May I say... that we are humbled to be part of such wonderful family that you yourself created?"

"How very kind of you. Is there anything you would want to change?"

"Perhaps somewhere bigger my queen. So we can feed on fresh humans rather than drinking cold blood that is rationed out."

"Yes, I agree. I'm afraid cold blood doesn't have the same taste or impact."

I stood and faced the room. "Do you all agree with Edward?" There was a moment's pause before anyone spoke, but general agreement was forthcoming.

"Then allow me to tell you my future plans. We will indeed move when we are ready back to the mainland. However, for now it is imperative that we survive and we are unable to do so at present. Rest assured though, that when the time is right, you will be able to feed freely, as promised."

I turned to the guard standing only a few feet away.

"Summon Lucas. I'll be in the Council chambers."

"Yes my lady."

He turned and marched out of the room.

"Good evening to you all."

Everyone bowed as I walked to the double doors at the back of the room and entered the chambers. It was time to think about the future, but first I must deal with John...

Chapter 18
The Pain

Amelia

I watched as Lucas entered the room and walked down to meet me by my throne.

"You wanted to see me Amelia?"

"Yes. I want you to gather the coven and then bring Jon here. I have a point to make."

"Yes, of course. I will see to it at once."

"And another thing Lucas. Don't allow him to get away."

Lucas nodded and walked quickly out of the room. I lay my head back against my chair and closed my eyes, listening to the trickling of the water from the pools in the chamber. I felt relaxed and in control of my emotions again. Jon didn't want me anymore and made it clear he wanted me dead. It was only right that I showed him the same contempt.

A few moments later my converts began to arrive with the human servants. I wanted everyone present on this occasion. I watched as the Council members came and took their seats, including Eleanor. Once everyone was gathered, I rose to my feet. The room went quiet, waiting for me to speak.

"Good evening everyone. I have gathered you here today to witness something which I will find quite difficult. You have all heard rumours of my past. Well I can confirm some of them for you. I was indeed married and I suppose I still am. The man I married found out about my true nature, our true nature. He killed my unborn child and has been seeking my death ever since, which he has attempted on two separate occasions. The man that committed these abhorrent acts is here today."

Everyone looked at one another and gasps came from the crowd.

"He has been held in the caves on my order and has been here for several days. You are all aware that Philippe was burned at the stake for his treason. That punishment would be handed to anyone who followed in his footsteps. But this man, my estranged husband, Jon, has tried to kill me and therefore he will be punished severely for his crimes. Lucas! Bring him in."

The crowd turned and watched as Lucas escorted Jon along with two guards into the Council chambers. Jon was bound behind his back and a rag appeared at his mouth. Lucas marched him to the foot of my throne and flung him down. Jon hit the floor and was lying on his side looking up at me. His eyes were red and swollen. I knelt down to him and placed my hand under his chin. He tried to shake his head from my grasp but I kept hold. I looked up at the guards standing nearby.

"Get him to his feet."

The guards dragged him onto his feet. I reached out and took the rag from his mouth and dropped into the floor. With his first free breath, he insulted me.

"You bitch!" he spat.

I watched as the guard behind hit him in the back of his head.

"You will never get away with this!"

"Look around you, John. I already have."

I reached for his throat and pulled him close to me. Ours eyes met for a second and I forced his head to one side. I could see the shock contort his face as my fangs descended. The vein in his neck started throbbing. I pulled him closer and slowly sank my teeth into his neck. He screamed and tried to move. A warm rush of liquid filled my mouth. Suddenly images of his life flashed through my mind. Most featured Catherine. I felt his body go limp and fall to the floor.

Not one image of me was in his mind. How had he managed to erase all traces of our life together? How could he? All I saw was his daughter. It shouldn't have bothered me but it did. I let go of him and watched him drop to the floor, blood spilling out of his neck and forming a small pool around him. I straightened up and walked back to my throne.

"Get rid of that."

I watched as the guards picked him up and dragged him out of the room.

I was angry. How could he hate me so much and have no memories of me at all? I knew then that I had made the right decision. He never loved me; he had just been making use of me for all those years. All he wanted was a male heir to carry on his name. I was so very angry that I allowed this man to get under my skin. It was a power over me that I had to stop.

Now I know why he didn't want the baby. He didn't want anything to do with me or what I was. For all those years I had battled with my emotions over him. Yet he spent his time plotting his revenge on me. If only I was able to read his thoughts then maybe I wouldn't have been put into that situation. I'm still not sure how I wasn't able to do that. In fact I recall I couldn't do that with his daughter. Perhaps she too could block me. Not that it's important anymore.

I could still taste John's blood in my mouth, but the normally sweet taste was not there. Instead it was bitter. I knew he hated me but could his bitterness have infected his blood? I ran my tongue around my mouth and the taste seemed only to get worse. My mouth was feeling odd too, as if it was going numb.

"Amelia? Are you well?" Lucas said as he walked back into the room.

"I feel quite strange, Lucas," I looked up at him and saw him react to the fear in my eyes.

"Amelia?"

My throat had been tingling but now it was starting to burn. I felt weak and thought I would faint. Suddenly a blinding pain shot through my body. I grabbed my stomach. The pain was intensifying and spreading throughout my body. Finally, I was in so much pain that I fell to the floor, groaning. My legs were convulsing as I started to retch. I couldn't breathe: I was gasping for air. The pain was all consuming. Black foam appeared at my mouth. My body was in tumult and I released a stream of black vomit onto the floor. My eyes began to fight against closing but it was becoming impossible to hang on to consciousness. I faintly heard someone shout to clear the room. All I could think about was the pain coursing through every part of my body. And then, darkness…

*

I awoke in the small cave under the Council chambers. I was laid in the blood pool. I opened my eyes to see Lucas standing at the edge. "Amelia?"

I coughed and slowly tried to stand but I was weak and kept falling back down. Lucas stepped into the pool and grabbed my arm helping me to my feet.

"Guards!" I heard him yell.

Two guards entered the room and all three helped me up.

"Take her to her chambers to rest."

I slowly looked at Lucas, worry spreading across his face, as I fell limp in his grasp. I had never felt so weak in my life. My energy was none existent.

All I remember is being carried to my chambers in the arms of Lucas. He laid me gently on my bed. I instantly fell asleep, which I had not done properly for so many years, a little when I was pregnant, but not fully since I was living with Grandpapa.

My body convulsed and shook as I lay there. Images of Jon's memory flooded my mind. My eyes were constantly losing and regaining focus.

Seeing the empty side of the bed next to me as I lay, I couldn't help but think about Jon, about our time together as husband and wife, many years before. I felt so weak I could hardly sit up. It felt as though any vitality had been sucked out of me. It was obviously something to do with Jon's blood. Even now all I could taste was a foul layer on my tongue. I couldn't explain it. Jon's blood had nearly killed me.

I heard the door open in my room and a hazy figure walked towards me and placed a cold, damp cloth on my forehead. I couldn't make out who it was … "Grandpapa…?"

"Amelia, can you hear me?"

It was Lucas. I tried to bring my eyes into focus on him but failed. I tried to speak but no words came, my mouth refused to move. My body tingled. My feet and hands felt as though they had been tortured with a hot fire iron.

"Rest, my lady..." was the last thing I remember hearing before drifting off into unconsciousness...

A few days later I awoke to see Lucas sitting by my bedside. He seemed to be snoozing. I turned towards him as he lifted his head and smiled.

"Amelia?"

"Lucas." I smiled, weakly. "What happened to me?"

"I don't know. You have been out for three days."

I did feel better, but still weak. Lucas lifted my head and placed a glass to my mouth. I felt my fangs descend slowly as the cold rush of liquid flowed past my lips and filled my veins. For the first time in a long time I was glad of this cold blood. Lucas laid my head back onto the pillow and placed the glass on the bedside table.

"Have you been here the whole time?"

"Of course, Amelia. I did not dare leave you on your own."

"You are very kind, Lucas."

"Shhh, rest my queen. You need plenty of rest and fluids."

"What happened to me?"

"It appears as though he was able to poison his blood shortly before we brought him to you."

"How?"

"We don't know yet. I am trying to find out."

I turned my head back and looked at the ceiling. Yet again, he had almost succeeded in killing me. I hoped against hope that his and Philippe's deaths would be an end to living in fear.

Still feeling weak, I closed my eyes and drifted off again. I knew that Lucas would stay with me no matter what. When I was strong enough again, I would find out who helped Jon to poison his own blood. Perhaps it was Philippe, before his demise. Perhaps he had known what I would do, in the event his plans failed. I would find answers. With Jon and Philippe out of the way I was safe to build my coven and secure a future for us all. I needed to regain my strength and quickly.

The next day I awoke to see Lucas still sitting at my side. His loyalty was second to none. It gave me the confidence to know that everything would be all right. He constantly made me sip my glass of blood to regain my strength and, slowly, I did. It was strange to be constantly falling asleep after so many years of constant consciousness, but the more I fed the less sleep I needed.

I knew that all it would take was time. And yet I had the sense that time was a luxury I could ill afford. So I did as Lucas wanted and remained in my chambers constantly under his supervision.

He sent orders down to the Council chambers. He ran the house like clockwork. I was very grateful and proud to have someone who looked after me so well. I spent the next few days resting in my chambers leaving everything to Lucas. I wasn't strong enough yet to deal with my duties but that never seemed a problem. Lucas was more concerned with me getting better than running the house. While I lay there though, I had the opportunity to think long and hard about what our next steps as a community needed to be.

Questions and ideas arose and passed by. I thought back to the minutes before the executions, to my sense of connection to everyone in the house and the wonderful feeling it gave me, and I vowed that this would be my number one priority. It arose in me a warm feeling, and with joy, I realised it was what I had always wanted: I would develop this coven until it truly felt like that which had been cruelly denied to me previously: a family.

Chapter 19
My Sacrifice

Jonathan Walker

I awoke to find myself bound by chains in the same cave I was in before. The whole of my torso ached from being hung by my wrists. I was in pain and weak. My head was hurting so badly from when they beat me, and my vision was blurred. I could taste dried blood in my mouth from where they had pulled out my teeth before I blacked out.

I couldn't see a thing in the dark except the bars in front of me. I had been able to get so close to Zanette before I had been captured. I didn't realise her kind had grown in numbers so quickly in such a short space of time. I couldn't see Philippe anywhere, or any of the men of our band. I wondered where Charles had ended up. I prayed that, when I had not reappeared, he had devised another plan of attack and was even now about to overcome the enemy. At the very least, I hoped he had escaped alive with the others. I didn't suppose they would easily get off the island unless a ship put in.

I had to hope they would tell everyone on the mainland what we had witnessed here and that an army could be raised. Lost in thought, I didn't hear the doors open. I looked up to see two tall guards approaching me. Before I could say a word, one of them struck me in the stomach sending a blinding pain through my body. The wind was knocked right out of me. I tried to gasp for air but the throbbing pain in my stomach wouldn't allow it. Suddenly a blow came to my head. It felt as though my eye was about to pop out. I knew they didn't have weapons but their blows felt like boulders hitting me from every angle. After the third blow to the face I must have fallen unconscious because I don't remember anything after that.

When I came to, my face felt ten times heavier and I could taste fresh blood dripping from my lips. I tried to lift my head but it felt weighed down like someone was hanging from it. I moved my tongue around my mouth to find pieces of broken tooth in some areas and holes elsewhere. I let out a sorrowful groan as I remembered they had tried to remove my teeth. I spat the pieces onto the floor. I could hardly breathe and my cough was making it harder to fill my lungs with air. I didn't notice someone in the cave with me. I looked up slowly to see a figure standing there. It was Zanette. She walked closer to me not saying a word at first. As she came in to focus, she studied me, looking intently at my face.

"You will never get away with this, Zanette."

She walked closer to me, never taking her eyes off me for a moment.

"My name is Amelia."

"Your name is Death," I spluttered. "Don't care what you call yourself... All those lives you ruined…"

"I have given them a new way of life John. They are happy."

I almost laughed at that statement. "They're not happy witch! They are ruled by you and must obey. Not the same."

Two figures stood behind her in the doorway. I couldn't make them out through my swollen, blurred eyes but they left on her command. She had brainwashed them all. She was truly evil. She turned to face me again and moved a little closer.

"John why have you come here? You could have had your life back on the mainland. You realise I cannot allow you to leave now after your attempt on my life."

"Life? Infecting others? Feeding on humans? Only the Devil's spawn could call this a life."

Life? She ruined that when she tried to kill my daughter. We argued and she stormed out. She threatened to bite my flesh and drink my blood so that I would become evil too. She wouldn't get the chance. I watched as she left and the cell doors were locked. I needed a plan.

She obviously wanted me alive for now. She had probably dealt with Philippe and now it was my turn. She wanted to change me into one of her demons and couldn't risk my dying too soon. Philippe had planned for that. He had given me a small rag, which he had made into a pouch, containing powders. He said that I should take it if I knew my death was imminent. He told me it was a poison, but did not name it. It was in my pocket and therefore impossible to get it to my mouth while my hands were chained. I had to think of a plan…

I ached all over now and was empty with hunger. I hadn't had anything to eat since I escaped. The men I had sent out to collect fruit and fish had been killed by Philippe.

I was very weak. I think that deep inside me I knew I wasn't going to see Catherine again. It filled me with dread knowing that I would never again see her face. I had been so preoccupied with revenge that I had hardly seen her in months. I had missed most of her birthdays over the years in trying to get ready for this battle and for what? Nothing. I had lost most of my men and ended up a prisoner about to be executed. Zanette had won. I would never see my beloved girl again.

I hadn't been prepared for the amount of people she had converted. They appeared faster and stronger and most seemed cold and distant. Perhaps that was the nature of this beast. She had victory, but maybe I could slow her down or perhaps take her down with me. If only I could get to that pouch.

"Wake up prisoner! Your time has come."

I awoke to see two guards standing either side of me. A black figure in the distance walked in and came close. It was the man who had been with Zanette at my house.

"You bloodsucking vermin. What do you want?"

"Is that any way to talk to a gentleman? Perhaps we need to give you a lesson in manners."

"What do you want?"

The figure moved closer to me, our faces only inches apart.

"The name is Lucas. I believe I have had the pleasure already."

I moved my head closer to his and spat in his face. He pulled out a white handkerchief and wiped his face.

"Ha ha. You still have a little bit of life left in you, then… Good."

"Take him down and be sure he does not escape."

I felt them tug on my arms as they released my wrists. I was in such pain, as if to return them to their natural position was a new torture. I went to take the pouch from my pocket but was stopped by a guard reaching for my wrists. I just managed to pull it out but it dropped to the floor. The guards had hold of my arms now and I went limp and staggered. At this, their grip on my loosened and I managed to slip free and balled up my fist. I swung. Lucas had me by the throat and crashed me into the wall behind. He pulled me close to his face again.

"A good attempt, but not good enough. You are a tiresome drain on our time. If it were left to me, I would have drained you myself by now."

He flung me to ground so hard I heard a crack in my shoulder. I fell next to the pouch and I grabbed at it with my teeth as I was hauled up, quickly hiding it in my mouth. My arms were held tightly behind my back as shackles were once again placed on my wrists. Not noticing the pouch in my mouth they pushed me out of the cave and up the winding passage.

I could just taste whatever was in the pouch. It smelt like garlic but the taste was of something very bitter. I was pushed through some doors into another small passageway leading down to thick wooden doors reinforced with iron.

"I'll take him from here."

I felt a hand on my arm as we approached the doors. The doors opened and in I was pushed. The room was crowded with people who parted to let us through. I looked up to see Zanette sitting on a high, hand-carved chair.

I was pushed to the front and watched as she stepped down towards me. She made an announcement and came close to me, pulling the pouch away from my mouth and, in doing so, releasing the contents into my mouth. I quickly swallowed and waited. She was speaking but I couldn't quite hear her and began to drift away as the powders took hold of me. It began to grow dark and I felt so tired all of a sudden. I may have made some flippant remark. I felt a searing pain in my neck. I screamed. The pain was terrible. I felt weaker by the second.

My vision was gone, and my heart seemed to be beating slower and slower. This was it; this was my end. I was…

Chapter 20
There is Light

Amelia

After a month I was still weak. I had managed to stand with the support of Lucas. Getting up was difficult but once up, I seemed to improve by taking a few steps. Lucas and Eleanor had been on hand to help me over the weeks as I walked further. Lucas would not permit others access to me until I was well on the road to recovery. I wasn't fully healthy but was improving each day.

I was surprised at how slowly I was recovering. I could hardly understand why this should be the case, when my powers of self-healing were normally so strong. I built up my strength gradually with Eleanor's regular blood offerings.

I finally felt ready to attend a Council meeting. I asked Lucas to take me to the Council chambers. Since the poisoning, I had not been involved in Council proceedings. I relied on Lucas to keep me informed of any particular aspects of government that were challenging, but he had not disturbed me much with the business.

"Amelia, are you sure it's a good idea to do this?"

"Yes Lucas. I am feeling much better now. Now, please take me to the Council chambers. I think it's time we decided what we want to achieve."

"Of course Amelia. As you wish."

Lucas led the way with Eleanor supporting me as we made our way down to the Council chambers.

They helped me to my throne before taking their seats. I breathed deeply, recovering from my walk. I held onto the arms of the throne for extra support. The sisters were waiting there too. Lucas stood and walked forward.

"It is good to see you recovered, my queen," said Borbala.

"We all bid you welcome back, my queen," offered Tanzeda, more formally.

I began to lead proceedings.

"Thank you for your good wishes, everyone. I am much recovered and almost back to normal. So, it is time for me to retake the reins of government. We have some important business that we need to attend to. As you will be aware, the weather is increasingly poor and the island has suffered many storms and now snow. We have received word that our shipment is unable to dock. They intend to send the supplies piecemeal by rowboat. We need volunteers to help."

"Send the humans," Borbala said from her seat.

"We cannot send the humans. Do not forget, we do not have enough to supply us at present."

"Are there no humans on board?"

"Yes, but they will not survive without our help, Borbala."

I noticed that Borbala seemed jaded today, and disappointed by my dismissal of her contribution to the meeting.

"Borbala, we will send out our guards: they can handle the weather."

"As you wish, my queen," she replied. I detected a slight tone.

"Before we move on…" I coughed, "we need to discuss what we are going to do about our future."

Lucas looked at me and walked forward. "What do you mean?"

"We cannot stay here without starving ourselves to death. We need either more ships on our fleet, or to move to a more populated area."

"But my queen, that is risky for us."

"Perhaps it is less risky though than living from hand to mouth as we do now, with the drips we can gather from the humans already here."

I coughed again feeling pains starting to form in my throat. I wondered if I had gone back to work too soon. I was hungry despite the fact that I had done nothing much more than drink for the past few days.

"Lucas, would you get me a drink?"

He looked at me for a moment, trying to gauge if I was unwell before turning to the guards at the back of the room to order the drink.

"Are you able to continue my queen?"

"Lucas, let us carry on. We must make progress. I am a little tired that is all, and we must resolve these issues."

"As you wish, my queen. The shipment is anchored off shore, so I will send men to help retrieve it."

"Excellent. Is there anything else before we move on?"

"Yes, my queen, Zach wishes to address the Council."

I sighed tersely and realised I was rapidly getting tired. "Very well." Lucas nodded at a nearby guard. The guard opened the chamber door and summoned Zach. As Zach walked in, I noticed he looked a lot older than I remembered, thinner and greyer. Although I was tired it really did confuse me. I looked at Lucas for an explanation. He just looked at me and shrugged his shoulders. I turned to Zach.

"What is it now, Zach?"

He moved closer, gripping his hands together looking at the floor.

"My queen I wish to know what is to become of the rest of us."

"Pardon?"

"Well, with less than ten people left, everyone fears for their life."

Unable to keep my eyes open any longer I simply looked at Lucas. He could see why I was looking at him and walked past Zach to the front.

"Allow me to explain my queen, our priority is your well-being and we were running low on blood from the blood pool. So we had no choice but to sacrifice some of the servants to keep you strong and indeed feed ourselves."

I didn't have the energy to argue so I simply nodded. I turned to Zach.

"No more will be harmed."

"But…"

I held my hand up.

"You have my answer. Now leave." I seemed to hear a slur as I spoke. I don't remember Zach leaving the chambers. In fact, I don't remember much after that, as I must have blacked out.

I awoke to find I had been placed on my bed again. I looked around the room to see I was on my own. I felt a little better but still so tired. I sat up gently and noticed that someone had placed a jug by my bedside. I poured myself a glass, watching the cold blood flow forth. I breathed in deep and took a sip. I turned to my door opening and Lucas appeared.

"You're awake Amelia. How are you feeling?"

"Lucas… I am feeling a little better. What happened?"

"I'm afraid you had another episode. Eleanor and I brought you back here. I fear your health is not fully recovered. Perhaps you should take some more time to recover."

I managed to stand and walk over to my dressing table. Placing the drink down, I held onto the table and steadied myself to sit.

"Lucas with all due respect I am perfectly capable of looking after myself." Even as I said it, I felt dubious, to be frank.

"Amelia, I am only looking out for your well-being."

I knew he was right and nodded. He was only trying to care for me. I looked into his eyes and we smiled.

"I'm very grateful for your assistance, Lucas. You have been so much more to me than my second in command. You are a true friend. Now tell me what is happening to our shipment."

Lucas walked forward and placed a hand on my shoulder. "They have arrived. The humans are being led to the cave as we speak and the rest of the shipment is being dispersed around the house."

I looked into the mirror seeing my face pale white, my eyes dark. I looked terrible.

"Lucas – summon Eleanor, would you? I wish to dress."

"Are you sure?"

"Lucas."

I turned to look into his eyes. Lucas smiled, knowing there was no arguing with me, and nodded. Before leaving, he looked over his shoulder at me with a concerned face. I watched as the door closed and returned to looking into the mirror. I knew it was going to take a while before I gained full strength again.

After taking a few more days to rest, I was feeling a little better. I managed to sit at my desk. My energy though was still up and down. It quickly retreated. It seemed I needed more blood daily to regain what strength I had lost. Eleanor would constantly bring me blood to drink and Lucas was never far away.

We held small meetings in my chambers as Lucas wasn't prepared to allow me to leave and I must admit I obeyed. I wasn't strong enough to make the journey down to the Council chambers.

We decided to stay on Fugloy Island and try to make it work. The island wasn't easy to get to and it was unpopulated. The only thing we needed to sort out was how we were going to establish a regular food supply.

Having only one ship was not reliable. It took weeks to travel from London to us, given the variable weather.

We decided we needed a second ship. There was a problem with this though in that I was the only one who could turn people and I was too ill to do this at present and I was not prepared to enable others to do the same. I was still so weak and turning any others would drain my power quickly. I pondered whether or not to give this ability to Lucas; I was in two minds. The question was: would I be able to control those who were turned by others? I couldn't risk it just yet, not until I was completely well again.

It was another wintery day outside and I watched from my bed as the snow flew past the window. The swirls of white fluff fluttering by my window sent me into a daydream, which was only interrupted by the door closing and Lucas standing there.

"Lucas, good, I am glad you're here. I wanted to talk to you about commandeering another ship to allow us to have only a short time between journeys."

"I have already thought about that Amelia and instructed our captain to capture another and bring its captain to the island as soon as possible."

"You have done well, Lucas."

He nodded and turned to leave. "I'm happy to see you're feeling a little better." He winked and headed back out.

I lay there for a while, watching the door, half expecting him to come back through it any moment. Since my illness, I was unable to tap fully into my senses in order to detect the others in the house. It was very odd to be without it. I had lived with it for so long that not having it fully recharged made me feel… well… normal, like I was before I transformed.

For so long, all I wanted was to feel normal and now that I had regained a sense of it, I felt lost. I knew now that I wanted my true self back – the self with all my powers intact. It was a revelation. I didn't want to feel what others called 'normal', I wanted to feel strong and part of my family again. My family! It still sounded strange to call the coven my family. I had been a wife and would have been a mother too, but that life was gone from me now. I had mourned it and emerged triumphant.

Here, I was in control and everyone obeyed me… well, almost everyone. Yet it felt like a home. In Lucas and Eleanor, had two very loyal friends who cared about me and did not try to restrict my life in any way. I had a wonderful residence and my status had been greatly elevated. I resolved that from then on I would embrace my life. It was not how I planned it, but I would make the best of my life on the island and not worry about the things it would be impossible for me to have.

Days had passed and I was still in my chambers, regularly drinking the cold dark liquid that was helping me to recover. Feeling stronger with every passing day, I managed to extend my senses to Lucas but only when he was in the room. It was a start. My strength was recovering slowly but surely. The intensity of my emotions was reducing, and the conflict in my head that I had battled with for so long was starting to fade. As the days passed, I felt stronger and more in control.

I could start to sense those in my house once again. I tried on occasions to summon all my energy but it failed, leaving me exhausted. I decided to leave it for a while and concentrate on getting back to normal before I tried to tap into my will again.

Lucas and I would go for walks around the island. He thought that a breath of fresh air would help me, and it did. The snow-covered greenery made our surroundings so quiet and peaceful. All sound was deadened and made me feel so relaxed and calm. It was from this peaceful place that I began to look forward to a new kind of leadership. I would create my own, different kind of family.

My plan would be to nurture the next generation here on the island and create a place where we would live happily without fear of being hunted down and killed. Deep down, I knew that it would take a lot of work, a lot of nurturing and wasn't going to happen for a long, long time. But nothing worthwhile ever came quickly. I knew the humans would never agree with our way of life. It was imperative that we kept our existence a secret. I would pass a law to compel our little family never to reveal our way of life to anyone, on pain of death. It would be a harsh punishment but one that needed to be enforced. If word got out, we could all be killed.

After speaking with Lucas I decided to hold a meeting with the Council members, to discuss my plans. I walked with Lucas to the chambers and, as always, he escorted me to my throne before taking his seat. I looked around the room to see Tanzeda, Borbala and Eleanor all seated, waiting for me to speak. I looked to Lucas who nodded and smiled.

"Council members, I am thankful that you have attended at my request. I have summoned you all here today to discuss a few things. First there is one item of particular importance to discuss, and when we have finished here, I will need everyone who lives here to be summoned to these chambers immediately. Is this understood?" Everyone agreed.

"Second, I have requested another captain and ship to supply us more frequently than of late. This should be running smoothly soon.

"Third, I am going to set new rules that will be absolutely critical to our survival, and I expect them to be obeyed at all times. Failure to do so will mean you will put to the fire."

I watched as the others looked at each other, not sure how to react.

"My queen?"

Tanzeda stood.

"Yes? What is it Tanzeda?"

"Are we still in control, or have you abolished the Council?"

I stared at her for a while.

"My dear Tanzeda, you all will be a big part of our future and, as far as control goes, ultimately I will always have the deciding vote. Do you understand? As Council members, you will assist me in the running and be given certain political powers but do not overstep yourselves."

"I was only asking, my queen." She bowed.

"Now you have your answer."

I stood and walked to the edge of the pools staring into the waters for a while before turning back to them.

"From this moment on, things will be different. We will grow our community and create stability. I have decided that, when the time is right we will send vampires out into the world to create havens in selected locations around the globe."

"When do you plan to do this?" Lucas was standing looking concerned.

"It will be a magnificent future Lucas. We do not yet have the resources to do this, but we shall."

I could feel my inner power and self-confidence rising like a phoenix from the flames of the past. I was physically weak but mentally strong.

"Over the past few years, we have dealt with a lot because of our own mistakes but this will happen no more. We have learned from this and we will not be put into those same situations again."

I wanted to inspire my followers to have faith in our coven. "We shall all be involved in bringing our community to life and in making it thrive." The reactions from the Council were positive and the rest of the meeting passed off without incident.

After the meeting, the Council members went to gather everyone. While they were out, I was alone. I sat thinking about our plans. I didn't want to admit it but something inside me said that I wouldn't be able to keep my word on things not going wrong. Something told me that a battle was coming in the future. Maybe it was just my fear rearing its ugly head. So I changed my thoughts.

It wasn't long before I watched the doors at the back of the chambers open and in walked my subjects, gathering at the back of the room. I was still amazed by the numbers we had. I knew it was in the region of 200 and seeing them all together in one place was certainly a boost to my faith in our way of life.

Once the doors closed, the Council members took their seats. Silence fell on the room as they waited for me. I turned to Lucas and asked him to summon a jug for me as I was going to need it to enforce my new rule. I knew once I tapped into my strength it would make me weak. Lucas did as I requested and sent a guard to fetch me a jug. I waited until he returned before continuing. I drank straight from the jug, my fangs descending sucking up the cold, dark liquid, which flushed around my veins. I instantly felt stronger but I had to act fast as it wouldn't take long before I would start feeling tired again. I stood from my throne and walked down to meet everyone.

"Good day to you all."

Everybody bowed, staying silent.

"I have brought you all here today to discuss a new rule. Although we are hidden away, and not many know about us I must insist that we keep it that way. My new rule is this. It is imperative that we keep the existence of our kind a secret. This will ensure our safety. If our community were to become known about on the mainland, an army would be raised and sent to kill all of us. Therefore the punishment for disobeying this rule will be an enduring and painful death. No question."

I began to feel my energy rising slowly, I knew had a limited time to enforce this. As soon as it built up I released it into the room covering everyone including the Council chambers. I forced my will upon them before it snapped back into me like a long string of dough breaking. I instantly felt weak and before I knew Lucas was at my side holding my arm.

"You need to rest, my queen."

He took me out of the room and up to my chambers to rest. He laid me on the bed and summoned another jug for me.

"Thank you, Lucas."

"Sleep Amelia. You did well today, but now you must rest."

I smiled at him before I drifted off. I knew it had gone well, but it would cost me a few more days' rest.

Chapter 21
Surprise

Amelia

Morning came and I was already feeling better. It was the start of spring on the island and the weather, although still cold, was slowly improving. It was a long process to recovery. Jon had been a zealot in his revenge, dedicated and, indeed, giving his life in making me suffer, and long had I suffered. But I knew I would have the last laugh. I had survived and it was just a matter of time before I was back to my full strength. He could not touch me now. I would reign supreme with no further interference from small-minded people who lacked true vision.

I slowly rose to the sun shining through my window. I gently got up and walked to the light. I pushed open the balcony doors and stepped out. The sea was calm and the sky was a light shade of blue, with whispers of clouds in the air, like feathers. My balcony was covered with sleet.

Although it shouldn't have bothered me, feeling weaker made me more susceptible to the elements. Yet the cold air on my skin was refreshing. I felt brighter today, more alive than I had been in the last few days. I stood there with the wind gently blowing through my hair.

Lucas came into my room and joined me on my balcony. He stood next to me watching the sea. "It's a beautiful day, Amelia."

"It certainly is."

I looked into his eyes as he turned to face me. A smile on his face, he gently laid a hand on my shoulder and turned to look at the sea. I watched him for a moment before returning my gaze outwards over the water. It was calm and having Lucas here next to me made me feel secure. He was always there for me whenever I needed him. I breathed in again and out slowly, feeling content. Things were beginning to feel good. I felt him gently squeeze my shoulder before letting go and turned to walk away.

"We must get ready for the Council meeting, Amelia."

"I'll join you shortly."

I watched as he walked across my room and to my door. He didn't look back this time but I knew he didn't need to. I could feel him. He felt relieved that I was on the mend. I even started to feel others in the house again. It was faint but it was there.

As Lucas left my room, Eleanor walked in with a jug for me. She placed it down on my desk and went to my wardrobe to gather my clothes for the day. She didn't say anything to me at first, just performed her duties with grace and her positive manner was mesmerising. She placed a long, black silk dress on my bed and waited patiently for me to enter the room so she could assist me in getting ready.

As usual Eleanor performed her task well and always made me look beautiful. I was so thankful she was in my life, and I believe she too was growing in her contentment. My hair was tied up with a black ribbon, with long curls down each side of my face. The dress fitted perfectly and had a short train behind it. I placed my locket around my neck and looked into the mirror. She had a real talent for making me look young, strong and beautiful.

We chatted for a while, about the weather and her role as Council member. With each passing day she seemed more confident and relaxed. She was truly settling into her new role. She advised me that the new humans had been placed into quarters instead of the cave and had been given duties.

The ship had returned to London and should by now have found another captain and vessel as requested. Things were getting better.

After dressing me, Eleanor and I went for a walk around the house. We walked through the main lounge where a few vampires where gathered, talking amongst themselves. The guards were stationed at all doors. Two guards accompanied us around the house. The new humans, busying themselves in their new roles, were overseen by Lucas. Half were promised work and security in return for their service. Our secret had been kept from them. I read their thoughts as I passed and found that fear and uncertainty about their future and work were the only things on their minds. It was almost as if any evidence of our true lifestyle was too fantastical to believe. Besides, they had enough on their minds: a new working life on a wild island in the middle of nowhere. Most were still in a state of shock. Knowing Lucas, I knew some type of threat had most likely also been made against them to keep them compliant. I knew it would take a while before they settled down.

Lucas kept eyes on them at all times. The other half were kept separately with all new arrivals. They would be used as food, drained and stored in the blood pool beneath the Council chambers. It was agreed that this should be done without the knowledge the other humans in order to contain any panic or resistance. In order to further ensure our secret was kept, Lucas had also placed certain guards and vampires to oversee the humans, along with one Council member who was put in charge. He called them '*les gardiens de la nuit*', the Guardians of the Night. I was to be nominal leader, although I would only get involved should I need to.

Lucas had certainly been busy organising the house and enforcing the rules. He had done such a good job. I was proud of him. Things seemed better than ever, a new start to our way of life. I knew we could only get stronger. We could not know our life expectancy, or if we would grow old or even die. That was yet to be discovered but for now I was happy to take each day as it came.

Eleanor and I walked around the house looking at the empty caves beneath the house and listening to the protests of men that were being sacrificed for food. I really did feel empowered, strong and, above all a queen. Vampires and humans showed their respect to me by bowing and bobbing. If anyone did not, they would receive a private lesson from Lucas. Screams could be heard from those who didn't. He was heavy handed but enjoyed his job. It was a new way for all of us, including me.

As Eleanor and I walked outside, the snow was melting on the ground and dripping from the treetops. Bright sparkles shone from the crystal dew that covered the fields. A light breeze awoke our spirits as we toured the perimeter of the house. Finally, we stopped at the cliffs towards the back of the house and watched the foam gently passing as it rode the waves. I had a feeling someone was approaching, and turned to see a guard coming towards us. The guards that accompanied us turned to face him.

"My queen," he shouted, "Mr Lucas requests your company in the Council chambers."

"I will be along shortly."

"Yes, my queen."

I watched as he used his power to run swiftly around the house in a blur. How quickly we moved was still amazing to see.

"Eleanor, accompany me."

"Yes, of course." We headed back to the house and into the Council chambers. Lucas, Tanzeda and Borbala stood and bowed on my entry.

"Yes Lucas, what it is?"

"We have a request from Zach my queen. He wishes to see you."

Now what? I thought to myself. I was rapidly tiring of Zach's bleating.

"Very well. Guards! Show him in."

Eleanor and I took our seats and waited for Zach. The doors finally opened and in walked Zach. I was losing patience with this one. "Zach, you had better have a good reason for requesting this meeting."

Zach walked forward and bowed. Looking into my eyes, he spoke cautiously. "My queen, I would like to request to leave the island in order to visit my family."

Before I had a chance to answer, Borbala stood.

"I beg your pardon? You summon a meeting for this?"

"Borbala," I said. "Allow him to give his reasons."

Borbala looked at him with fury before taking her seat again.

"Go on, Zach."

"Well, m–my queen, I have received news that one of my family is unwell."

I tapped my fingers on the side of my throne. "Who informed you of this?"

"Elizabeth, my queen. She is a new servant here and I knew her before on the mainland."

"What does she know about us?"

"Nothing, my queen. I told her nothing."

"Very well… Which family member is unwell?" Out of the corner of my eye, I saw Borbala rising from her chair.

"You can't seriously be considering this my queen? This man is human and they are not allowed to leave this island under any circumstances."

"Borbala, please, take your seat. We will discuss this in private once I have found out more information."

She did as I requested. I could feel the anger coming from inside her.

"Try and control your emotions, Borbala. I do not wish to feel your anger."

I turned back to Zach. "Continue."

"It is my little sister, my queen," Zach spoke with building emotion, his eyes filling with tears. "She has the wasting disease and, from what I have gathered," he paused to regain his composure, "she does not have long to live…" He broke off, overcome, and wiped his eyes.

"I'm afraid Borbala is right, Zach. We have rules on this island. We cannot break them for situations like this. I'm sorry."

"But my lady – she is all I have left in the world, I'm begging you…"

I took a deep breath and released it slowly. "Leave us. We will discuss your request. You will be called once we have agreed on an answer."

"But…"

"Leave now Zach!" I raised my voice.

"Yes my queen."

We watched as Zach shuffled towards the doors. Borbala stood and walked off the platform and towards where Zach had been standing. She turned to face me.

"We cannot allow him to leave. If the mainland gets wind of our kind, we would be in mortal danger, my queen."

"I agree," Lucas said.

I turned to Tanzeda. "What are your thoughts?"

She looked at her sister for moment before answering.

"I say let him go… under very close supervision, of course. We cannot become animals with no compassion or concern for those who work for us."

"Tanzeda, you can't be serious!" Borbala snapped at her sister.

"Please, ladies, keep your composure." I turned to Eleanor "What say you?"

"I agree with Tanzeda, my queen. We should show compassion and trust."

"Trust? Are you mad? If that man leaves we will be signing our own death warrants and will have nothing but trouble from the rest of the house."

I listened to them arguing amongst themselves. Finally I said, "Enough! I have heard all of your reasons, and I find that two speak for either side of the debate, therefore, it is down to me to cast the deciding vote. Now take your seats. Summon Zach."

I watched as the guard opened the door and shouted for Zach to quickly enter. He came forward and stood in front of me. "After careful consideration Zach, the Council remains undecided. The casting vote is left to me. Should your request be granted, how do you plan to get back to the mainland? Our ship has already set sail for London and will not be returning for weeks."

"I know, my queen. I would have to wait for the ship to return." Zach's eyes filled up, and his tears finally fell.

"You realise your sister might not survive until you get there?"

He nodded, and drips fell onto his fraying shirt. "Yes my queen. But I have to…" he broke off and took a breath. "But I have to try, for her sake."

I straightened up in my chair placing my hands on the arms of the throne. I took a deep breath and sighed. "Very well. You can go."

"Oh thank you, my queen. Thank you so much!"

"I'm not finished. You can go on these conditions. First, two guards will accompany you to the mainland and watch you. Second, you will have one week and one week only. Do you understand?"

"Yes my queen, thank you."

"And third. You are to tell nobody where you come from or anything about us. Should you break this silence, I will grant the guards the power to clear the mess up and that will include ending your life, as well as the lives of those close to you. Do you understand? It will not be tolerated."

"Of course my queen. You may rely on my silence."

"Then go and prepare yourself. The ship should be with us again in two to three weeks' time. I shall instruct Lucas to find you suitable company."

"Thank you once again, my queen." He bowed and left the chambers.

"Borbala, I sense your frustration but please calm yourself." I stood and walked to the Council doors. Outside my guards were waiting.

"I'm going to my chambers."

I arrived at my door and asked the guards to wait at the bottom of the stairs. Having them stand outside my door was making me feel like a prisoner. They did as requested and left. I opened my door and walked in sighing.

"Humans." I said to myself. As I walked in, I noticed my jug on the floor with its contents spilled all over. I could see that from behind my desk, lying still on the floor, a man's legs emerged. I turned around to the creaking of my door, before I could shout for the guards, I froze. I looked down to see a knife plunged into my stomach. I slowly looked up into the eyes of the intruder...

"Catherine?"